In the Cold Cold Winter

Keshia C. Willi

House of Honor Books

House of Honor

Copyright © 2025 Keshia C. Willi

All rights reserved

The characters and events portrayed in this book are fictitious. Any similarity to real persons, living or dead, is coincidental and not intended by the author.

No part of this book may be reproduced, or stored in a retrieval system, or transmitted in any form or by any means, electronical, mechanical, photocopying, recording, or otherwise, without express written permission of the publisher.

ISBN: 978-1-68596-097-1

Printed in the United States of America

Published by House of Honor Books.

Harvest, Alabama

DEDICATION

To the ones who broke me...
Bandages heal wounds, but scars will never forget.

Tha dioghaltas na mhias as fheàrr le fuachd.

PART ONE

SPRING

1953

Vengeance is mine, and recompense, for the time when their foot shall slip, for the day of their calamity is at hand, and their doom comes swiftly.

Deuteronomy 32:35

Moonstone
(Hecatolite)

a pearly white semiprecious stone, especially one consisting of alkali feldspar

creates balance and sparks the intuition to life

awakens the body to an awareness of mind and spirit, allowing guidance from the hereafter

the wearing of a talisman or charm will guide the wearer to choose the path that is right

1 Moonlight Man

That spring, I wanted to kill him.
I heard the tall grass of the high fields taunting me to do it. The cool spring that ran along the house trickled out the words, *"Kill him."* The thought was everywhere around me, clinging to the air, tainting my heavy chest, my aching heart, and head.

One day, I took a long, hard listen. I let the words sink in like mud within my veins. The words felt good there. So, I let them sink in deeper.

"Jaelle," my husband gasped out as I rolled off him onto my side of the bed, sinking low into the lifeless cushion of the old mattress. That was all he said, as he clung to me with a death grip and fell into an exhausted sleep.

I didn't sleep. Spring had brought an early heat, stifling and dry. My head was still aching dully from where his hand had lent its weight, and my temple had met clumsily with the wall. I had forgotten to wash his lucky shirt for his big poker game with the boys the next night. Silly me. I knew better than to turn my back on him. My broken body knew better. The rest of the night was a sickening blur, a flash of simmering images in the late April heat.

As I lay there in the quiet of the late night, sweat slid down my neck to my chest, dampening my faded blue nightgown. It stung the burns there from one of his many fits of rage brought on by my refusing to sleep with him. I had been feeling awful sick and refused him. I was awakened that night to a searing pain on my breasts, the smell of cigarette smoke, and burning flesh. I kept my mouth shut in the darkness as he pressed his stub of a cigarette, burning red hot in the night, into my skin. I heard the skin sizzle and pop, but I didn't scream. Didn't even cry. There was no making noise when Jeremy was teaching you a lesson.

    I had learned my lesson that night, that was certain. When he said he wanted me, I came. I loved on him like a passionate lover should, and when I thought he was satisfied, I lay awake and hated myself for doing it. Like tonight.

    Jeremy knew how to make you feel small, inside and out. With a flick of his cigarette butt, or that wicked half-smile that always seemed to curl across his cracked lips, he could school you in what you really were. With the back of his hand, he could whip you into shape and make you forget everything but him. He was good at that.

    That night, the heat was so thick that even my lungs felt the weight of it. I took deep breaths in, keeping quiet, because God knows you didn't want to wake Jeremy from a dead sleep. I turned carefully onto my side to watch him sleep. Sure, he was handsome or had been when I first met him. His sharp cut features had long ago blurred behind his mask of scruff and dirt. He stank of booze and sweat and manure from the farm. I breathed him in, trying to remember the scent that he had carried with him ages ago. What was it then? *Moonlight Man.* That was it. The cologne he used to wear.

    In the back of his car, as we kissed, he used to whisper, "That's right, baby, I'm your moonlight man. I'll sweep you off your feet and dance into your dreams. You'll never be rid of me."

    That's what I feared most. His promise in that beat-up old Ford truck. I knew that he meant it. He would always be with me. Always.

    That's when those thoughts came rushing up on

me again in a wave of luxurious, frightful fury.

If my husband's not going to let me leave, then he's the one that's gotta leave.

My own voice in my head seemed to float up from my chest, through my mouth that I'd clamped shut, and out on to the air. I watched it float there like a shadow and take form in my Great Ma's old rocking chair. It was me. I was staring at me as I sat there rocking as if the sound wouldn't wake up Jeremy. Daring him to stir. The phantom image of myself stared at my husband lying in the bed next to me, before it turned toward me with a look of wide-eyed rage.

Make him leave, Jaelle. You gotta make him leave, the phantom me said without moving her lips.

I could hear her voice as clear as day. I answered her, whispering breathlessly in the dark. "How?"

…him, the phantom me said.

She sounded like a radio signal coming in and out, all full of static and noise, and I couldn't understand the first word.

"What?" I mouthed to her.

She looked frustrated now. Furious. Enraged. Her eyes stared me down, glaring sharply. Suddenly, she was out of the rocking chair. In an instant, she was at my bedside, leaning over me. A shadow deeper than the shadows. She glanced with hate at the man asleep next to me. He stirred in his sleep, clutching me tighter until I couldn't breathe.

Kill him, she hissed.

I shook my head in answer, though my heart and head were leaning toward her every word.

Kill him.

"No," I squeaked out, feeling his hands all over me. I squirmed beneath his touch, his hands feeling like the burns he'd given me. Searing, scorching, red-hot and wild.

The shadows shifted and phantom me now stood

on the other side of our old bed, hovering above Jeremy, knife in hand. The knife loomed far above her head; her hands were not trembling, but certain. Then they came down on Jeremy's chest.

I screamed, and the shadow of me was gone. Jeremy grumbled in his sleep.

"Quiet your screaming, bitch. Just one of your damn nightmares."

I was trembling all over, not like the shadow I had seen of me. She was sure and certain. Unafraid. She could do what I couldn't. I felt his hands pull me close, hungry for me again already. The booze on his breath burst into my face. I clamped my mouth shut again, my teeth chattering even in the heat. I wanted to be sick, to retch and scream all his disgusting words right out of me. All the words and angry love he had fed me for so many years.

I felt it rising from my stomach, rising higher and higher to my chest. Up, up, to my throat. I peeled myself out of his arms to his grunting and groaning, and I ran to the bathroom, barely there in time to be sick in the toilet.

I clung to the toilet after it all came up. In the silence, I could hear his voice mumbling above the night sounds just outside the window, skirting across the air with such poignant precision that not a syllable was missed.

"Damn bitch. Good for nothing, not even my bed."

I clung to the toilet, sweating and full of violent chills. The words of my shadow traced delicately across my lips. Over and over again.

Kill him.

2 Saturdays

In the backwoods of West Virginia, the weather was as unpredictable as Jeremy's old truck. Maybe it'd do what it was bent on, maybe it wouldn't. Just like, maybe it'd rain and water the endless fields of corn and soy, and maybe, just maybe, it wouldn't. Maybe instead, it'd dry up all those fields and kill the crops.

Last year, it rained when the soil was thirsty and staved off storms until harvest. This year, the weather was as fickle as a scorned lover. The winter had been good to the farmers with rich rain and sunny days to make the farmers feel safe and praising God for another good year. Then it turned on them with such ferocity, those men just stood in the middle of their fields, scratching their heads, mystified and thoroughly stumped. There hadn't been rain for over a month.

My husband didn't own the land he tended it. It belonged to his daddy. My husband wasn't rich enough to own his own land, smart enough to bargain for it, nor thrifty enough to save his own money to claim it. His daddy wanted him to make something more of himself than a disappointment and a drunkard. On our wedding day, he gifted Jeremy the use of an old orchard that hadn't borne fruit in years, a rundown old farm, and a house that hadn't seen a body in it for many a year.

I busied myself making that beat-up old house a cozy home, while Jeremy worked himself to the bone trying to bring the orchard to life again. In the eleven years that we'd been married, Jeremy hadn't reaped a single harvest. To make money, Jeremy was a bootlegger. Selling cheap liquor was our mainstay, and despite himself, it was Jeremy's pride and joy.

Any money he got would go straight to his own booze habits and his damn stamp collection. Those stamps were worth more to him than me, the land or the house we called home. Every Friday he would come home late, full of booze, drunk off his ass, carrying with him a small little bundle of fresh new stamps for his book. By the light of the kitchen lamp, he would sit up late into the night pressing them ever so delicately into sturdy pages. Then he would stare them down all laid out before him like his own little trophy case. I didn't touch his stamps or his precious book. I didn't dare.

On Saturdays, we would head to town. I'd dress up in my finest plain dress and do up my hair. I'd stare at myself in the mirror with Jeremy yelling and hollering for me outside in the truck. I would tremble with excitement at the thought of the ride. And...*people.* I longed to see people. It didn't matter if I knew them or if they knew me, I just liked the idea of them. I liked to watch them and imagine what it would be like to step into their shoes. Walk a mile in their lives. Far, far away from mine. I wasn't allowed to talk to them, not while Jeremy was with me. He got awful jealous if anyone said a word or looked at me an instant too long.

One particular Saturday, we were to go to my mama's house. I didn't waste time dressing up fancy for her. I ran my hands through my wind-swept hair and took a glance at my sun-kissed, freckled face in the mirror. It wasn't anything pretty to see now. I had been pretty once but life with Jeremy, life in these high fields, had turned my hands to leather and my skin to rot. Even my crystal blue eyes that used to sparkle and shine were dead and dull, the life in them swept away with the great winds that rolled across the valley.

All I had left was the memory of me. The me before Jeremy.

"Damn it, Jaelle! Get a move on!" Jeremy's voice clattered in from the open window of our bedroom, disturbing my solitary thoughts.

I hurried. I grabbed my purse from the ragtag dresser that his mother had given us at our wedding. I scurried out of the room, down the rickety stairs that screeched and whined under every step, and out the screen door as it wheezed out a gusty slap behind me.

I could see Jeremy's eyes. They were simmering and angry. Always angry. But this Saturday morning, there was something else festering inside them. I looked at them long and hard while making my way toward him. I tried my best to see beneath that angry look of his. To see what I was up against that morning. Whether I should make light of everything and smile my way through it, or steer right clear of him entirely.

Still perplexed, I chose to smile kindly at him. I must have done it wrong. His answer was a wallop to my face with the back of his hand. My head reeled; the breath stolen from my lungs in one fell swoop. I didn't turn to him. I didn't want to look at him. I knew he was staring me down with all the hate in the world.

"That'll teach you to keep me waiting."

I managed to gasp out, "I'm sorry."

He chuckled deep in his throat until my blood ran cold and my stomach lurched. "Sorry don't cut it, honey. Those're just coward's words. I'd like to think you were more than that."

He leaned close to me until I could smell the vomit, the tobacco and the rankness of leftover booze lurking about his mouth. My stomach lurched again, but I swallowed hard. Our eyes met long enough for me to see him muster up a sneer.

"Lord knows I ain't married to a Hollywood glamour girl, but I'd like to think you was a little better than this."

Something sparked inside me as he headed to the driver's side of the truck. That little spark of fire blinded my insides, leaving me empty and open.

"You don't think I'm pretty?" I muttered to the wind.

He heard it. Damn it, he heard it. I trembled where I stood, clutching tightly to my purse and the open truck door. He slid into the truck and turned to me with a sickeningly sweet smile, gesturing for me to get inside.

"Get on in, sweetheart. You'll be late for your mama's."

I gripped the truck harder, feeling the hot metal sizzle under my touch. I didn't trust that easy smile of his. I hadn't known that smiles had layers until I met Jeremy. There was that easy smile, so cool that it chilled me to the bone. Behind that easy smile was his cold and vacant sneer, one that I couldn't quite capture or understand. I knew it was trouble. I didn't want to get in that truck. I didn't want to sit in the seat beside him. There was no option but to go along. Mama was expecting me, and Jeremy didn't like leaving me alone. Thought I'd get into trouble. I secretly imagined that he was afraid I'd run. I never did. Not once.

Cautiously, I slid into the seat next to him, my eyes glued to him. I quietly closed the door. Like a whip, his hand shot out to strike me—but it stopped just an inch from my face. My stomach was in my throat, ready to burst. I winced, prepared for the blow. It didn't come. A stunted sigh tumbled out of his rotten mouth as he pulled his hand away.

"Nah," he muttered angrily. "I'll not lay a hand that your mama can see. Not a damn finger. I'll not have her hexin' me."

With that, the truck jolted to life, and we were headed on our way.

My mama lived on the outskirts of town, away from

the life that carried on in bursts of vivid colors and clouds of chatter. It was quite a way to go in that truck with Jeremy. He didn't say a word to me. Immediately out of the driveway, he flipped the radio to the only country station that the truck would pick up way out there. It blared it the entire ride.

Jeremy knew every word to every song, wailing and whining along with the twangy music. Jeremy couldn't carry a tune, but boy, he could whistle. When he got winded, and grew tired of singing, he would chirp out a whistle along with the song. The sound was pleasant enough and listening to it almost made me forget the unpleasantness of the trip.

Sometimes he forgot himself in the moment, and he would turn to me and smile. Finally, I'd smile back, fearful of what might happen if I didn't. But my smile was unnatural, and he could read right through it. His smile quickly faded with a disgruntled groan, and he turned his eyes back to the road.

I sighed, grateful that his attention had skirted past me. Feeling the heavy air between us shift and lighten just a little, I moved my eyes warily to the window. Endless empty fields sped by in a blur of dusty haze. The leftovers from last year's crops peeked up from the arid earth, the once vibrant stalks and leaves now a putrid sight of rot. It made them look like corpses. I sighed silently.

"Fields'll be nigh on useless if we don't get some damn rain," my husband muttered as he spat a wad of tobacco juice out of the open truck window.

"If the rain comes—" I started quietly.

Jeremy stepped in with a grunt. "Rain ain't coming." Another glob of spit out the window. "Daddy says our harvest should be plentiful and good this year. But we've had nothing but bad luck with those damn trees since we got 'em. I don't reckon we'll get anything but a scattering of rotten, bitter crab apples for all my trouble. Nothin' can help them trees save for a miracle."

I looked at him with surprise. "You believe in miracles, Jeremy?"

He huffed and snorted, giving the side mirror a long, fitful glance. "You know me better than that, sweetheart. God and me ain't exactly friends."

I stared nervously into my lap, folding my hands there. "Even if you don't believe in God, that don't mean you don't believe that somehow, some way, unexpected things can happen."

He thought about it for a moment. I watched as a single glint, a miniscule spark of recognition and understanding lit up his dull, dark eyes. As fast as it came, it faded. He gurgled out a laugh

"Bullshit."

And that was that. We didn't speak anymore. He glared down the road, gritting his teeth and gripping the steering wheel so tightly his knuckles burned white. I stared out in front of us, watching the road come rushing at us in a blur of dust and dirt. Slowly, my eyes drifted closed, and I dreamed.

Blood. All I see is blood slipping and sliding through my fingers. It is everywhere. All over the bottom of my best dress, down my legs and my weathered white shoes, and the floor beneath me.

I am crying. No, screaming. It echoes along the stained-glass windows and white-washed walls of the small church until everything is silent, listening to the sound of my cries. I can feel their eyes on me. All of them turning in their stiff Sunday best, peering over their pews to look at me with wide eyes. No one comes to help me. No one even gets up.

I'm standing in a puddle of my own blood, feeling the pain surge through my insides in rushing waves. And I can't stop screaming.

Suddenly, I hear, "Jaelle."

I turn to see Jeremy sitting beside me in the blood-

stained pew. Not a drop of blood is on him, but I know he's the reason. He's the reason for the pain and the blood I'm losing here at this moment. He looks up at me with a look so stern and strange that I immediately go quiet, my mouth still gaping open in silent rage. He just stares me down in that way of his, and I suddenly feel stupid and embarrassed. I'm trembling all over, slipping in my own blood.

He says, "Stop your fussin' and sit down." He yanks me down into the pew. Hitting the hard pew sends a new wave of pain shivering through my body. Jeremy leans close to me until I breathe in the cloud of whiskey hanging from his lips.

"Still believe in your God now?" he sneers with a throaty laugh.

I stare ahead of me, my bloodied hands lying lifeless in my lap. The preacher's eyes are on me from the pulpit. Staring hard and judging me, as if he could see every dirty, sinful thing I've done. Things that Jeremy's made me do. I can feel the blood seeping through my underwear onto the floor.

"Where is He?" the hissing words haunt me as an echo on the walls of my mind.

I drift away into black, and the white-washed walls and stained-glass windows draped in red vanish in a gust of shadows and whispers. And then...

I awoke with a start as the truck choked to a stop. Blinking, I tried to get my bearings. We'd arrived at my mama's, the dust of the road billowing behind us.

Without a word, I pushed open the truck door. Jeremy didn't utter a word. He just watched me like a hungry hawk as I made my way to my mama's dilapidated front porch. She was waiting for me, brittle but strong, sitting on the front step, muddled in with its vines and wild ivy like a wild thing herself. She was full of that unearthly fire that fueled her body to live on, ignoring the pull of age and time. She was old, having lived to be a mite older than her mother before her had lived.

"Gone around the sun a time too many," my mama would always say. "I expect the next'll kill me."

It never did.

I turned back just as Jeremy's truck sped off down the dirt road, a cloud of dust clambering behind it.

"That boy's gotta lotta nerve lookin' at me the way he does," Mama mumbled under her breath, just loud enough for me to hear as she spat upon the earth.

I turned to her and tried to give her my best smile, but everything inside of me cringed to look at her. Age had not been kind to her once ethereal beauty. A hard life in the mountains had long ago worn away that loveliness to something both harsh and cruel, while still retaining that frigid otherworldly essence of the woman she would always be.

My mama was not a Christian woman. She was born of the earth and the air, the water, and the fire of the sun. She worshipped what begot her, the magic and the gods of the backwoods. In her youth, she had been well-known in these parts by people who believed just like her. To them, she was both midwife and healer, wise woman and nigh on a goddess in her own right. To the truly Christian people of our little corner of this great world, she was a witch.

As a child, I watched my mother carry out her rituals and ancient ways. I saw it save the lives of breech babies that were too stubborn or too terrified to enter this world head first. I saw it rescue farmers from disease and rotted fields. I watched it consume mama and all those her witching touched, way down deep to the root of their souls, until they could believe nothing else. As for me, I was different. I was not my mama.

When I was young, I had been entranced by the white-steepled chapel at the edge of my existence of vines and earth that stretched in every direction from my mama. Every Sunday, its bells seemed to call me, sweetly singing in the distance. It was a captivating song that I could never seem to understand with the clang and clatter of my mama's voice pounding in my head. For a long time, the bells and my mama's whispered words of spirit were at war within me, battling for a soul I could not comprehend or see. But I felt it.

Mama wasn't against the Christians or the little Baptist church that lay as a backdrop against our land. Lord knew, the two often ran together. But she simply didn't care for them. They were needy and judgmental of her ways. They would come round every Christmas and Easter, asking for alms in exchange for their blessings and prayers. Mama would stand barring the door, a smile spread across her lips that only I understood. Her smile was neither warm nor kind. It was a warning.

"Send your prayers to the dust, for unto it you shall return," she would say sternly and nothing more.

The door was closed on those well-meaning Christians every time.

My mama would turn to me and say, "Their god ain't ours, girl."

That was all that was said until the next season. That wasn't enough for me. I wanted more than whispered words to earth and air. More than offerings of fire and elemental meddling. So, I gave myself to God. The God of Abraham and Isaac. I was baptized on a clear, bright Easter morning, and when I stepped out of that murky river water with the rest of those believers, I felt clean and clear and bright on the inside. Like a new penny must feel just out of the mint. It felt good to belong to the Light and the day.

The preacher looked at me with a beaming smile, and said, "You take care of that spirit of yours. It's the Lord's now."

Mama, of course, didn't come to my baptism. From

that day onward, she was cool to me. We rarely exchanged words until the day I married Jeremy and left her for good.

Then it was only for her to mutter under her whiskey-tainted breath, "Not mine anymore."

I looked at her now, cantankerous and sour, curdling in her blood-red rage like a festering boil. I smiled, and she glowered. The longer she looked at me though, the stranger her look became.

"Somethin' strange upon you, girl," Mama croaked, her voice a raspy echo of the soothing tones of her youth. "Be like a cloud of shadow has passed across your face. What troubles you?"

I didn't want to say anything about the troubles or the heartaches that were mine. I knew that she already saw them.

Still, I said quietly, "Nothin', Mama."

She spat upon the earth and grumbled loudly. "Liar! I'll not chastise you for a lie, but *your* god surely will!"

A smile crept across her cracked lips, trembling with palsies. It was the same smile that had met the goodly Christians who dared to step foot over her threshold. My stomach sank to my tippy toes to see it spent on me. I felt as if I were five years old again, standing before my mama to be punished, her watchful eyes burning black as coal as they judged me with the weight of the world.

"Well, girl?"

I cleared my throat, clinging tightly to the secondhand clutch purse tucked under my quivering arm. "I came as always to help you, Mama. That's all. Nothing more."

Mama snorted and nearly choked on her own spittle as she laughed. It was a cackling sound, groping in the air to smother the lovely notes of spring that sang quietly there.

"That husband of your just wants to dump you on

my doorstep a while so he can do his business. And you—" she glared at me as she spoke. "You only come to bring me Jesus."

She grinned a toothless grin, her gums stained nearly black from tobacco and years of neglect. It was a revolting smile, and I swallowed hard. She pushed up off the rotten front stoop with a groan and headed toward the door. As she reached the threshold, she turned back, that smile still painted across her dark features.

"Shall I refuse Him again, or shall you give it up, and come in?" she said.

I said nothing. With a sigh, I made my way up the porch steps and followed her into the house of my childhood.

The inside of Mama's house was as wild and shadowy as the outside. The vines and ivy that blanketed the house's skeleton had long ago made their way into its earthen heart, twining and twisting about its ribs and cavity which made up its inner sanctum. It was holy to those that found solace and sanctuary there. Even now, I could feel the pull of those vines at my heartstrings, tugging at my memory until I recalled my many years within these walls. Despite the house's darkness, there was joy within its shadows, safety amidst its rooms. The memory of it steadily forced itself to the forefront of my mind. Here, I was created and born. Once I had lived here. Inside, it was as if I had never left.

My fingers traced the familiar cracks in the plaster walls. Every one had a story; every one a memory. I breathed in the fragrant musty scent of old earth and dusty jars of pungent herbs and flowers. I reached out to touch one as I passed. A bundle of lacy white flowers was inside. They were lovely and strange little things. I started to undo the top of the jar.

"Don't you touch them flowers, girl!"

Mama glared at me from the shadows. "Hemlock.

Them is deadly to the touch. Best you keep away from them."

I put the jar back and looked no further. As I followed my mama deeper and deeper into the house, I caught the rank smell of her. She was not one to bathe. Not one to wash the caked-on dirt, the sweat, and the blanket of dust from her skin. She believed it bore its place on every inch of her and kept her from illness. It only added to the sour smell of ancient grime that rose from every corner of the place.

Mama sat herself down by the fireplace, the fire only embers now. There was a chill in the stale air that shivered up my spine. It had been pleasant and warm outside. In Mama's house it never seemed anything but frigid. Her fire burned almost year-round; it was odd that now it was nigh on dead.

She motioned for me to sit across from her, and without a word, I did. Her clouded eyes never left me, looking over every inch of me. The small, rickety table between us was a godsend. It felt as if her gaze could rend me to shreds and render me naked right there before her. It was so easy to see through the slender façade that was my body, riddled with the scars and the track marks of Jeremy. She could see it all, every unwanted shadow in my eyes. I squirmed nervously beneath her all-knowing stare.

"Your husband done took his hand to you, eh?" she said. It wasn't really a question.

I said nothing. I sat eerily still, trying with all my might not to reveal anything with my eyes. My body seemed to tell her so very much already. She smiled, as if the nakedness of my soul was something humorous and easy.

"But you like it, don't you? And you stay—"

"Because I love him," I was fast to lie.

I could tell that she knew it was a lie. She gurgled out a laugh as she dipped her hands into a wooden bowl full of ashy powder. She brought her hands together as if to pray and blew the powder into the dying fire. Instantly, it burst into life, its flames licking the mantel above. Mama settled with pleasure into her seat.

"A wise woman sees love for what it is," Mama said. "A foolish woman sees it only for what it could be and settles all her hopes, her life, her faith, in that." She cocked her head to the side with a vicious smile. "You a wise woman, girl? Or a fool?"

Instead of answering her directly, I said, "I heard tell of a new preacher comin' to the little church in town. He comes this spring with much promise, so people say."

I said it just to spite her, and she knew it. Her face scrunched up in a look of pure disdain and condemnation. It was as if I'd said the Lord's name in vain, only that wasn't her god. She likened herself not to a woman made in the image of the Lord, but an animal, keen and wild as the earth, made in the likeness of its secrets and power.

There's deep power riddled in the roots and soil, she'd say every spring as she dug her gnarled fingers into the rich sod. Maybe she was right. Though I never let on, I could always feel a presence as I stood out in the green and growing land. With my feet sunk down deep into the sun-kissed soil, I could feel a little niggling of power seeping through to my toes. It always gave me an inkling of hope and strength, as the darkened folds of winter scattered in the sunlight. Yet even if Mama was right, that wasn't God's power. It was something else entirely, and I wouldn't let it sink in. Not ever.

Mama grimaced as she busied herself with a teapot, resting it on the hook in the fire to boil.

"Promise ain't the same as piety, so I gather," she murmured as she waited. Her eyes rose sharply to me. "You stay clear of that preacher man. You understand, girl? Thems not your kind. They'll never be, no matter how hard you try to make 'em fit. You'll not be accepted into their fold unless you stop your very heart from beatin'. Stop your soul from breathin' in the fire of the light. They've got a mind to kill you from the inside and make you look like them, act like them, inside and out. Watch yourself! You hear?"

I sighed out, "Mama—"

She wasn't listening. Her eyes were far away, staring into the crackling fire. The teapot was already spitting; its low humming whistle just cresting the steaming spout. From Mama's dry and crusted lips came her own soft murmuring hum. Low-spoken words that I had to lean close to hear.

Over the hum of the teapot, I heard, "Fire in the trees. Blood. B-b-blood in the snow."

I could feel the prickling fear of my youth trail down my spine. It was one of Mama's visions. She was wont to have them when the air was crisp and taut with shivering new life. I told her long ago they were from the Devil's hand, but she never listened. It was easier, she'd say, to listen to the sounds of spirit than that holy fire of the Church. One was a clear bell on a quiet morning. The other was a death knell.

I never did like when the spirit took her. Her visions frightened me to no end. They always circled around death and darkness, dark shadows from the depths of her muddled mind.

Growing frustrated, I said again, "Mama!" Louder this time, just as the teapot began to sizzle and hiss and holler. The sound nearly made me jump out of my skin.

Mama's dark, clouded eyes turned glassy and bright as she looked up at me. The spell was broken. Her gaze was none too happy upon me. I squished down deep into the rickety wooden chair I sat in. It was a fool's prayer that somehow this would hide me from her watchful eyes. Mama hissed at me like a feral cat and glared sharply.

"Don't you squawk at me, little girl. I'll not have you raisin' your voice in this house."

It was a house, not a home.

Quickly and well-rehearsed, I said, "Sorry, Mama."

She nodded, licking her lips with a serpentine flick of her tongue. Satisfied, she busied herself with the tea, pouring the piping hot water over the crisp, dried tea leaves in mismatched cups. She shoved a cup in my direction, the tea sloshing out and spilling over the sides. Little rivulets of brown water ran along the wood grain of the table.

I watched them move steadily toward me, a hypnotic dance of fluid motion that captivated me and drew me in until my mind retracted. Back, back, and back it wended. I stared down the darkness of my own mind. Buried deep within its folds, there was an eerie glow, a glint of scattered white. It fluttered faintly and a whisper arose from it. One I couldn't make out. I felt myself creep closer to the light and the sound. Closer and closer—

"See somethin', now, did ya?"

My mama's voice ripped me from the darkness and the muddled voice. I trembled all over from the journey, finding myself once more in that dark kitchen with *her*. She was looking at me with a venomous sneer, her eyes alight with a hint of mischief and wicked amusement. I shook my head, but my body couldn't lie. I was shaking violently. I shook so much that I dropped my teacup on the floor, where it shattered.

My mama just sat there, watching me.

"What is it you saw?" she demanded, her voice croaking like a ghastly river creature.

I was quiet. A roll of distant thunder rumbled outside. She huffed and scooted off her chair. Shuffling slowly, she reached up to the mantel coated in a dusty black from years of smoke and constant fire. Atop the mantel, there was a small wooden box.

She brought it down, placing it on the table before me. With a toothless smile, she cracked open the box. Her grubby fingers poked inside and brought forth a moonstone amulet hung on a worn and rusted chain. She reached over the table and placed it around my neck.

"Don't you take this off now," she warned. Her eyes met mine. "It'll protect ya from the comin' storm."

I said nothing.

"Ya hear?" She was adamant now.

I nodded.

It was threatening to storm as Jeremy and I drove back to the farm, but I knew the rain wouldn't come. I could feel it. I was quiet the whole way home, my nervous fingers toying with the moonstone dangling at my breast. I could feel that inky blackness, that earthy power seeping from the thing, but my fingers couldn't help but touch it. It was danger and comfort, old ways and new ways, battling to reach my troubled mind. All I could think of was Jeremy as the thunder rolled overhead with a vengeance. And how I wanted to kill him.

3 And the Lord Sayeth Unto Me

"They say Brother Wise was the pride of the seminary back in Lynchburg. I've heard his wife Prudence is of good Baptist blood herself. Her father was the preacher Brother Abel West that we've heard tell of since we was babes in cradles. Word amongst the elders is that our little congregation is headed toward its very own renaissance of sorts. A 'jubilee of the spirit', they called it. After all our community went through, what with Deacon Johnston's speedy departure west and Brother Wallace's unnatural death, it truly feels like God is shining down on us again.

"Word amongst the nosy congregation was that Deacon Johnston had been keeping tryst with the likes of one of the farmers' wives. No one knew who this harlot was, but Deacon Johnston was swiftly swept away to the west, and not a word more was said."

I took a breath, though I hadn't said a word. My good friend, my only friend, Missy Temple, could talk her way clear through the Lord's second coming if she was allowed. She was a pleasantly plump and vivacious middle-aged woman, fair-skinned with rich blonde hair. She had a smile that seemed to brighten up the shadows like the sun and I liked that about her.

Her husband's farm was only a few miles away from ours. Every Sunday, she would sit in the last pew of our little church with me, chatting away endlessly, despite sharp looks from the preacher. She was inclined to visit me some days when she knew Jeremy was away. She didn't like Jeremy and Jeremy didn't like her. With a mutual agreement of disdain, they avoided each other; silent ships passing in the night that wouldn't budge an inch.

    I didn't mind. I liked having Missy all to myself in those brief moments when we were alone. It was a breath of fresh air rushing toward my stagnant soul that made me feel alive and more than just useful. I was wanted, and that was enough. At least, that's how Missy made me feel. Though she rarely talked about anything other than herself and the gossip she had caught while sitting with the other church ladies at the sewing club or evening Bible study. Things I was never allowed to take part in, so sayeth Jeremy. While this sort of talk was not my cup of tea, the way she told these snippets of delicious somethings was interesting enough. I'd smile at her vibrant and colorful stories, although at times I couldn't help but blush at some of the unspeakable stuff she thought to say.

    Today was no different. She had just finished a salacious little tidbit about one of the elders' sons, before getting sidetracked with all she knew about the coming preacher, Brother Wise. The entire congregation was all aflutter with excitement at his coming, but also a little apprehensive—him being from a neighboring Southern state and all. Our community was tight-knit, and after the trouble with the northerner Deacon Johnston the year before, it was also very, very cautious of outsiders.

    Missy paused long enough to gulp down the remainder of her tea. But mid-swallow, she recalled another slice of information with a full-bosomed shout that nearly made me jump right out of my seat. Seeing me surprised, she giggled like a silly schoolgirl into her cracked teacup. A bit of shame split my smile in two. Oh, how I wished I had nicer china, the finer stuff that matched with not a crack or chip in sight. That would suit Missy better. She deserved finer things, but this would have to do.

She set down my sad little chipped cup on the threadbare tablecloth which hid the rotting kitchen table I was equally ashamed. I was in luck, because Missy talked so much that she never seemed to have time to notice these little imperfections. She eyed me with a look of delightful naughtiness, as if she were about to burst with the weight of her forbidden words. I could already feel the judgment of God glowering down upon us as she leaned her head in closer to whisper. Instead of her usual gossip, she started with—

"Has he come to call on you?"

My wicked little smile faded, and immediately, I felt guilty for the pleasure I had expected at the possibility of more delicious gossip.

"What?" That was all I could muster as my head dropped, my eyes falling to my folded hands in my lap.

Missy wiggled happily in her chair, ready to speak before the word had barely rolled off my tongue. "Brother Wise means to visit every family in the church *personally* to show his utmost respect and gratitude. It is a great honor to be visited by such a holy man."

She kept smiling, her bright eyes shining brighter than the sun. But I didn't feel their warmth any longer. Brother Wise had not come to call on me and my house. According to Missy's mindless chatter that followed, he had already been to the Anderson farm not a mile north and the Samuels' house just one farm over. I could feel the awkward edginess on the air as Missy looked back at me with pity. I didn't want that; her pity was no good here. Not when I knew why the preacher hadn't come.

It was Mama and her witching ways. It was Jeremy too, who to the rest of our small Christian community had sold his soul to the devil of drink. Oh, yes, there was talk. There was always talk, thanks to big-mouthed gossips like Missy.

It didn't matter how good a woman I was, or how much I loved the Lord. To them—to all of them—I was a wicked, no-good, mealy-mouthed little sinner. Wife of a sinner. Daughter of a sinner. That wasn't to be tolerated, not here in this quiet valley of God and the good. I kept my head hung low and Missy finally grew quiet. For that, I was thankful. My quick-beating heart couldn't take anymore of her fast talking.

I felt her hand gently lay atop mine with a soft pat of reassurance. Instantly, I felt a flash of vision overtake me.

The color red. Bodies shifting in the dark, twisting and twining together in a knot of passion. And a name—a name—but I couldn't—

A sharp and unexpected wind rushed in through the open window behind Missy, startling her. The blustery breeze flitted across the table. Missy's hand shook violently as she gave a cry, and her cup tumbled to the floor with a crash. Missy jumped, her eyes dropping away from me and her cheeks flushing bright red.

As swiftly as the wind came, it fell away. The air between Missy Temple and I was strange and cool and eerily quiet. Missy cleared her throat, her eyes timidly meeting mine again.

"Surely, he'll come. Jaelle. Think nothin' of it."

She nodded as if to reassure herself. She went to pat my quivering hand again, but she thought better of it. Her own hand quickly withdrew to her lap.

"He'll come. It'd be an awful disgrace to show ill favor on one of our congregation now. Brother Wise would do no such thing. I have it on good authority, alright?"

Missy had it on good authority, because she had already met this Brother Wise and his wife. It seemed he had made many of his visits earlier in the week and Missy's family farm had been one of the first. I knew her family was treasured and well-respected in the community, especially at church. Many of the church's renovations were paid for with their charitable donations. I knew they were well-loved for their money as much as their kindness, just as I knew for certain that Brother Wise and his wife were not going to come.

Missy quietly took her leave, and I sat in the silence of the soft evening sun on our porch. The creaking ebb and flow of my rocking chair soothed my aching head, though my thoughts were racing. Mindlessly, my fingers played with the amulet around my neck, its faint vibrations twinging on my skin like tiny firecrackers. It comforted me to feel its tender pull.

My weary eyes turned to the road as a gust of blustery wind scattered the dust and dirt into a billowing, blinding cloud in the distance. I watched the cloud as the wind carried it closer and closer, the setting sun staining it a rich, bloody red. All I saw was red, and my eyes could not look away. Like the pull of the amulet's touch, something in the air was tugging at the spirit and the life in me. It was a trembling, funny feeling that I couldn't shake. I looked on until from in the red-stained cloud, two shadowed figures emerged.

It was as if those two shadows walking toward me came from the dust itself. I stood and trembled, confused at the feeling of wanting to run toward them full-fledged and free, as if freedom itself arose from the shadows. They emanated a warmth that only a holy fire could bring. Then I tasted the change they brought with them on the wind—a sweet-veiled essence tinged with something sour hidden in that fiery humidity. It fell thickly upon my cotton-dry mouth and filled me with fear. Something was coming.

I wanted to run, no longer toward the shadows and the light, but to the safety of my dark house and the tall pines at my back. The heat of the evening was too much for me, those shadows were getting closer. Shuffling quickly back to the house, my fumbling fingers tried desperately to grasp the handle of the screen door. My deep breathing quickened; my heartbeat raced until my ears ached with the pressure. Through its deafening sound, I heard a whisper in the air come rushing toward me with the last of the wind as the dust coated everything around me.

Ruith.

I managed to pull the door open, when my fear was interrupted by a loud, clear call from behind me.

"God's blessing upon you, Sister!"

That sourness in the air sank heavily to my tongue and I could not answer. I turned cautiously, my heart sinking to the pit of my stomach as I saw a man who I knew must be Brother Wise. He was dressed fancy-like in his crisp white dress shirt and colorful suspenders. Red, they were red. A deep red that stood out like a sore thumb in the evening light. His suit jacket was neatly folded over his arm, but seeing me face to face, he quickly donned the jacket, fiddling with his tie to make it just so in the reflection of the front parlor window. His eyes hung there on himself for an instant too long for my taste.

A little vain, I thought to myself.

Satisfied with his appearance, he smiled and grabbed the hand of the woman next to him with a prideful gusto. The woman beside him seemed uncomfortable.

Must be Mrs. Prudence Wise, I thought, as I eyed her with a beam of jealousy in my wide-eyed stare.

Mrs. Prudence Wise was dressed in the fanciest Sunday best I'd ever seen. Most folks in these parts made the clothes they wore. Earthen colors suited to the seasons were their wear, but this woman was nothing but store-bought finery, every inch, and every stitch of her. And bright, bright colors too. Nothing like us, nothing like the people here.

Brother Wise smiled placidly up at me, teeth glaringly white. His eyes sparkled with a strange sort of gleam. They made me shiver.

"Mrs. Jaelle Bennett," he said in a rich, warm tone that seemed to slither on the air to me.

It was soothing and sweet but underneath lay a note of something deeper and darker, a bit like muddied earth and roots. It did not sit well with me. I had the wherewithal to smile back and nod. Brother Wise smiled all the wider and took off his wide-brimmed hat, tucking it neatly under his arm. Gently, so that he wouldn't crush it.

Nodding, he said, "Sister Bennett, my name is Brother Elijah Wise. The new pastor of The Narrow Way Baptist Church. It's a pleasure to meet you."

He held out his hand to me. I nudged myself to the edge of the porch and took it. As our hands touched, skin upon skin, I felt a fluttering flash of shadow pass from his fingertips to mine. With the shadow, there came a flicker of fire that quickly spread into a blaze in my mind's eye. All I saw was fire in his eyes.

I pulled my hand away, nearly fainting where I stood. I held onto the porch railing to steady myself. My other hand trembled at my side, but he didn't notice. His gaze was strange and distant, as if he had also seen that same fire. The air grew eerily still, and no one spoke for a long while. Gaze met wary gaze, but that was all. Finally, I watched his cautious eyes shake off their fright, and he smiled at me, sweet and wide.

"Is your husband at home? I was hoping to meet all your family on this fine evening."

I was still trembling, but I heard the words slip casually from my lips. "Jeremy ain't home. It's just the two of us on the farm."

Brother Wise seemed disappointed at that for the briefest of instances, but he was quick to recover.

"This is my wife, Prudence. I do hope that you and Prue will cultivate a great friendship, as I hope all the ladies in our church will. After all, fellowship is a blessing given us by the Lord as well."

Prudence Wise said nothing. She merely smiled and gave a nod of her head. She too had an air of strangeness about her that I couldn't quite understand. I smiled back at her with little conviction. She noticed, as did her husband.

Brother Wise cleared his throat, and with a nervous crack in his voice, he said, "I've heard you are a very devout member of our church, Mrs. Bennett."

Is that all you've heard, Brother Wise?

He tried to smile off the awkwardness of my silence with more talk.

"That is very pleasing to my heart. I only wish that all those in our community were as pious and loving toward the Lord."

A sharp dig at my husband, to be sure. I was beginning to dislike this new preacher very much. The longer I looked at him, the more his sharp-edged, reddened face with its five o'clock shadow and scouring pock-marked cheeks seemed anything but holy. I could feel his judgment from where I was perched on the edge of the porch. It took all of me not to bellow and wail and send him away.

I gripped the railing so tightly that the crumbling paint beneath my fingernails began to chip and fall to the ground below. The remnants poked at my skin like little daggers, awakening a rage in me that I had never known. I could tell that he was uncomfortable in the quiet, and though manners declared that I must ask him in, I knew I couldn't allow that. He didn't dare to enter. This was not a place of God in his eyes, and he wanted nothing to do with it.

"I best be getting inside. My husband will be home soon, and I've not started his supper yet."

I spoke slowly so that they could hear every disagreeable syllable, every note of the disruption I felt at their coming. Brother Wise nodded and replaced his hat atop his head, his face flushing all the redder with what I gathered was embarrassment. With that, he took his wife's hand and turned away, back toward the dusty road from whence they came.

As I watched them begin to leave, a sudden pang of guilt sprang up in my breast. I called after him.

"Brother Wise—"

Almost reluctantly, he turned back to me. His wife kept her eyes on him with a note of unease.

"Welcome."

I had said all I wished to, and I had done my duty. With his welcome received, he smiled his last and went on his way. I watched Brother Elijah Wise and his wife disappear into the gloomy darkness that had begun to creep up from the distant horizon. When they were far from sight, I turned my eyes away and went into the house, slamming the door behind me.

All I can see are the apple trees. Rows and rows of them, dead and dry and begging for the flame that is rising quickly to their hungry boughs. The fire engulfs them with a steady whoosh. The trees disappear, and all I see there in the shadowy whiteness of the snow is the fire.

I awoke in the middle of the night, shivering in the stifling air. The scent of smoke and ash still twinged in my nostrils, my skin still flushed from the nearness of that phantom fire. But it was a dream. Only a dream.

Jeremy slept beside me, clinging to me so hard that I couldn't get up or move. I stayed, peering out into the darkness with fear. I prayed, but silence was the only thing that answered.

4 Blood For Blood

There was no blood come Saturday. Or the next day. Or the next. Nothing all week. My time of the month hadn't come for quite a while. Up until that day, I hadn't paid much attention. Come Saturday, I knew that it wasn't going to show.

As I peered down at my pristinely white undergarments in the early morning light, my heart fell straight down into my empty, aching stomach. It sat there churning in the rotten dread I now carried. A child had always been what I desired, even before I married Jeremy. After losing five babies before I could even hold them in my arms and give them proper names, I had long ago given up the notion. Jeremy was all but done after the first dead child. Since I'd lost so many, he swore he'd leave if I couldn't carry another.

A flutter of delight leaped up to my chest at the thought of a child inside me. I quickly quelled it and buried it deep down. A child wasn't promised, and even if I was with child, there would be no joy. Not if Jeremy knew. I shivered in my fleece-lined slippers and quickly wrapped my robe around my body. In a daze, I pulled on some clothes and shoes, my mind bent on only one thing.

I had to get to Mama's. She would know what to do in a moment like this. I knew I didn't. My nerves were afire with little lightning sparks, and my body was trembling.

I could hear Jeremy calling for me from down by the truck. He was anxious to get moving and I was dawdling away the morning in worry. I made my body stop stuttering and quaking, and rushed down the stairs to the truck, where Jeremy waited. He was sober this morning, his eyes bright and bent on me. He was looking me up and down with some kind of hunger. I shivered beneath his stare, and he smiled.

Most of our rides together were full of noise, the racket of the radio and the sounds of the truck as it sped down the dirt road. The ride that morning was quiet. So silent that even the truck's rickety axles seemed to hush just for us. Just for us not to talk, to let the quiet sink in.

Jeremy seemed like he was tied up in a bundle of nerves. I wondered if he knew that I might be with child. Perhaps he could smell it on me, like a dog or a wolf, sniffing to destroy any sign of new life. I turned to him and almost spoke, but the words jumbled up on my lips and would go no further. What would I have said anyway? It was not the time then to spout out such things. Besides, I might be wrong.

Jeremy's truck stopped with a jolt in front of Mama's house. Instantly, it seemed as if the warm sun had slipped into a sliver of shadow and crept away. Nestled beneath the mountain and the wide valley below, it was always cooler at Mama's house.

Jeremy cleared his throat. That was my cue to get out. I took it and slid out of the patchy leather seat, the bare skin of my leg catching on the jagged edges of its holes. They scraped me, but I let them. It woke me from my troubled thoughts. Before I shut the door behind me, I took one last look at Jeremy before he left me.

A flash of red. Bodies intertwined. And a muttered name, a whisper in the dark I couldn't understand.

There he was, sitting in all his funk and glory, his ratty white T-shirt full of stains wrapped around his flabby body. Nothing to look at. Nothing to tempt me. My mouth went bone dry, desperate to scream at him, to revel in my hatred for this pathetic creature before me. Instead, I slammed his truck door shut and turned my back on him. It was the least that I could do. He didn't seem to notice my little act of rebellion. My silent scream of rage. He just skidded off without a glance or a word. I didn't watch him leave.

Mama wasn't waiting for me that day. I swallowed hard, anxious and afraid to see her. I had to have my wits about me to try and tell her. With a deep, unsteady breath, I made it to the door of her shack. Through the tattered screen, I met my mother's face, her gnarled features already scrunched into a grimace.

"Mama," I gasped, startled by her sudden appearance. I could feel my cheeks flushing wildly. I gripped my purse tightly. Breathless, I said, "Please, Mama, can I come inside?"

With a bestial grunt, she shook her head, eyeing sharply every inch of me. I didn't care to be held under her microscope and so I lowered my eyes. The door opened a crack.

From inside, I heard, "When was you gonna tell me that you was with child?"

I stumbled on my words. "I-I don't know if I am."

She spat a muddied wad of chewing tobacco on the porch at my feet, chuckling with a gurgling hiss as she wiped her mouth clean.

"Nonsense that is," the old woman snarled. "A woman knows. *You* know. Besides, I can smell it on ya. It be the scent of new life. Of a soul bent on this world with a wild fury."

Her eyes drifted away, listening to the distant bird calls and the waves of wind. I waited in silence for what seemed like hours. Waited for her to drift back to me with her words of wisdom. As a Christian, I no longer listened to her soothsaying, nor bent to her magic touch. Yet here in this raw, unyielding moment, I allowed myself to lean eagerly toward her. Hungry for her words, her truth, whatsoever that might be.

"I'll have the child?" I stammered out.

She shuffled her deep-stained tongue across her cracked lips and said nothing.

"It'll live?" I asked.

Her eyes narrowed, and she hesitated. Our gazes met, and I saw the faintest sliver of fire resting in her eyes. Like the fire I'd seen in Brother Wise's eyes only the day before. It frightened me.

"The child brings with it the breath of life and the touch of death. Be wary. For a veil rests upon that child that even I cain't pull back. It rests in shadows where the light cain't reach. Darkness follows you at its comin'."

My heart sank with fear.

"What're you saying, Mama?"

I pulled the screen door open wider, standing before her at the threshold. She grabbed hold of my hand, gripping it tightly. So tightly, I couldn't pull away. I don't know what she saw in her mind's eye when she touched me, but her gaze was wide with fear. Her hand trembled in mine, the tendrils of her lifeforce seeping into my fingertips, teasing a power I couldn't quite grasp.

She pulled away with a gasp. I had never seen my mother so terrified. This was no ordinary fear, but something much deeper and darker. I could feel it dripping from her, seeping into the wood beneath my feet and tingling up my toes.

"Blood for blood, Jaelle," she said. "Blood for blood."

Then she was gone. Fluttering and flitting among the shadows inside. I stood in the wake of her at the front door, breathless and shaking. My hand fell gently to my aching belly, as if to calm the child inside. Yet it was really I who needed a soothing touch, a calming word. Slowly, I entered and closed the door behind me, a smile creeping upon my lips.

A soft darkness overwhelmed me, and I felt safe.

The smell of smoke and pungent earth from my mother's kitchen played about my senses, coddling me and urging me to stay in that chamber of quiet and stillness. That twilight between sleep and wakefulness. But I couldn't stay there.

Fuil na talmhainn. Eirich.

I heard my mother's voice in the twilight, stirring the stillness with a quake of thunderous surety.

"Till up the earth. Prepare your land. Mix yourself some honey, milk and yeast and pour it into the four corners of your land. As you do it, say these words, "Fuil na talmhainn. Eirich."

My eyes fluttered open at those ancient words. They rattled from my mama's lips like satin and silk, easing me awake. I had heard such words all my childhood as she tended to the needs of the farmers and their families. Though I didn't understand them, they filled my heart with comfort.

I was nestled in a dark corner of the kitchen on my mama's small cot nearest the fire. On the other side of the room, I saw Mama with a crotchety-looking old man. A farmer, for sure and certain, by the looks of him. His clothes were moth-eaten and old, stained like his hands with the blood of the earth, the mud and manure that made up his livelihood.

He stooped over Mama's worktable as she prepared a talisman. He looked less than pleased with her. Still, she took her time, her hands slow and shaky in their work.

"And that'll bring me goodly crops? Make the rain come?" the old man croaked, itching with impatience.

My mama's eyes were alight in the flame of the fire. She looked up at him, handing him the talisman.

"You'll have your goodly crops, Ismael."

He snatched up the small leather bag.

My mother eyed him sharply. "If you do as I say."

He grunted, turning away. "It better, woman. Else."

"Else what?" My mama's voice was all arsenic and sweet poison, as she looked up at him with a sneer, challenging him silently.

He glanced back with a shiver. It seemed that he thought twice about whatever threat hung heavy on his lips.

He simply said, "It better."

Then he was gone. I sat up quietly, rubbing my eyes gently and blinking in the dim light. Mama looked my way with a huff.

"You sleep like you was dead, girl."

"Didn't know I was so tired."

She stood and put her box of charms back on the edge of the blackened mantel.

"It's the babe in your belly. It'll suck the life right outta ya, as well as the youth from your bones."

Her words struck me hard. She seemed a little displeased with the idea of a child. I could only wonder what Jeremy would think when I told him.

"Drink this."

A wooden cup was pushed in my face. Mama stooped down low with it to meet me eye to eye. It smelled foul and tasted even worse.

"Go on now. Drink it up. It'll get that baby growing good," Mama said.

I drained the cup dry, and Mama nodded, satisfied. She took back the cup and shuffled to the fire, staring into it. It was quiet for a good long moment.

"You watch yourself telling that husband of yours 'bout that baby. He's liable to kill it. *And* you."

I shivered a little where I sat.

"Yes, Mama."

I waited for her to turn back to me, but she didn't.

I made Jeremy's favorite supper that night, just to please him. I knew the news I was prepared to give him would anger him enough. Maybe, just maybe, a good meal in his belly would help him to forget. Maybe, just maybe, he would be happy this time.

I laid the vittles out on the table with care, just a minute to spare before he was set to be home. It was lovely, if I do say so myself. I even lit little candle stubs and placed them around the dishes, and a vase of spring flowers from the garden in the center. I smiled just a little at my own genius.

I looked up at the cuckoo clock hanging on the wall above my fine feast as it began to strike the hour. The little yellow canary inside its workings peeked out from its perch and gave a shout at me.

It's time! It's time! It's time!

Indeed, it was time.

Placing myself at my usual spot opposite Jeremy's chair, I waited. I waited until the sun had long since set and the stars were blinking in the sky, blotting out some of the grim darkness with their sweet fairy lights. The only light in the kitchen was the faintly fading candles on the table, the wax pooling lazily on the tablecloth. The food was stone cold, and the house flies were swarming low over my platter of chicken.

Let 'em have it. Let 'em have it all.

In the flickering light of the candles, I sat before the feast I had made, staring into the shadows until my eyes flashed with weariness. Tears welled in them, ready to burst at the brim, but I didn't let them come.

Jeremy!

A woman's voice carried down the hall. A cry of ecstasy and passion. It made me shiver and shake, but I knew there was no one there.

The cuckoo clock chimed the late hour. My heart sank low and deep. There were only two reasons that Jeremy would ever be this late: he was out running his liquor, or he was out with the boys drinking up every last dollar he'd made bootlegging over the weekend. The weekends were for bootlegging, which meant the weekdays were for getting drunk.

A sickly sour taste of bile crept up into my mouth at the thought of him coming home so drunk he couldn't stand. The mess he'd make. The rage he'd let out on anything in reach, including me. Usually, a numb sort of acceptance would settle over me in times like this.

Just keep quiet and stay out of the way.

Fear was useless. Only silence would keep me safe. But now there was a child to keep safe too. My hands again flew to my belly, eager to feel the life inside tickle at my fingertips. A twinge of the deliciously sweet sense of something real growing just below the surface of my skin. That power was there, faint and fluttering, but it was there. The power of life inside me. It soothed me in the darkness, until I heard the raucous sound of Jeremy's voice just outside.

I sat still, not moving and not breathing. I listened as his loud, clumsy footsteps climbed the front porch steps. The screen door creaked open and slammed shut with a *whoosh* of foul air that rushed toward me. Step by step, he moved in the dark. Then he was there, standing in the shadows of the doorway, his dark eyes glowering down at me. Jeremy swayed on his feet, squinting in the dark to see me.

He looked—disappointed. He shuffled to the table and plopped down into his seat. Tucking his napkin into his shirt collar like nothing was amiss, he looked at the spoiled bounty laid before him and smiled.

"Woman, you must've done somethin' mighty wicked for to have cooked such a fine meal on a Saturday," he slurred.

I said nothing.

He huffed under his rotten breath and plunked a drumstick onto the empty plate before him. A mountain of mashed potatoes was added, his eyes on me alone. He was watching me with the precision of a hawk. Drunkenness made some men sloppy and disoriented. It only made Jeremy all the sharper and more accurate. And he knew it.

I knew I should keep quiet when he was like this,

but I was awful tired, and my back ached from sitting in that hard wooden chair for hours. In my weariness, the words tumbled out of my lazy lips.

"Jeremy—we're gonna have a child."

I regretted those words as soon as they fell out of my mouth. Jeremy's full mouth stopped mid-chew and hung wide open. His eyes glared with a fiery rage that the candlelight only seemed to accentuate with hellish delight. He was silent for a long while before a smile slowly crept upon his lips. He began to laugh, low and churlish-like, and the grating sound wouldn't stop.

I couldn't hold back my tears. I turned my head away as they fell down my flushed cheeks.

"You think you're gonna keep it?" he demanded. He wiped his mouth with the back of his hand. It wiped the smile off his face too. "You'll kill it just like the rest. Your insides are 'bout as welcoming as a graveyard. Everything dies there."

He thought that was awful funny and leaned back in his chair to bellow with laughter. He nearly fell out of it, but that didn't stop him.

Suddenly, his face turned pale green, and all that chicken and potatoes came up and out in a slurry onto the table. The vomit flowed out of his mouth until I thought his stomach might fall out with it. When he was finished, he wiped his mouth and gave me a wicked smile. Then he got up from the table. He disappeared noisily into the shadows, while I sat in his mess and let the tears come.

5 My Cup Runneth Over

Early in the morning, long before Jeremy was awake and stirring, I was up. I hadn't slept a wink all night. My mama's words had run round my head until they were all I heard.

Fuil na talmhainn. Eirich.

I didn't know what they meant, but I could feel the power in them bleeding into my flesh and bones, seeping into the air I breathed, until I really felt them. Mama believed there was power in those words. The old man at her door believed there was power in them, enough to pay Mama just to say them.

At the Narrow Way, they preached against such things. Charms and spells were the devil's playground, and you could lose your soul if you gave them power. Surely, if the preachers feared them, they held their own sort of strange power. A kind of magic born of the earth that settled into the hands of believers like my mama.

I wondered then what kind of power this magic really had. If it only worked in her hands, or if anyone could capture it. Hold it. Contain it. And use it.

God help me for having such a thought.

I said that over and over again, as I carried a pitcher of milk, yeast, and honey in one hand and a spade in the other, out across the fields to the orchards. I came to the first corner of our land as the dawn light pierced the sky with its purples and pinks. I meant to use the spade, but something didn't seem right about that. Instead, I knelt to the ground and used my hands to dig up the earth. When it was deep enough, I dampened it with my mama's concoction and whispered those mysterious words over it.

Fuil na talmhainn. Eirich.

They felt like blood dripping from my mouth. Life and something else flowing from each syllable as I said them. Something full of its own power, giving it to me as I stood over the offering I had made. I trembled in that power. Trembled all the way to each of the other three corners of our land and did the same. The sun was rising fast as I finished and headed back to the house. Still, I couldn't stop shaking, even as the house came into view, its faded white shadow looming in the near distance. I was afraid. Afraid of what I had just done and what God would think of me.

As I entered the house, I saw Jeremy standing unsteadily with his backside to the stove. He must have been cold, because he was shivering from head to toe, his face white as a sheet. He turned to me with a frightful look when I came into the kitchen with my pitcher in hand. He looked plum confused at my mud-caked hands and stocking feet.

I made my way straight to the sink and pumped a volley of water on my shaking hands, washing them clean of the spell I had conjured out in those fields. I looked down at my glistening, wet skin in the light of the morning sun. It gleamed like a newborn babe in the river Jordan, fresh and full of life. Maybe, just maybe God wouldn't be so angry. After all, I did it for Jeremy.

"Where the hell you been at the crack of dawn, woman?"

I gave him as innocent a look as I could and turned to walk away, my bare feet padding along quietly past him.

"Prayin'."

That night, the rain came, plentiful and steady. The air drifting through the open bedroom window smelled of good earth and musky sweetness. Thunder rolled softly overhead, rumbling across our tin roof. It woke me from a troubled sleep. There was silence in the bed beside me, so I crept my hand across the cool cotton sheets to feel for Jeremy. All I felt was the moist indent where his body had been, and nothing more.

Bang!

Downstairs, the screen door slammed shut. I sat up straight in the bed, staring out into the pouring rain. Jeremy was out there. After the other night, I wouldn't have cared where he was, but something just didn't feel right. The rain lulled my weary eyes to close again. Yet the air was fraught with a strange sort of electricity that tugged and pulled at me until I opened them again. There was something out there in the night that I needed to see.

My bare feet touched the floor, and I slipped out of the bed, too distracted by the pull and tug outside to put on my slippers. I crept through the hall and down the stairs, and I stopped at the screen door. There was Jeremy outside, blubbering like a baby while he leaned his head against one of the small pillars that held up the porch awning. He stood there, crying, rivulets of snot and saliva dangling from his face and dripping like honey to the ground below as he watched the rain. I'd never seen a man cry, least of all Jeremy. He hadn't shown the slightest bit of emotion save for lust and anger since we'd met, oh so many years ago. He was a man of very few words and even fewer feelings. He was what *he* liked to call a "modern man" of the world, born and bred to till the earth, nursed on liquor, and schooled in black and white and rage. He was his father's son, who was his father's son, who was the man that everyone feared, even in death. There was no failure, and there certainly wasn't any crying for a man like that, the man he was meant to be. I kept quiet and still at the door. Not daring to move or even breathe, lest he turn around and whoop me something good.

A flash of lightning streaked clear across the sky and settled its illuminated roots right down in the middle of the orchard. It was quickly followed by a thunderous crash. The light and the sound startled me, and I nearly jumped clear off the ground. I gasped. Jeremy heard. He whipped around with a reddened face full of spite and something else I couldn't understand. His eyes pierced the night, glaring though they were far away and eerie. The lightning flashed in their dark centers and made him ghost-like and frightening. Even more so than he usually was in my eyes.

We stared at each other for an endless age, not speaking. Finally, he had sense enough to wipe away the wetness from his eyes, sniffling hard.

"What you want, woman?" he snarled.

Bidh an spiorad a 'fàs leis an talamh.

I didn't quite hear him. Something else had called me, from way out in the fields of gnarled apple trees. Past Jeremy's yelling, past the thunder and rain, a voice that wasn't quite a voice whispered from the trees. Calling for me. Calling my name. I looked past Jeremy, and without a word, I followed that voice. Off the porch. Out into the pelting rain. As soon as my feet hit the muddied earth, I could feel that pang of power surging through my skin. Through all of me, leading me.

Jeremy yelled for me, but the din of the storm was too strong for his rage. It drowned out his voice with the swiftness of an ocean wave. That strange voice on the wind was all that I heard now. It had grown from a faint flicker of sound to a crackling crash louder than the thunder. It led me into the orchard, past rows and rows of dead and rotting trees. My feet knew where they were headed, though I didn't.

A wave of dizziness came over me, and I stumbled over to an apple tree, resting my trembling hand on it to steady myself. That same power that rose up from the earth to meet me now played about my fingers, pushing at my palm to wake me to its gentle stroke of life. Yes, there was life there within that deadened tree. I felt it. In the pulsing flashes of lightning, I glanced up at the tree's low-bent branches, and my eyes grew wide.

Jaelle.

The life-breath and the power called to me. I pressed my hand hard into the bark of the tree to feel it.

"Jaelle!"

Suddenly, I was whipped around to face Jeremy. Now drenched, breathless and furious, he looked fit to be tied, and the spell was over.

"What's the matter with ya?" he screamed.

My mouth parted, but not a word tumbled out. My hand was still planted firmly on the bark of the tree, fingering its gentle grooves, its sacred pattern. Slowly, my fingers rose up, up, up, to point to the highest bough of the tree. Jeremy's eyes followed to find the little bursting bud peering down at him from the tippy top of the branch.

His eyes grew as big as saucers, wide with delight and disbelief, and a sigh tumbled out of his mouth.

"I'll be damned," he whispered.

There wasn't time to say anymore. He was gone, dashing from tree to tree in the rain, looking for more hopeful buds. And there they were. Every tree was dressed and decorated with fresh life. As he ran, he began to whoop and holler, dancing amidst the shadows of the trees. Then he looked back at me with something akin to pleasure, a look full of light and hope and happiness. The first I'd seen on his face in quite some time. He smiled at me, wide and toothy, and I smiled back.

Under my breath, I whispered, "Thank you."

I wasn't sure if it was to the Good Lord I gave my thanks, or to the earth that had answered me. My body flushed with fear as I said it, but somehow, it seemed right.

PART TWO

SUMMER

Behold, children are a heritage from the Lord, the fruit of the womb a reward. Like arrows in the hand of a warrior are the children of one's youth. Blessed is the man who fills his quiver with them!

Psalm 127:3-5

Dandelion
(Cankerwort)

a widely distributed weed of the daisy family, with a rosette of leaves, bright yellow flowers followed by globular heads of seeds with downy tufts, and stems containing a milky latex

helps to improve psychic powers and intuition

the root can be used to call spirits and grant wishes

6 A Church Man is a Dead Man

I'm dreaming. There's a young girl dressed in a pale baby blue dress with a white pinafore. Her hair is the color of fresh summer wheat, and her eyes are dark brown like rich soil after a rainstorm.

"Siuthad!" The little girl yells as she rushes ahead of me into the orchard, which is now growing wild and full of life.

"Lean mise."

She laughs as she dances between the trees. They are heavy-laden with new fruit and bright green leaves. Their burdened branches creak with the weight of the fruit in the soft breeze.

I let the girl run ahead of me.

"Lean mise."

Let her dance. Let her play. There is not a shadow in the sky, and the day is bright and warm.

The girl turns back to me and smiles. My heart leaps with tender joy and aches all the while with a niggling of fear. As if all of this could vanish in an instant. The girl doesn't notice my smile fade. She hops up on her tippy toes and reaches for a ripe piece of fruit. Though it hangs low on the bowing branch, she cannot grasp it with her small, eager fingers.

I rush to help her, plucking the fruit with ease and handing it to her with a smile. She smiles back and takes a bite. Her face grows pale as blood drips from her lips. The apple is rotten inside, rotten through and through. Worms poke out of its decaying flesh. The girl stares me down, her eyes black as midnight, and she screams.

The walk to church on Sundays was a lonesome time for me. Jeremy had long ago given up what little faith he was brought up with, and for the life of me, I couldn't get him to come with me. I used to ask him in the early days, but his answer was always, "A church man is a dead man."

His answer always frightened me. It was too near to my mama's own feelings about the Christians. Too near to that godless rage that permeated every shape and shadow of my mama's world. For all their dislike of one another, my husband and Mama were more similar than they would ever admit. But I saw it.

I couldn't drive, and even if I could, Jeremy would have never let me borrow his truck. I didn't mind though. The walk was peaceful and nice. I set out at dawn to walk the seven miles to the Narrow Way, praying to God Almighty that my feet would carry me there fast enough for the service at nine.

These days, though my feet knew the way like the back of my hand—the flesh was willing, but the spirit was weak. I had seen Brother Wise's grand entrance into our fold. I'd seen him rush into our lives like a spiritual storm, all frightful winds and lightning. It was enough to drive a body mad.

Our old pastor, Brother Wallace, had been a good man, and his sermons each Sunday were like Jesus come down from the Mount to preach to every one of us. Leaving services on those Sunday mornings felt as if I'd been to Paradise, like stepping off a cloud to the earth below. I felt its power all through me, and it was peaceful and good.

I couldn't say the same for Brother Wise or his sermons. I didn't much care for either. There was a touch of fire in that man's eyes when he looked at me, something maddening and unholy. The words he spat out from the pulpit every week were full of nothing but burning brimstone and hellfire. A body would feel awful low and frightened stepping out of his church, as if the Lord knew your every sin, and the sky would fall if you hadn't laid your heart down to repent.

Repent! That was Brother Wise's favorite word. To the ladies of the sewing circle and the evening Bible study: *repent!* To the simple-minded farmers who could barely make their mark on a legal paper: *repent!* To the little children scattered in the fields and fluttering through the grass with laughter: *repent!*

To me...well, at first, he didn't speak much to me after that first evening on my front porch. He did ask me once about my husband—if he attended our church, or if he had fallen away from the Lord. After my muddled answer, he came to the swift conclusion that Jeremy and I needed God more than any other members of the congregation.

After that, the eyes of Brother Wise were always on me—*on us*. As my belly grew, so too his gaze grew even narrower on me in the last pew of that small church. Every Sunday, its walls closed in a little more, and the air grew thinner until I could barely breathe.

This Sunday was no different. The walk to the service had been less than easy. I couldn't seem to catch my breath. All the while, the church choir sang its familiar hymns, ones I knew by heart. I couldn't sing along though, not this time. My head felt faint amid my shallow panting breaths. I closed my eyes, swaying in my seat like a drunkard on his last drink for the night. A heavy veil of sweat blanketed my forehead. It was so thick I could feel every last drop slither and slide in a serpentine path down my temples to my neck. With my eyes shut, the world went black, and I dreamt of cool darkness.

I slip down deep, deep, deeper still until the darkness is a hole. A deep, dark hole at the bottom of the world, at the end of everything.

I realize I am dead in that hole. Dead and gone if I

don't scramble my way back out of it. So, I do. My slowing heartbeat pounds in my ears as I claw at the walls of the hole. The hole is made of damp earth and deep roots that spring out from everywhere. It smells of death and decay, like a dead animal left out in the sun. Only now, I realize that the hole is a grave.

Looking up I see the entire church congregation hugging the surface of that deep, deep grave. At its head is Brother Wise, his fiery eyes gleaming down at me, an angry sneer on his lips. Mrs. Prudence Wise stands at his side, her green eyes flashing like levin fire. A smile creeps across her blush-pink lips. Her fist is clenched tightly at her side, holding onto something. With a deep breath, she tosses that something into the hole with me. My amulet, but on my flesh it becomes a slithering snake.

Brother Wise speaks, and the word from his mouth sinks its way down to me with the foulest of winds.

"Repent!"
"Amen!"

The roaring resonance of the church choir singing those final notes startled me to a shattering wakefulness. I gasped loudly in the sudden silence. I looked up in a fright as heads began to turn in the pews ahead of me. Up, up, up to the pulpit of Brother Wise, who was himself looking in my general direction with a glowering, dark stare.

The room was deathly still. So still that every blessed child fidgeting in their seats made such a noisy racket that it echoed like thunder through the whole church. You could see every father and mother flinch at the sound. I didn't flinch. I was staring straight at Brother Wise, and he was staring straight at me.

Ruith.

There was that innocuous voice again, spinning around in my head like a broken record. It was sharp this time, ripe with purpose and urgent intention. Still, I didn't understand it.

I glanced up at the giant wooden cross hanging high above Brother Wise's head. The sun hit it just so, making a harsh shadow across his red face. Then my eyes fell on Brother Wise. Oh, how he looked at me. As if the devil himself were at my back taunting him, raising a storm of hellfire that would rush to his feet.

I couldn't breathe. I just sat there, gasping for air while my hands clung tightly to my belly. Everyone was watching me. Everyone and Brother Wise. A chill shivered and burned down my back. My flesh was on fire, and he knew it. Knew that I was burning before the eyes of he and God. Burning, burning, burning.

It was Brother Wise who broke that eerie silence.

"Sister Bennett?" his voice echoed thickly on the air.

Sweat poured down my face as I gulped hard, jumping to my feet. For a moment, I only stood there, anxiously avoiding all those wary eyes upon me. There was one pair of eyes I couldn't shake. There at the head of the congregation was Mrs. Prudence Wise, her vivid green eyes flashing violently in the bright sunlight beaming down on her. She was watching me. Watching me so closely I felt she could see down to my very bones. I couldn't bear it any longer. I pushed past Missy, whose face was redder than a summer burn with embarrassment. She tried to pull me back into the pew.

"You're makin' a right spectacle of yourself, honey," she hissed low, her grip on me hard.

But I was stronger. I felt a prickling surge of something powerful run straight through me, settling in my frail fingertips until they burned. A shocking spark flew from my fingers to Missy's hold on me. She cried out, and the service abruptly stopped. With that searing force behind them, my fingers peeled her hand away from my skin, and I was free. Above me, I heard a crack. A bit of dust and crumbled ceiling tumbled to my toes.

Missy looked frightened. Everyone looked frightened. Everyone but Mrs. Prudence Wise. She just kept staring as if she could peel away my skin to see the power in me. I hurried away from those watchful eyes, that looming shadow of the Lord and Prudence Wise. I ran out.

As I hit the steamy morning air, my mouth burst open, gulping it in. It didn't soothe my aching lungs, but a hot breeze brushed damply across my face and urged the stuttering breaths from my lips, drying the drops of sweat from my brow.

I waited for someone to come for me. To come shouting and carrying on about what a spectacle I'd made of myself. No one did. From where I stood, I could feel the heavy shadow of the church's steeple weighing on me. I stepped away into the shade of the tall dogwood trees. It was cooler under those trees, their shadows caressing my burning skin. I could feel the very essence of their curling, outstretched branches, heavy-laden with lush leaves, reaching for me. I reached out to them to feel that spark of life play about my eager fingertips. A brush of something real on my skin that awakened and refreshed me. My breathing slowed and my body cooled.

A rustling in the tree above my head caused me to glance up as leaves fluttered down to meet me. There I saw the little girl from my dream, clinging to the barky branches of the dogwood tree, her face a myriad of shimmering sunlight and shadows from where she was perched. In the glistening light, she smiled at me. I smiled back. The sharp crack of the tree branch upon which she sat rippled through the leaves down to me.

Crrraaaaaaack!

I could see the tree branch ripping beneath her hold on it, but she did not look afraid. She did not look anywhere but at me with a smile.

Crrraaaaaaack!

The little girl sank lower as the branch hung on by a sinew of barky flesh. Still, her smile didn't fade from her lips. Her eyes never left mine.

I woke from my dumbfounded stupor and called out to her, as I tried to climb up the tree. The bark was slippery beneath my Sunday shoes and my hands were shaking too much for me to grab hold of the high branches. Again and again, I tried, as thread by thread the branch broke free. Try as I might, I couldn't get up to her.

Grounded and shaking, I called up to her once again. Her smile grew wider, unnaturally wide. She lifted both her hands from the branch. In that instant, it gave way, and she came tumbling down toward me. I stepped back and closed my eyes, too frightened to see her hit the ground. I covered my ears so I wouldn't hear the sound. And I waited.

Nothing came. No sound. No shudder beneath my feet. Nothing. After a moment, I got up the gumption to open my eyes. I searched the ground around the tree. The girl wasn't there, not a hint of her. I gasped out loud, the fright that had built up in my chest tumbling out of me like a flooded river after a long rain.

"Sister Bennett?"

I shut my mouth up tight, bottling up all that fright once again into my heavy chest. My body shivered. For the longest time I didn't dare turn around. I knew who I would see.

It was Brother Wise. The service had ended, and people were barreling out of the red double doors into the hot morning sun. All of them eyeing me. Brother Wise looked at me with wary kindness. A wry smile that seemed to wrap around his entire face made it eerily comical and wrong. He edged closer to me, his hand outstretched. His hands were soft, supple, and pink, not like the dirty and callused hands of the men in his congregation. Even the women here had seen hard labor, their own hands scarred, their nails brittle. Beauty was not in them. I just stared at his manicured, pink hand for a long while, while he cooed at me to come to him. His voice was velvet and suede, subtle and warm, but beneath that sun-kissed mask of gentleness, I heard a quiet hiss. It shivered up my skin until I was cold. Deep, deadly cold.

His eyes bade me to take his hand, a look like the Lord Himself come down from Heaven on his face and a golden halo of light about his brow. Yes, he looked like Heaven, but his eyes were full of hellfire. His smile was intoxicating, a sliver of a peaceful promise, and I took it. I took his hand, and he quietly led me away to the parish house.

It was a small house painted bright yellow with deep green shutters flung wide open, as were the windows. I imagined that the hot summer sun painted crisp white walls inside with nary a shadow in sight. I was sure that God would not allow dust or darkness in a place like that. A place for His beloved servant and the woman that he loved. I imagined that Mrs. Prudence Wise never had to clean the fluff around the baseboards or wash the Sunday dishes. Never had to scrub guts and grime out of her husband's undershirts. Never had to pick at the dirt beneath her fingernails from a day of work and toil. Surely, the Lord would send His angels to aid her so that not a speck of dust or dirt spoiled her snow-white hands. For sure and certain, Mrs. Prudence Wise was living in Paradise in that little yellow house with the dark green shutters.

Before I knew it, Brother Wise had led me to the front door, painted the same deep green.

Click.

The door swung open. It didn't squeal or whine like my rusted-out door with its chipped white paint and dirty half window. That door swung on its hinges like butter, smooth and sweetly silent. With the door wide open, a delicate smell wafted toward me from inside. The scent was familiar, lavender and spices. My house smelled of aged wood, pickled vegetables and my husband's funk. Didn't matter how much I cleaned, how much I wore myself out on my hands and knees scrubbing, the smell was always there.

With a gentle hand on my back, Brother Wise showed me into his house. Just as I thought, it was bright white and full of sunshine. There was not a shadow to be seen, a speck of dust, nor a thing out of place. It was perfect. Pristine, just as it should be. In the corner of the open space, Mrs. Prudence Wise sat basking in the daylight, a flowery china teapot in her hand as she watched me approach. Her eyes watched me carefully when Brother Wise led me to her small table and had me sit. I sat across from her, her gaze sharp and judgmental. Flashes of green glinted in her eyes, a spark of jealousy perhaps, as they settled on my plump belly.

I kept my head down, my trembling hands folded tightly in my lap. There was an awkward silence. I knew they were looking me over and shifting in their seats. The clanking of fragile teacups and the quiet lapping of tea from its pot told me so. Still, I didn't look up. I could feel the sweat on my brow gently cool in the soft breeze floating through the gauzy curtains toward us. The sunlight shone down on us, but it too was cool and calming. Even the sun was different here.

"Jaelle?"

The use of my front name instead of the usual formal greeting startled me to wakefulness and I glanced up with wide eyes. There was Brother Wise and his wife, smiling down at me with that wary sort of kindness again. As if they feared me. But what was there to fear? I was a good Christian woman, born again in the Lord long ago. Did I not deserve the same place at their table, the same kindness as those chits who spent their mornings, noon days, and nights gossiping about the very man that sat before me?

I blushed, surprised at my own anger, my own weakness in the face of pride and jealousy. I was a better woman than that.

"Jaelle?" Brother Wise said again, sharper this time just to get my attention.

From the look on his face, he seemed to regret that sharpness as soon as it flew from his mouth. But he got my attention this time and my fierce thoughts faded away. I looked at him with as innocent and kind an expression as I could muster. I was a good Christian woman. He had to see it. He had to see that I was worthy of God's love, worthy of this child still growing in my belly.

"Yes, Brother Wise?" I whispered, my voice weaker than I intended.

He smiled, that wariness fading from the corners of his lips with the mention of his name. His eyes grew kind. Without a word, he gestured to his wife to pour me a cup of tea. It was more of a command than a respectful request. I watched her eyes fall in answer. Quicker than a jackrabbit, she had that tea poured and pushed toward me. It sloshed a little into its accompanying saucer. She winced, glancing up to see if Brother Wise saw. He did but said nothing. Only the corners of his smile cracked a little and fell. Mrs. Prudence Wise noticed that. Her hands folded timidly in her lap and her eyes fell fast to meet them.

Brother Wise turned to me and said, "Please, take a sip. It's chamomile. To ease your tired nerves."

I did as I was told. I didn't want that smile to crack and fall for me as it had for his wife. I didn't have a notion as to what he might do if I did not obey. I had seen a man lose his temper before, lose his mind in some kind of wild rage that would drive even the Devil to fright. I had seen anger and ire, and what delved even deeper in a man's soul: hellfire and sin. I didn't want to see what lay inside *this* man.

The tea was good. Even in the heat, it felt nice on my insides and filled me with a warm fullness that seemed to calm me. I realized as I sipped away that my eyes had never left the preacher. Haply, he still gazed at me, curious and a little frightened. Finally tired of his staring, I set my teacup down, sweeping my hands across my skirt with a restless motion.

"Thank you, Brother Wise," I said.

He was quick to answer. "Please, call me Elijah. I was never one for formality. Not here inside my home at least."

"Elijah," I repeated.

The word tasted sour on my tongue. I caught a flash of a look from Prudence as I said it. I wanted to spit it out in that blue floral teacup set before me, but I held it in.

"I'm sorry for the scene I caused. I was feeling unwell is all. But I'm better now," I added.

He smiled, wider now, a glint of some shadow flickering out in his eyes. "You gave us all a tremendous fright, Mrs. Bennett. That I will say. I was beginning to think that perhaps the spirit took you or perhaps—"

He stopped himself. He and his wife shared a glance. I knew why. No, it wasn't the spirit taking me that worried them. They feared something darker. Something devilish and wild, something that only a witch would bring. But I was not my mother.

I'm a good Christian woman, Brother Wise, and nothing more. Don't you see it? Or does it pale in comparison to the blinding halo of your wife?

Again, I blushed at the rage that seemed to be conjured in this man's presence.

"It wasn't the spirit that took me. Only a faintin' spell. The heat is unbearable today is all. I'm sorry that it brought your sermon to a stop. If I'm unwell again, I'll be sure to stay at home."

Brother Elijah Wise cleared his throat and fidgeted

uncomfortably in his seat. He didn't like that idea, I gathered. The chair creaked under the weight of his solid body. His wife's smile had all but faded now. She sipped her tea quietly and didn't say a word.

"Surely, we wouldn't want you to miss a Sunday service," started Brother Wise. "But if you are unwell—" he paused to clear his throat again.

With all his hemming and hawing, it was a wonder to me that he ever got a single word out in his Sunday sermons. How could this man, who was said to be so educated and smart, be so clumsy with his tongue now?

Another throat-hacking stutter, and then, he said, "Can your husband bring you on Sundays? Mrs. Temple has told me you travel all this way on foot, and in your condition, Jaelle, I can only fear for your safety and that of your child."

When he was able to spit out his words, they ran as swift and soft flowing as a river, flooded and burgeoning with life. They made me want to obey, to run home and tell Jeremy that he was to take me to the house of the Lord, because the Lord Himself said it should be so. Brother Wise made me feel like God Himself had come to speak to me, and me alone. I could see now why the congregation believed him to be a blessing.

I dropped my head low, staring into my lap once again. "He won't. He ain't right with the Lord. He'd likely think the steeple'd fall right on 'im if he walked up to them double doors."

Brother Wise chuckled, I guessed at my ignorance, but I knew my husband. He didn't. Faith was not something you mentioned to Jeremy.

"Surely, that isn't true, Jaelle. The Lord is not a frightful person. He's ever-loving and kind. He invites all his children to come unto him on the holy day of rest. All his children, that is. Your husband must see that. Must know that he is loved and forgiven."

Every time he spoke my name, my heart beat a little faster. My face would have blushed were it not already burning. This man made me feel unsteady and unsure all in one sweeping breath from his lips. I felt carried away by them, somewhere far away, as if he'd put a spell on me. But a Christian woman shouldn't think such thoughts about a married preacher man.

With every word from his mouth, I was certain the Devil himself would catch me in some ungodly sin of worshipping this man, his honey-tongued laughter and the light that seemed to wash over him as he smiled on me.

Dear Lord in Heaven, help me.

I had walked into this house wary of the man. My mama had warned against him. Jeremy had said as much himself. My own heart had bidden me to stay away. Yet here I was in his house, taken by him, captivated by him. My heart skipped a beat as I stood. Still weak and unsteady, I swayed on my legs, but I quickly grounded myself. Looking at the couple in the sunlight with my bleary eyes.

I said, "I'll not speak ill of my husband here in this place. Not with the eyes of God watching, His angels above listening, and all of 'em judging me for what wrongs you want me to put upon him. My husband is a good man. A good man. And I know that there will come a day when he's right with the Lord again. But I'll not judge him. Not before you or God. I won't."

Brother Wise seemed taken aback. I didn't care. I was woozy and tired, and the road to home was long and far away. He gave me a weary half-smile, his eyes full of disappointment. At least, it seemed for the moment. He glanced at his wife, their unspoken words rubbing me the wrong way.

With a sigh, he said, "These walls are safe, Jaelle, and within them, we speak only good."

His words were godly and well-meaning, but still, I didn't trust them. Not when they came from that ever-smiling mouth of his that kept taunting me. Luring me into its sweetness and guile. I had to get away. I nodded without saying another word and made my way to the door. I was almost gone, almost out, almost free of the whiteness and the brightness and the sunlight. Away from the clanking of perfection and those saccharine-sweet smiles and those watchful, condemning eyes. My hand was on the doorknob, willing it to open of its own, so I could burst out into the hotness of the day and wake from my sickening daze.

"Sister Bennett?"

I didn't turn. I froze in my tracks, listening to Brother Wise's heavy footsteps approach me. His pansy hands slipped past mine and opened the door for me. His hat was on now, his red suit jacket draped neatly over his arm. There was that wide, open smile again. Beguiling and dangerous. Quickly, I looked away.

"Please, let me drive you home. In this heat, you're liable to faint upon the road."

As if against my will and swept up in the devilry of his godly selflessness, there I was in his fancy car speeding down the road toward my home. The ride had been quiet so far with not a peep from Brother Wise. His face was shadowed by the visor. Even in the shadows, it looked consternated and pickled with a pruned frown. It made me feel at ease somehow. His smile unnerved me.

He pulled his car up to the front of my house with its yellowed, peeling paint and sagging roof. It was nothing like his paradise back in the shadow of his church, but it was home to me. I cringed as the car came to a stop and the dust of the road swept up to blanket the lonely walkway leading up to the farmhouse. I couldn't help the sigh that tumbled from my lips.

I didn't want to go inside, but I didn't want to be

here with him either. My mind was on fire with indecision. My body made the choice for me, when his hand settled softly on mine within my lap. The breath in my lungs caught up in my throat, closing tighter with every second that passed. My head turned as fast as a spinning top to look at him. He was looking back at me with those eyes of fire, wide, full and blazing now, as if all of Hell were in them. All of Hell, and Paradise too was wrapped up in his eyes. I was breathless as they swept me away.

His mouth parted and a wispy breath whistled from his lips, as if the words he wanted had collapsed there at the back of his teeth and wouldn't come.

"Jaelle," he stuttered out.

Bang! The sound of the screen door broke the spell we both were under. I turned my head, and there was Jeremy coming up the walk. He was fuming, his face beet-red and burning. His eyes were bent on me and Brother Wise.

Brother Wise's hand shot back to the steering wheel with lightning speed. He gripped it tightly, swallowing hard. I could tell that he was frightened by the mountain of a man that was storming toward his car with an axe in his hand. As much as I didn't want to get out of that car and face the wrath of Jeremy, I couldn't stand the thought of unleashing that kind of rage on this man of God. I quickly gathered up my purse, and without a look back at the preacher, I scooted out of his car, slamming the door behind me. Jeremy stopped in his tracks and looked at me. I had at least distracted him for a moment. As soon as he saw me though, his rage ignited, and he raised the axe up.

Oh my god! He's going to kill me!

He swung at the preacher's car. Brother Wise's headlight was smashed to smithereens. Jeremy went for the other. I screamed and his eyes came for me, weapon raised high above his head. Waiting for more.

With a squeal of his tires, Brother Wise drove away in a flurry of dust and noise. I watched his fancy car dash down the road and disappear amidst the trees and brush. I turned toward the house.

It was quiet again. Quiet behind me where I knew Jeremy stood. So quiet that I could hear the rustling of the summer leaves on the trees around us, the hissing of the long grass. The dulcet sounds of the afternoon tumbled out like a voice.

Run, it said.

I didn't listen. Next thing I knew, Jeremy's hand hit me hard against my face, and everything went black.

7 What Came to Me on the Breeze

With the joy of the child, I had forgotten the hellbent desire to kill my husband. I had forgotten how cruel and harsh his hand could be. How his eyes on me, like death and darkness, could make me feel. I was as good as dead to him. Dead and gone and buried beneath the earth, or so he wished. In the hope of Spring, I had forgotten what I was to him and what he was to me.

Now, I remembered. I wanted him dead more than anything in the whole wide world. God help me, I wanted him dead. I would give my very soul away to see it done. Sure, I'd always been a Christian woman, a good one at that, but maybe I wasn't so good. Maybe I was something else entirely. Something that only Mama and the earth could understand. Something that grew up from the sod, clawed, and crawled its way up from the roots and the mud, and bloomed like a summer flower in the harshness of the sun. Maybe, just maybe.

It was a Sunday. I sat curled up in the rocking chair on the front porch. The early twilight stars poked out of the blackening velvet sky. It seemed I'd been sitting there practically all day. Jeremy kept me from going to Sunday services at the church.

"I seen that preacher man looking your way. No woman of mine is gonna stand under the same roof as that devil," he told me.

I did as I was told. I stayed. Now I was wrapped up

in the growing night, feeling nothing, my mind a blank and empty place. I pulled the faded, raggedy quilt around my shoulders with a sigh. A fluttering breeze tickled my face, waking me just a little from my nothingness. I winced as it brushed against Jeremy's handiwork, the scrapes and bruises on my cheek.

It wasn't cold, but my body couldn't seem to soak in the heat of the day. If it weren't for the blanket, I would have been shivering. Ever since that Sunday with Brother Wise, I had been sick as a dog. It felt like something had got hold of me, into the very blood and bones of me. It pushed and pushed up through my stomach, to my heavy chest until it hit my throat and lodged there, pressing to get out. I wanted to vomit, to scream, to do anything to relieve that pain inside of me.

The amulet about my neck felt heavy there, burning against my skin. The burn burrowed deep into my flesh, tugging at my ribs to reach my heart. My weak heart pounded almost out of its chamber to reach that tugging pull of power.

There was a feverish feeling in my aching head. A feeling of dread and a sickening rot in my stomach as if it were on fire. That fire had slowly spread to my chest, beating against my heart like a drum. Beating with a flush of passion and desire at the thought of Brother Wise. It was a feeling I was well ashamed of but could not shake. The way he looked at me on that day, the way his eyes were always on me. The touch of his hand on mine left me wanting more. Something I could never have—never.

I told Jeremy that something was wrong with me. I told him again and again, but he didn't listen. He didn't care. There weren't going to be any doctor's visits, no well-meaning calls from the ladies of the church. There would be none of that. Jeremy made sure of it. I was alone.

Jeremy kept himself scarce these days. There

wasn't enough liquor in the whole of these United States for him to gulp down or sell. I'm sure he was making good money with his bootlegging, but I never saw any of that. Sure, he tended to the orchard by day. The fruit was growing good and wild, but as soon as that sun set, he was gone. I didn't know when or where he slept. When I'd wake in the night, he wasn't there. The bed beside me was empty and cold. I should have been grateful that he no longer touched me. No longer ravaged my body in the dark against my will. But the more he left me alone, the more I felt alone. Like a body drifting out to sea, I was waiting to die on its treacherous waves.

The more I was left alone with my thoughts, the more I wanted that awful man dead. Dead and gone and buried beneath the roots and rocky ground. Dead, so the worms could slither through his skull and twine around his bones. Dead, so that not a soul would remember him or say his name. Dead, so I would be free. Those were the thoughts that rambled through my brain on this late summer evening. They had trembled and roared in my mind all day long like a coming storm. Now, as the darkness overwhelmed the sky, they came headlong into me. Too tired to fight them off, I listened. I let the waves of hate and tremulous fear sweep over me, drown me. I realized right then and there how strong that feeling of hate had become in me.

I hate him!

"I hate him," now that I finally spoke them, the words floated quiet-like on the wind.

As much as my heart cringed at them, they were swept up on my lips. With their coming, I imagined a flood of other words rushing from my mouth like crashing waves of filthy waste. All hateful, ugly words vomited up from the very pit of my soul. All of them black and full of pitch. Rotten. Putrid. Spoiled. They were evil words, and I knew if God heard them, He would smite my body down in an instant.

Let Him, then. I was ready to die right there.

"Kill me, then," I said into the wind. "Strike me down. Go on."

God didn't answer.

The wind did. It gusted and billowed over the land outstretched before me, picking up the dust as it swept up to my feet. With a hiss, it slithered and coiled about my legs, up my torso, until it caressed my battered cheek, and brushed softly against my lips. This wind was deathly cold, an icy touch of winter at its heels, though winter was a long way off. The bitter cold of it pinched my flushed face into a raw and angry smile. A rush of whispers fell upon the wind as it wrapped around me, coaxing me, calling me. My feet seeped into the wood of the porch so deeply that I swear I could feel every fiber, every grainy strand of its flesh. It was a part of me, and I was a part of it.

Slowly I stood, trembling and weak, a fever rushing through my body like an unbidden storm. My feet led the way, down the creaking porch steps to the dusty ground. My toes sank into the earth, sank down good and deep, until I was part of the soil. I was the sky, and the sky was me. I was the earth and the air, and they were also me. My heart climbed up and out of my chest to meet them, welcoming it all.

I sighed, peaceful and still. My spirit no longer ached and my body cool. God had not come to me, but the earth had. It had bundled me up in goodness and set my body to heal. Something God had never done. I shivered as the thought quaked through me in the silence. This is what Mama worshipped. This is what she lived and died for. I had never truly felt its power until now, seething through my fingertips and toes, deep into the very blood and bone of me. I accepted it, I knew that. I could feel the folds of my childhood faith, the bond with that wooden cross of the Lord, fading. The Lord was a shadow, and this new thing, this old way was the sun.

I was afraid. Afraid of my eagerness to turn away from the only God I had ever known. The ache in my heart was too great, the sadness too deep, and deep inside, I knew that God couldn't heal it. I could feel this new something prickling at my fingertips, poking at my flesh to get in. I was hesitant, my breathing wild and frantic. My hand slowly rose to my breast, where my mama's moonstone lay beating like a heart against my skin. It breathed; its gentle breaths matched my own. As I listened, my eyes fluttered closed. I could feel my body sway on my feet. It was like dancing and the wind kept time. Like praise and worship in the house of the Lord, I raised my hands to greet the wind and the earth and the sky.

"Jaelle."

A voice off in the distance called to me. It was eerie but familiar. The wind pushed me forward and the earth beneath my feet was willing. I went down the pebble-stone path from the house, through the high grass of the fields, to the orchard with its ripening fruit. I walked down the rows and rows of trees, peering here and there for the one who spoke. I knew that voice. It was my Great-Aunt Millicent's voice, one of my mama's people. I had known her well when I was just a young'un in pigtails and pinafores. She had always been kind to me.

"Jaelle!"

My head turned with a leap of my heart, and there she was, Miss Millicent Fairchild. She was just as I remembered her, pale blue shift dress baggy on her small, bent frame. Her shoes were off her feet, her hammer toes sinking deep into the tall green grass. Her frosty white hair was cut short, framing her round, puck-like face. She looked so much younger than her eighty-two years. She smiled and I saw the wide gap between her two front teeth. Her tongue clicked on them with a chuckle as she laid eyes on me.

"Ah, Jaelle," my name breathlessly flew from her lips as she laughed.

She sat on the grass in the shadow of one of the taller apple trees. It was indeed the tallest and it sat at the center of the orchard on a little hill. I could always see it from the house, standing tall and proud in the sun.

Aunt Millicent bade me to come and sit beside her, so I did. The evening shade was cool, fresh, and sweet. I smiled back at her when she turned to me. We were quiet for a long while, just enjoying the coming nightfall. The old woman reached up to a low hanging branch and picked a ripe red apple from the tree. With a smile, she took a big old bite, juice running down her chin speckled with white whiskers. Her fat tongue rolled the chunk of half-eaten fruit to the pocket of her cheek.

"Good is the fruit from the vine, the flesh from its branches," she said.

She offered the apple to me, and I took it. Hungrily, my mouth made quick work of the fruit she had not eaten. Wiping my mouth, I laid the apple core on my lap with a smile. It was the first thing that had tasted good in many a day.

"Seeps up the poison in ya," she said softly.

I smiled wider, but she didn't smile back. A raspy, crackling sound rose up from her chest.

"Sweet is the flesh. But beware, what lies beneath can turn as rotten as a dead thing."

That choking, gagging feeling returned, pushing up into my throat, as if something vile was going to crawl out. I clamped my hand over my mouth to keep it in. I heard the old woman sigh. It was a weighted thing that tumbled from her chest like a rockslide.

"Well, that spirit done took ya, Jaelle."

I looked at her. Her eyes were serious, her face sullen. I saw age sweeping swiftly into every crevice and wrinkle. I had never seen her look so old. Ancient as if the weight of the world lay in her bones. Her blue eyes were almost black now as they stared me down.

"That," she spat out through gritted teeth, "ain't your god. Your spirit ain't its own. It is not yours to give away. Do ya hear me, girl?"

She hissed the words out now. "Give it back! Give it back! Or blood will buy only blood. Do ya understand? Blood for blood, Jaelle."

The chain felt tight around my neck, choking me. I grabbed at it, trying to rip it off. The old woman wailed out as she lunged for my throat, reaching for the amulet. She desperately tried to grab hold of it, clawing me as she did. But she wasn't trying to save me. She was trying to keep me from removing the charm. It took all of me to pull away from her hold.

Falling back into the grass I kept my eyes closed tightly, holding the amulet to my breast with both hands. I waited for her to come for me again. The air grew silent and still.

Lifting myself up, I opened my eyes to find myself alone beneath the apple tree. There was a bitter taste in my mouth, something burrowed in my throat. I coughed and choked until it flew from my lips into my hand. A bit of bloodied earth and apple lay in my palm as I sat breathlessly in the shadows.

Aunt Millicent was gone. If she was ever there. She had been dead for some ten odd years. Dead and buried back in Kentucky. She was a ghost from my memory and now a specter on my land. I trembled where I sat and stayed until night had come, and all the light was gone.

8 Millicent

Come, Jaelle. The stars call to me.
    I remember my young'un days, before the white chapel called to me. Those were wild days, full of long forgotten things and secrets of the earth. The air was ripe with whispers, and as a child, I listened.

Mama always said that Millicent was a woman that was broken by design. Her mind was a touch too slow for most people, her manners often childlike, and her heart was crudely sewn upon her sleeve for all to see and ruin as they pleased. She never married, though she had a beau once in her youth. That man was a brute. He treated her something awful. He died when Millicent was but twenty years old. He fell into a gorge on a late summer night. Folks reckoned he was drunk. Mama knew better. Millicent had simply had enough.

"She may be a mite slow," Mama would say, "but she ain't dumb. The mountains are high, and the earth is deep, girl. They can swallow you whole if you ain't careful. Even a child knows that."

I believed her, and I believed Aunt Millicent when she said she was better off without that bastard of a man hanging on her apron strings.

As I said, the earth was full of secrets.

Millicent was a child of the earth, bound to its roots by blood, her spirit as wild and unruly as any summer storm. As my mother and the rest of the women in our family had always done, she learned the old ways. But she believed in the Lord too. Singing praise to Heaven and Earth as one, the Book of Psalms was her grimoire and a source of her power. She believed that the ways of God and those of our ancestors could exist together in one body.

Come, child. Come.

As a child, I spent many of my summer nights by her side, dancing among the dainty fireflies and fields of red clover while the sun burned the skies as it fell to sleep. Despite her age, she danced right along with me, singing her songs of praise and worship for all that she believed. I sang with her in those young'un days, feeling those spirits of life and death and everything in between flow through me. Beneath the shadow of the stars, I felt the pull of ancient roots beneath my bare feet as they steadied me and brought me to life in ways I can still remember. I breathed in nightfall and starlight, and it filled me full.

I remember Millicent on those nights. I remember the way the starlight shone like fairy dust upon her youthful face, her smile as wide as the crescent moon hanging low in the sky.

"The stars call to me," she whispered in my ear.

My body tingled with a delight I cannot describe. I was part of it, the great secret of the earth and the sky. Millicent understood. Beneath the moon, she led me along the mossy, fern-lined paths of the open land.

"The stars will guide us. They will. To a better place."

Through the dew-dappled forest, we crept on our tippy toes, so as not to disturb the night critters. They watched from afar, the doe-eyed deer, the pesky opossums and coons. The fireflies fluttered around our heads, settling in our hair. Millicent glanced back at me, her smile as bright as the sun.

"You gotta crown, Miss Jaelle. A crown of fire."

I giggled and she hugged me tightly. We traipsed our way in the darkness until the ground beneath our feet was no more. We stood at the edge of the gorge, the very one her beau had fallen down all those years ago. I shivered at the remembrance, looking down into the depths of the blackness. The magic of the night had grown cold, and all that was left was a deep and pungent shadow of death.

With tears in her eyes, Millicent whispered on the wind, "Feel it, Jaelle. Even the dark's got its secrets. Way down deep, where none can ever find them."

She wept then and sang a woeful song, her voice carrying out into the darkness of the gorge.

"It calls to me, Jaelle. It calls for me to come. He calls to me."

The night and her lover never answered back.

9 What I Dream is What Will Be

Eisdibh. Everything is dark behind my eyelids as my mind drifts between that veil of wakefulness and sleep.

Eisdibh. The voice in the dark wraps its strange and tenebrous vines of mysterious sound around my mind, slowly tightening its grip until I listen. At first, I hear nothing.

Smash! Crash! Crunch!

The sounds of a car crash tear at my insides, ringing in my ears with such violent force that I can feel my body jolt. The silence afterward is haunting. It is quickly swept away with a wave of whispers that rushes toward me. The whispers come, ebbing and flowing to my ears. There are shouts in those whispers, rising higher and higher. One of them is a voice I recognize as well as my own—Jeremy. He's screaming and carrying on at someone I cannot see.

I can't see anything in this dark. His voice wraps around me and chokes me tight. I can't breathe. Can't scream.

Jaelle!

I awoke to the evening sun glaring in my face as it set. I heard shuffling somewhere in the room. Jeremy was poking through my things in the dresser, looking for money, no doubt. I knew he meant to go out. I sat up in the bed, clutching the thin blanket over my body.

"Don't go," I whispered, just loud enough for him to hear.

He huffed and half-turned toward me, as he pocketed what little change I had.

"What's it matter to you?" he grumbled. "That babe in your belly should be company enough. You got what you wanted, woman, now let me be."

He headed for the door.

"Something'll happen, Jeremy."

He stopped, his back to me.

"Something bad...if you go."

He breathed deeply, his shoulders rising and falling as he balled his hands into fists. I didn't think he would, but he turned back to me. Glared me down.

"None of that talk now. Sound just like your damn mama with her witchery and devilish dreams."

"But—"

He didn't let me finish. He held up his fist and that was all I said.

"Damn woman. It'll be a cold day in hell before I believe that shit."

He walked out without another word.

I sat up listening to his truck rumble to life in the yard below. The sound slowly faded away as he drove off. When I couldn't hear it anymore, I lay back down, settled into the lumpy mattress and fell asleep.

Bbbbrrriiinng. The telephone downstairs shivered to life, echoing up the long flight of stairs to reach me.

It was night, and my bedroom was draped in deep black. Despite the heat, I clung to the blanket wrapped around my body and listened as the silence was shattered by that blasted phone. Jeremy's daddy had put it in for us last year, along with the indoor plumbing and the bathroom upstairs, but I hated the thing.

"Times are changin' and we gotta move with 'em, Jaelle," so sayeth Jeremy.

I wasn't like my mama, clinging so tightly to the old ways that nothing could come between her and the past. Still, I hated the shrill ringing of that damned contraption. It broke the peaceful quiet of my little world and brought the busyness of the outside with it. That was something I couldn't bear. It never brought good news. It was a harbinger of ill omens and bad news, a death in the family, or the mortal illness of a friend.

I wasn't allowed to answer it while Jeremy was home. I didn't mind, but the lack of freedom when it came to that thing was awful irksome. It was still ringing as I sat there in the dark, wondering if I should make my way down to answer it. Jeremy still wasn't home, I knew. I guessed he must be running around with the boys.

Maybe it's about Mama.

The thought shook through me with a flood of fear. With the speed of a jackrabbit, I was up and out of bed, scooting down the shadowed stairs so fast that the old steps didn't have time to make a squeak.

The telephone hung on the wall right at the foot of the stairwell. A big, black monstrosity that cut away the beauty of the subtle floral wallpaper I had picked out especially for that hallway. That was the one thing that Jeremy allowed me to do when we were fixing up the farmhouse. I picked that design. It was the cheapest I could find. I thought the colors were delicate and bright. Deep down, I think it reminded me of Mama's place, with its climbing vines and fields of flowers. It was a bit faded with age now, but it was still pretty enough to look at.

I stood before the big black telephone and watched as it rang away. The sound was all the louder and more earth-shattering as I stood next to it. My hand rose to pick up the receiver. An inch away from my skin and I could feel its tingling vibration. Hidden in that tremulous ringing, there was a trickle of that otherworldly something. like I'd felt with Aunt Millicent, and tonight in my dream. It tickled about my fingertips as they brushed the receiver's cold metal with such a sense of foreboding, I nearly pulled away. But like a moth to a flame, that same something pushed me closer and brought my fingers to the telephone. I picked up the receiver and put it up to my face. I listened for a long second, waiting for some ghostly voice to answer my silence.

"Mrs. Bennett?"

It wasn't Mama. And it wasn't Jeremy.

The local sheriff, Roy Weber, spoke again, this time using my front name. "Jaelle?"

If Roy was calling, it could mean only one thing. My voice sank low and deep.

"It's Jeremy, ain't it?"

There was a brief emptiness. Roy sighed, "Yes, ma'am."

"An accident?"

My heart leapt at the words as they left my mouth. Maybe, just maybe this was it. No more old Ford truck. No more Jeremy. No more—

"Yes, ma'am."

My breath left my body in a trembling jolt.

"But I don't want you to worry none."

What?

"Jeremy's fine. Just a little shook up is all."

My body nearly collapsed to the floor and my heart sank down to my stomach with a sickening thud. I held on to the wall with all my might.

"But Jaelle, I have to tell ya, Jeremy's done got himself arrested. Got caught speeding clear through town, drunk as a skunk in spring. And that ain't all."

My breathing sputtered shallowly from my lips. Still, I did not answer.

"Jaelle?"

The cloud of shadow passed from me, and I jolted back. A deep breath struggled out of my mouth, and I said, "I'm comin', Roy."

There was silence on the other end of the line for

an instant. I imagined that he knew all he needed to know about Jeremy. The whole town did. They knew he was rotten to the core, that he was no good for me. No good for anyone. But instead of stopping him, there was always this deep and heavy silence.

"Alright, then."

The telephone line clicked. Roy was gone. I was alone again.

It took a moment for my mind to conjure up a plan. I picked up the receiver once more and flubbed my way through talking to the operator. I waited while the phone rang and rang.

Mrs. Ethel Samuels muddled through a hello on the other end of the line. I heard her husband's muffled cussing in the background. They must have been sleeping. Only then I realized I didn't know what time it was, but from the look of the darkness outside, it must have been late.

"Hello?" Mrs. Samuels said again, annoyed now.

"I'm sorry, Ethel. I...it's Jeremy, he's been in an accident."

I heard Ethel clear her throat. Once, twice, three times, before she sighed out, "Alright, Jaelle. Alright. We'll be there to fetch you."

She hung up. I hung up too with my own weighted sigh, only mine was heavier, because Jeremy was still alive.

I waited on the porch for over an hour in the dark. I felt the night begin to stir, the shadows slowly lifting, the blackness changing its hue to the varied shades of opal blue and orange. The sound of wings fluttered all about the treetops as the birds awoke and the wind picked up to a steady breeze that brushed against my hot cheeks, cooling them.

The fear I should feel after the dream that wasn't a dream hadn't hit me yet. Mama had visions. I had never had one of my own. My mind was weak and drowsy in the wake of it. There was another deeper sense that rippled below the surface, a power that seemed to throb against my beating heart and echo across my skin to my mama's little amulet wrapped around my neck. Though I was afraid, I liked the sensation. My fingers found their way to the necklace lying across my breast and wrapped around it tightly.

A plume of dust and the stark white beam of a car's headlight coming up the road broke the amulet's spell. I watched as a big black car came toward my house. It stopped just where the gravel met the grass. I tried to peer through the windshield to see who had come. It wasn't the Samuels' truck and the large shadow moving around in the driver's seat wasn't a familiar one. The car door opened. The shadow inside shifted—Brother Wise.

It was Brother Wise. I saw the busted headlight then as the dust scattered and my heart sank down deep. The wind hissed at my back as I watched him walk up the little path to my front porch.

A warning, it must be.

Up one step he went, and then another and another, until we were eye to eye. That warning wind whipped up to my face with his approach, bringing with it the scent of his cologne. Sweet earthy cedar and orange, a rich fragrance that toyed at my nostrils with the accidental pleasure of its smell. Bold and sensual in a way that made my toes curl and my soul quake. His smile was stunted and strange, his eyes so deep brown they were as black as midnight. They looked me up and down, with such intensity that I was amazed they didn't fall right out of his head for looking. My body trembled and my skin felt like it was on fire. I turned my gaze down to my feet, just as his smile faded.

"I'm sorry," was all he got out.

There was an uncomfortable silence as his gaze fell.

"Ethel Samuels was to get me and take me to the

jail," I stuttered out. "Roy's got Jeremy locked up and if I don't come soon, he's liable to be awful mad."

Brother Wise nodded, his eyes dropping just a little, like he was deep in thought, or just looking at my bare legs peeking out from under my dress.

Damn. I plum forgot my stockings in all the hubbub.

I felt dirty as the thought crossed my mind, but I met his gaze anyway.

"The Samuels were not able to fetch you. They called me, asking for help, and so I've come to take you. If that's alright?"

He spoke in such a glorious tone, like he'd come to save me. Like a hero from some old-timey fairy tale. But this was no fairy tale, even I knew that.

Sure as hellfire and brimstone, it isn't.

I blushed. This man shouldn't make me feel any sort of way. Yet here I was acting like a bashful schoolgirl, squirming at every glance, and every whit of a smile he beamed my way. There was a kindness in his eyes that never wavered. A kindness that would wrap up all my troubles, bend and pull them into a pretty little bow, just so I would smile back. Or so I reckoned.

I knew that God was glaring down on me for the feelings bubbling up into my chest, but they were beyond my power to hold back. I didn't really care. For whatever they were worth and whatever they were, they were there, and nothing was going to stop them.

I nodded in answer. He held out his hand to me. I wanted to take it, but amid my pleasurable acceptance of this feeling, I heard that singular voice again.

Ruith.

My heart jolted back in its gutted chamber with a slap of pain. It was like I was struck by a powerful force of lightning. Though I didn't understand the voice I feared.

Jeremy. He came to take me to Jeremy.

I reminded myself of that over and over as I

avoided his hand and hurried down the porch steps. He followed fast behind me, reaching the car just ahead of me so that he could open my door.

"Thank you," I muttered.

I kept my eyes down when he sat in the seat next to me, the warmth and the nearness of his body oh so near and tingling on my skin. It unnerved me, the fire that came off his flesh next to mine. This man was fire and heat, and it set off something wild in me. I cleared my throat and turned my eyes to what lay outside the window. Without a word, Brother Wise started his car and pulled out of the drive. We soared down that dusty dirt road, the fields and trees rushing past us. Everything was basked in that pale early light of dawn. I heard gentle voices swiftly sweeping past us as we drove. They were the voices of the trees, the air, the earth. I smiled to hear them.

He must have seen my smile, because out of the silence, I heard him say, "Hope in a new day is a gift from the Lord."

I dared to turn to him. He was looking straight at me.

"It's good that you have hope in a new day, Jaelle."

The sound of my name on his lips broke the smile on my own. Hope for a new day was not something my body bore, because every new day was full of the same as the last. Every day was tiring, painful, and utterly useless. But somehow, hope on his lips meant something different. It was brighter, cleaner, and it really meant something. I gathered that was that word of God I had so often longed to understand but never could. From his mouth, it seemed to make so much more sense.

That was the power of Brother Wise, not the Lord. He was a good salesman for the Spirit, but the Spirit wasn't in him. At least, I couldn't feel it on him. Something else drifted over Brother Wise. Like a deep, dark cloud of a coming storm, it was bent on sweeping me away if I let it. I wouldn't though. I wouldn't.

I gave the preacher an odd sort of smile. "Hope in God ain't somethin' I lean on no more, Brother Wise."

"Please," he interrupted. "Call me Elijah."

I would not be calling him Elijah. Front names were too personal, intimate, much too intimate for the likes of him.

A consternated look spread across his smooth face. He had shaved just to fetch me, and in the shallow sunlight you could hardly see the pockmarks. Though the windows were wide open, not a hair on his head was out of place. Despite the early hour, his clothes too were impeccably clean and put together, his red suspenders glaringly brightly in the burgeoning dawn light. He was the picture of pastoral perfection.

He cleared his throat. "Sometimes the Lord God gives us trials and tribulations to test our piety. Our...faith."

If that was God's way, it was a wonder any of these mountain people had any faith at all. They had seen trials. They had seen tribulations. They had seen cruel summers of dearth and winters so bitter and harsh that a body was lucky to survive with all their fingers and toes. Hundred-year floods, sickness, hunger, death and the kinds of plagues only Moses would understand. It was a wonder these people believed at all, and no wonder at all that some of them turned to the old ways.

It was a comfort when God only scorned them for their trouble. God didn't fill their bellies or save their crops. He didn't raise their children and babes from the dead. He showed the least of these the hardness of his hand, and from that, they rose up strong as the rocky ground and steady as the wind, giving thanks to the earth.

As if he could understand my silence, he went on. "I know that coming from a man like me, who hasn't shared in your labor and your pains, these words leave little comfort. However, I assure you, they are not my words, but the Lord's."

He glanced my way with a look of woe manufactured just for the occasion. It was nothing he felt, nothing he would trouble himself over enough to really feel. His words were as distant and cold as a winter wind. I just stared him down. The heaviness of my silence made him uncomfortable. It was a look I'd stolen straight from Mama. She would have been pleased.

"Does the Lord also say that women should be silent in the face of violence and adversity?"

That was also my mother.

He cleared his throat again, fidgeting in his leather seat. He tried to keep his gaze on me while struggling to watch the road. It was a desperate gaze, searching and wild, and it delved into the very depths of me.

"What have you seen, Jaelle, that makes you despise the Lord so?" he said quietly.

Almost a whisper, it tickled my ears so much I pulled away. I was awful quiet for a while. The thought of answering him sent shivers down my spine. Jeremy wouldn't want me to answer. Jeremy wouldn't want him to know. If I were to utter a word about him or our life together. There would be whispers. Big-mouthed busybodies, those women in town were. Not a one of them knew how to keep their fat traps shut. Yet there was something about the way that preacher man looked at me. Something that drew me in like waves onto the seashore.

"I've seen a good man turn rotten and everything he loved turn to rot right with him," I said.

I sat in the wake of those words, waiting for them to settle and stain the bittersweetness of the day. But they didn't. Emboldened, I dared to speak further.

"It's like watchin' good earth that you've tended and sown get swallowed up by poisonous vines and choked with hemlock and the like. Doesn't matter how much you stomp them out, that good earth is never good again."

I watched him ponder that image for a while, letting it sink in deep.

"You're a good and godly woman, Jaelle. Know that."

His hand rested on my arm long enough for me to feel the hotness of his skin. So much heat radiated from his body it seemed as if he were on fire, but his face was cool and pale. There was no outward sign that he felt this heat the way I did. I blushed. He noticed. I glanced down at his hand on my bare skin. When he saw that I noticed it there, he quickly pulled it away. It rested back with the other on the steering wheel.

He cleared his throat once again. a nervous habit it would seem. I waited for another godly lecture, but it didn't come. I heard him sigh softly.

"A good woman."

That was all he said. His look turned sour and sullen, and it pulled his young face into a look of guilty sadness.

We rode in silence the rest of the way to the jail. The jail wasn't much to speak of, to be sure. It was a tiny rectangular building right at the edge of town, just a few yards away from the post office and Mr. Tillman's market. The sheriff would usually sit just outside of it in a rickety old chair and whittle away the hours with a piece of dry wood and a pocketknife. He was there now. Only this time his eyes were watchful, like he was waiting just for me.

Roy jumped out of his seat as we pulled in across from the jail. I hesitated to get out of the car, but Brother Wise was eager and hopped right on out in a hurry. I followed, slamming the door behind me. Only then did I realize that I hadn't brought my purse. In my flurry of excitement and worry, I had misplaced it. Surely it was still sitting on the dresser or the table next to the front door.

"Jaelle, you oughta come with me now." Roy gave me a serious look, shadowed by the awning of the jail entrance.

My heart just about dropped to my toes. Jeremy would be so angry if I couldn't bail him out. Not that it mattered about my purse. There wasn't anything in it but a couple of pennies and a dime. It wouldn't have been enough anyway.

"Jaelle," Roy nodded in my direction for me to follow.

I nodded back, my face flushed and my eyes barely skirting past him as I approached.

"Alright, Roy," I said quietly and turned my gaze downward.

I watched my feet plod one step in front of the other into the jail. Brother Wise trailed close behind me. So close I could feel that heat of his brushing up against my backside. I moved a little faster to keep some distance between us.

The humid air inside was nigh on unbearable. The county couldn't afford much, but with "Sissy Roy"—as he was called behind his back more often than I could count—in charge, a lot had changed in the jail. That included new cells he said were certified escape proof. Roy was delicate for a man and more sensitive than a woman. He was particular and couldn't stand the heat. He said he'd be damned if he was going to suffer the likes of hellfire just to babysit a bunch of delinquents eyeing for trouble.

Roy was eerily quiet with the preacher there. His bug-eyed look of surprise and constant glances back to Brother Wise and me were enough to realize that something was really wrong. We passed a couple of cells full of roughnecks. All of them were angry, all of them were watching us. There was a shadow hanging over every one of them. I could feel it. I could see it curling about their bodies like smoke, poking at their insides as if it wanted to get at them where it really hurt. My hand rose to brush against the metal bars of a cell I passed, and the shadow swooped down to touch me. It was a nasty cold thing when it clipped my skin. Quickly, I pulled my hand away, clutching at my belly to protect my child.

As Roy led us through the maze, he tried to speak low so only I would hear. But Roy was deaf in one ear, and he was anything but quiet.

"He's in a hell of a mood, Jaelle. Son of a bitch crashed clear through the Temples' brand-new barn." A side glance from Brother Wise and Roy was quick to add. "Apologies, Preacher. Don't mean to offend, but I'm not a man to mince words, and this fella here ain't one to lose a fight."

"Fight?" I muttered, but neither man heard.

A flash of color and something wild ran through my head.

The color red. Bare skin on bare skin. My husband's face in ecstasy like I'd never seen him with me. And then, from in the shadows below him, there was Missy Temple.

I cringed but said nothing. Roy was still talking away.

He explained matter-of-factly, "I'd forgive a man for being drunk once in a while, but he had a beef with Mr. Temple evidently. Instead of dealing with it like a man, Jeremy duked it out until Sal's barn wasn't the only thing busted up."

I watched Brother Wise's body flicker with a glint of inspiration. Where he had been oddly silent and uncomfortable a moment before, now he seemed to sense that the services of the Lord were needed. His bent form began to straighten. He held his head high and folded his well-manicured hands before him. He looked like a menacing angel, captured crudely in stained-glass, all jagged lines and mismatched colors. A bit of the Divine and a bit of something else. An oddity here, especially in this place.

"Perhaps I should speak with Mr. Bennett?" Brother Wise was all too eager to chime in.

Roy looked him over before hands on his hips he smirked. Roy wasn't much for praying, and he had little time for God and the hereafter.

"Nothin' personal, Preacher," said Roy. "But I wouldn't let you touch ol' Jeremy there with a ten-foot pole in the state he's in. He's liable to tear your head clean off your neck just for lookin' his way."

Brother Wise looked plum embarrassed at that. His face flushed bright red as he stepped forward. "This man needs the Lord."

Roy nearly smiled and held up his callused hand to stop him. "God's not what he needs, Preacher. What he needs is a strong cup of coffee and a good kick in the damn pants."

Brother Wise gritted his teeth, but he backed down and said no more.

Satisfied, Roy turned to me. "He ain't asked for ya, but we thought it best if you came down. Maybe you can settle him down, Jaelle. I sure as hell can't."

My heart was beating fast. Brother Wise held back and watched as Roy led me to the last small cell along the hallway. I could hear my husband before I could see him, cussing and carrying on so loud that the empty concrete walls bellowed with the sound. I turned, my heart in my stomach, and there was Jeremy, butted up right against the bars. As soon as he saw me and Roy, he screamed in our faces all the louder.

My ears rang sharply, but I stared him down. He glared at me and rattled the bars like a wild animal in a cage. That's what he looked like now, an animal. Wild and dangerous, and oh so very deadly. Low in his belly, I heard him rumble and growl, until he roared.

"Damn you, woman! Damn you!" he retched out the words with such violence a shower of spit flew his lips.

His eye was swollen shut, his face full of stubble was cut and scratched all over. His nose was broken, blood still trickling down to his mouth. Roy tried to quiet him down with his hand of authority, holding it up in front of Jeremy's face like it was some kind of secret weapon. Jeremy only sneered at him and spat at him. The glob of spittle landed on Roy's pristine uniform shirt. Roy's face got redder than a beet. Roy hated anything but a clean shirt.

"Now, Jeremy, I told you that's enough."

"You shut up, Roy! That badge of yours don't mean nothin' to me. You can wave your hand at me all you want. I'll not stop. Not while that whore of a woman is standing right there!"

That shut Roy up fast. All eyes were on Jeremy now, and he knew it. He gripped the bars of his cage with bruised and battered knuckles. I could have sworn he had the strength to bend the metal cage. He stared straight at me with all the hate he could muster, and I prayed that metal cage would hold him in.

"You nearly killed me! You and your witchy ways!" he screamed at me.

I stepped back and Roy's hand stopped me. His hand was gentle and cool, not like the touch of hellfire and a hint of desire of Brother Wise. I was safe with Roy, at least until he opened that cell.

"What the hell are you talkin' about, Jeremy? This is your wife we're talkin' about here, not some backwoods medicine woman."

It was a stab at my mother, but I let it slide. I clamped my mouth shut tightly and let Roy do the talking.

"Jeremy, I've a mind to just leave you in here, charges or no, till you done sobered up."

Jeremy slammed his fist against the cell bars. I heard a loud crack come from his hand, but he didn't seem to notice or feel any pain. Roy used his cool, gentle hand to pull me back a few more feet away from Jeremy's cell.

Jeremy pointed his finger at me through the bars

"You're as jealous as the moon," he yelled. "Ain't enough that you gotta roof over your head and food to eat. Ain't enough you got that babe in your belly and a man that'll bed you. No—just like your mad mama, you need more. So much more that you'd do me in to have it all."

"Jeremy—" Roy started, but Jeremy didn't let him finish.

I could feel a rage start to rise within me. My chest was so tight I couldn't breathe. That prickling feeling began to pang at my fingertips. No longer playing there, it burned. Instinctively, I grabbed hold of Jeremy's hand holding onto the bars of his cell and held it tight. He looked at me, his dirty mouth hanging open like a fly trap.

He got his wits about him enough to say, "She's what damn near killed me! It's her that should be in this cell, not me! She dreamt it and she made it happen."

He tried to pull his hand away, but that feeling had a hold of him now too. I felt the burning leave me, felt it seep out of my skin. Jeremy's eyes got as big as saucers, and he screamed.

Roy moved up to the cell ready to fight. "*Jeremy!*"

That shut Jeremy up. He blinked wide and empty-like, as if he were just waking from a nightmare. He trembled all over. Without a word, he plopped down onto his cot looking frightened. Roy looked at me and my swollen belly, and his face changed to something like pity.

"I'll be keepin' him, Jaelle. I'll not send you home with that man today. Not as drunk and disorderly as he is. Can you get home alright?"

Brother Wise stepped up beside me, grabbing a

gentle hold of my arm. "I'll be taking her home, Sheriff Weber. I'll see that she's safe and sound."

Roy eyed the preacher's greedy hold he had on me. Finally, he nodded. "That'll be fine, Preacher."

"Elijah," Brother Wise corrected him. "Just call me Elijah."

Roy only nodded, not to be bothered with niceties or proper names. He pointed us down the hall. Away from Jeremy and those shadows and that smell of rot and sweat. I stopped at the door, something on the air catching my ear. It was Roy, still nestled between the long hallways inside. He and his deputy Harold were speaking low and as soft as Roy could manage.

"I best keep an eye on that preacher man," said Roy. "I don't like him lookin' at Jaelle that a-way. And in front of her husband too. That man may say he's from God, but he's got the hungriest damn eyes I've ever seen."

I turned my head to listen further, but Brother Wise tugged me until I came away with him. Away from the whispers and those wicked words.

As we hit the fresh, warm air of the morning once again, I gasped out loud, gulping it in with each deep breath. Brother Wise was still clutching tightly to my arm as he led me to the car. It was as if he wanted to squeeze the life right out of me. I was glad of it.

10 Deep, Deep Down in the Hole of Sweet Sin

As we stepped out onto the sidewalk, I waited for Brother Wise to say something about what had happened between Jeremy and me. I could feel the remnants of that power tingling and sputtering on my fingertips, like sparks of electricity before a fire. But the fire was inside me, pushing to get out. Anger had settled in my chest, one so powerful that I could barely contain it. It made it awful hard to breathe, and to think. I stumbled my way down the street next to Brother Wise.

We were silent. We just kept walking past all the shops and parked cars. I didn't know where we were headed. I don't think Brother Wise knew either. I turned to look at him. His face was set dead ahead of him, his eyes narrowed in thought. He was thinking alright, probably about what a terrible man I was married to and what a terrible woman I was for staying with him. I could hear the sermon on Sunday already.

"Jaelle," he began.

I knew I was in for it. A man like that wouldn't let an opportunity to lecture and sermonize go, even now. He stopped and reluctantly turned to me. Here it was. I knew it. He looked behind me into the big window of the diner where we'd stopped. I glanced behind me. Eyes were watching us, big wide eyes with whispering mouths.

Brother Wise looked nervous. He gently led me away from those eyes and nasty words.

"How long have you been married, Jaelle?"

By then, my feet were hurting something awful. I stopped to take off my shoes, while Brother Wise watched me all the while. His gaze was heavy and deep, conscious of my every movement. I felt my skin burn beneath his stare. I was quick to pick up my shoes and plod once again beside him on the dirt road.

"Would you believe I don't right remember how long?" I said with a timid blush and a smile. "It seems like it's been Jeremy and me just about forever."

"Have they been happy years, Jaelle? Are you content?"

I laughed bitterly, my smile turned jagged and sharp. "Life ain't about being content. And life with Jeremy ain't about being happy."

I could see the troubled expression on the preacher's face. He didn't understand. He never would.

"Jaelle, life is more than toil and tribulations. Life is beautiful. It's joyful and..."

His voice trailed off with an exasperated sigh as his eyes wandered past me. His mouth thinned to a decisive frown. I followed his gaze down the road to see what had made him so on edge.

It was Missy. She sat alone at the bus stop, a suitcase by her feet. Her chubby figure was squeezed into her fanciest dress, reserved for Sundays and special occasions. She must have had somewhere important to go. Her hair was all done up fancy-like, her plump, doughy face and all its chins were done up too in cheap makeup. A little too much for my taste. A little too much for Brother Wise's taste too from the expression on his face. As we approached her, she stood to meet us. Beneath that veil of color, she was as pale as a ghost. She gave us a saccharine-sweet smile, her eyes flashing at me with a spark of fear. I let it slide.

"Brother Wise, how are you?"

She didn't acknowledge me. She just kept smiling at the preacher like the Lord himself had come down from Heaven just to see her fat self busting out of that ugly damn dress.

Brother Wise smiled back. A flash of envy quaked inside me. Thankfully, no one noticed. No one noticed me at all.

"Sister Temple, a good morning to you, and God's blessing," he said. His words were stunted and cold, like for once he didn't mean them.

Missy smiled extra-wide at that. She glanced at me with pride for an instant. It spilled out with every bat of her eyes. My chest burned even more; my body flushed with anger. She didn't notice. No one did.

"God's blessing on you, Brother Wise," she said in return.

Then she looked straight at me with all the ire she could muster. Something wasn't right.

"Jaelle, I—" she started, reaching for my hand.

She quickly thought better of it. Her hand retreated back to her side with the swiftness of a slithering snake. She didn't say it, but I already knew. I knew about her and my husband Jeremy. About the brawl between her husband and mine. From the look on her face, she knew that I knew.

A rumbling roar came up from behind us on the road. The bus squealed to a stuttering stop. Missy took a deep breath that shivered on her lips. The weight of it pushed the air around us into a flurry of anxious unrest.

"It's a right shame about Jeremy."

Her eyes avoided me now. They glanced down to the cracked sidewalk that seemed to separate me from Brother Wise and herself. The line in the sand had been drawn, and I was on the wrong side.

"My husband should have known better than to let things come to this. He knew—he—"

A flash of color. Red. Missy's husband, Sal, standing over his wife, her nose bloodied and her face red. Her suitcase sits in the shadowed corner.

Brother Wise's eyes narrowed. "I'm sorry, Sister Temple. I don't think I understand."

Again, Missy's eyes were on me. A look of guilt. A look of shame. Then, back to that crack in the sidewalk that kept her safe.

She smiled at Brother Wise, a soft and weary smile. "Just women's chatter, Brother Wise. Nothing more. You know how it goes. Men make fools of themselves, and women talk."

All I could see in my mind's eye was Missy wrapped up in the arms of Deacon Johnston, sinning in the dark. Heavens, how they talk. Suddenly, it all made sense. Missy cleared her throat and held out her hand to Brother Wise with a plastered smile I knew she didn't mean. She snatched up her suitcase.

"It's a pleasure to see you, Brother Wise. You take care now."

She turned away without a word to me and boarded the bus.

As the bus set off down the road, I watched her hurry to a seat. She never glanced back.

Brother Wise gently laid his hand on my shoulder with a look of concern.

"Women may talk, Jaelle, but God reads hearts better than sinful mouths and false words."

He glanced harshly at the bus as it rounded the corner and disappeared. A look I was glad of, so much so that I nearly smiled. Then his black eyes were upon me, burning deep and dark.

"God knows better," he said again, slow so that I might remember. I would remember. Even if it were the death of me.

***

The door to Brother Wise's house swung open. Home, it was a home. A place of rest and peace, not just a house. Not like my house of shadow and rage. It was cool inside. He led me by the arm into his wife's sitting room. I sat as he commanded, expecting Mrs. Prudence Wise to appear at any moment with her pruned smile and glaring eyes.

"My wife Prudence is away," I heard him say from the other room. "Please forgive the mess. I'm terrible at keeping house without her."

The house was anything but a mess. Everything seemed in its place as I glanced around quietly.

He's probably too afraid of her to touch anything, I thought with a chuckle.

A moment after, Brother Wise came stumbling in with a tray of iced tea and some sandwiches. The tea had ice, and the sandwiches were fresh and cool. I realized how hungry I was as he motioned for me to take one. I did, keeping my eyes down, for I felt his gaze upon me. I heard him chewing on his sandwich. He was loud and the sound filled the silence with a disturbing squish that seemed to resonate in my stomach with a foul churning. As hungry as I was, I put my sandwich down.

Smoothing out my skirt and brushing away the pesky crumbs that lay in my lap, I dared to look up at him. He was watching me, those black eyes beaming at me. Hungry, it was hungry and not for the food laid out between us. Here I was, pregnant and another man's wife, a witch to some and a whore now too. He looked at me like that. Like he hadn't had enough desire and flesh and passion to sate him. I had seen a look like that in Jeremy's eyes on nights when he was too drunk to stand. It usually meant trouble and pain. There was no pleasure in a look like that.

I believe Brother Wise saw my discomfort and his expression quickly changed. There was warmth now where a moment before there had only been a fiery lust. His hands were fretful in his lap, twisting and wringing until they were red. Trembling, his hand reached for mine. Reached so slowly that I thought he'd never get to me. But he did.

His hand was too warm. It burned my skin as it touched me, so sizzling hot that it felt like the Devil himself held my hand. At first, his hand only brushed mine, gentle-like as if the touch of my roughened skin was something he treasured. As if he had waited for just that very touch to soothe him, his hand stopped trembling. He clamped his fingers around mine and held on tight. So tight I couldn't have pulled away if I'd had a mind to do so.

My heart began to race. I held my breath. He didn't say a word. He just held my hand, his thumb softly tracing the lifeline of my palm before settling into smooth circles across my skin. His touch burned, but it sent shivers from my fingertips up to my chest, my breath catching on my tongue and trembling there on my lips. He noticed and smiled, seeming proud of himself that he'd done that to me. Still, he said nothing. The air was thick and quiet, full of wild anticipation and a stroke of danger that I did not like.

The longer he touched me, the more it burned, but still I let him. How could I not? He wanted me, the same as every other man I'd known. Once a man wanted you, there was no denying him. I sighed as my body relaxed within his hold. His arms were around me now, a hungry grasp that I could not escape. He knew it, and he knew that I wanted it. I could hear his heavy breathing and feel it crawling on my skin. My heart was so loud in my ears that the silence was no longer silent.

I closed my eyes when he looked at me deeply. I couldn't look at those black eyes sinking into me, seeing every part of me. Knowing me in ways that only God could ever know me.

"Oh, God," he groaned.

He kissed me hard. A kiss so ravenous I could barely breathe. I felt his hand sweep across my shoulder, down my arm, and restlessly tug at my skirt. I let him. I kissed back with as much desire as he showed me. I began to fall into his arms, into the darkness that surrounded me. Deeper and deeper. Within that darkness, there was fire and snow and blood. The sound of his breathing and my own clouded the air, drowned out the screaming and shouting that was coming closer and closer in the dark. It was coming for us.

"After desire has conceived, it gives birth to sin; and sin gives birth to death." I opened my eyes, startled by that voice, and trembling in his arms.

A low shadow in the darkness of the hall caught my eye and disappeared just as quickly.

"Elijah," I gasped out. He stopped and gazed at me with a look almost of shame—almost.

Slowly, he peeled his arms from around me. He returned to his seat without a word. Without making a sound. His furniture was new, it didn't whine and screech when I moved. His eyes dropped to his hands in his lap, once again fretful and wringing, desperate to cling to me.

After a long moment he said, "Jaelle."

I looked up at him and forced a smile. Tears I hadn't asked for were now brimming in my eyes and skirting across my cheeks.

"Elijah," I said, and he sat up straight at the sound of his name on my lips. "Please take me home."

I didn't go home. Instead, I stood on my mama's porch in the setting sun and watched him leave.

Elijah, his touch still burned all over me. It felt good, and I let it remain there. But that voice—the fire and the blood and the snow—stopped my pleasure cold in its tracks. Something was coming. Something in the deep black of that preacher man's eyes. It was coming for me.

11 The Moon and the Mustard Seed

And the Lord said to them, "Because of the littleness of your faith; truly I say to you, if you have faith the size of a mustard seed, you will say to this mountain, 'Move,' and it will move; and nothing will be impossible to you."

O, ye of little faith.

My mama had welcomed me with as much warmth and kindness as a blizzardy winter day. Her face was all storms and angry lightning when she saw me step out of Elijah's car. By the time I'd reached her stoop and watched the preacher leave, she was fit to be tied. While we stood there in the wake of dust made from his big black car, I could tell that Mama couldn't stand it any longer.

"I couldn't go on home, Mama. Just couldn't."

"What you doin', girl?" she grumbled.

I didn't answer her. She grunted with displeasure under her breath, loud enough for me to hear.

"You think they won't talk?" she said bluntly.

I whipped around, glaring at her, but she didn't back down. She smiled.

"Ah, you see, I'm not blind yet. I can see right through those baby blue eyes of yours. See down deep into the flesh and bone of you. To the heart of you. You think you can hide the sin inside, the blood-red lust that consumes you for a man not your own. But it shows all over you like blood on a white smock."

She wouldn't stop talking, and so I stopped her

with the back of my hand to her face. It got eerily quiet in the wake of that slap. My little flash of violence, something I had never entertained before. My hand echoed with the weight of it, panging with the sort of pain that wouldn't leave when my flesh had recovered. My heart, my body, ached at the hate I had shown my mama.

Her answer, of course, was to slap me back. My head reeled, but the ache of guilt in me was satisfied.

"An eye for an eye," she grumbled. "Isn't that what your god says? An eye for an eye?"

Mama's words made me dizzy and sick. I tried to speak, words pushing to break forth from my lips. Instead, the world went black.

My eyes shot open, but there was nothing to see. It was pitch black and the air was silent except for the peepers' song dancing in the darkness. I blinked and the blackness began to shift with shadows and light. The room took shape before me, my mama's kitchen. I lay on the cot near a fire that was slowly dying. There was a chill in the air. I shivered, wrapping my arms around my body. My head still felt faint. My stomach was full of butterflies and knots. I didn't dare sit up just yet.

A shuffling creak let me know that my mama was close by. She scooted into my sight and tended to the fire. As if by magic, the flames grew high and bright, licking the underside of the mantel with a hiss. Red waves of heat rushed at me and my body eased its trembling. My mama stooped over the fire. She stared into its flickering, ever-changing flames, immersed in a silence that I had never known from her.

"Mama?"

Silence was the only answer.

"Mama?" I called again, my voice now desperate and wild. Tears streamed down my face and pooled there in my lap.

Still nothing.

"Mama," the name fell faintly from my lips. Barely a whisper in the grim darkness.

From the darkness, I heard her say, "Your husband's done smacked you upside the head one too many times, girl, for you to be thinkin' you can raise your skirts to that preacher man for a little fun."

"I-I ain't done nothin', Mama."

Her eyes darted toward me.

"You take care. Your soul be slippin' into the gloomy depths, the muck and the mire, and you seem to like it."

Anger vibrated in the very pit of me. Something wild and unruly. Something dark.

"I ain't done nothin'," I said firmly.

"But you wanna."

"No," slipped quietly from my uncertain lips.

"You wanna crawl right into his bed. I see it there on your face. Wicked lustful thoughts ya have."

I wanted to scream at her. To rail at her. But the only thing that would come out of my mouth, quietly and barely above a whisper was, "No, Mama."

"Dirty, vile woman! The same dark rottenness as my ma before me."

Mama had never spoken much of Great Ma, but the comparison was not lost on me. "I'm not," I said.

"Dirty and full of shadows."

"No."

"You want him. You want the preacher man more than life itself."

She was coming toward me now. Barreling toward me with all the venom she could muster in her frail and ancient body.

"Say it! Say it, girlie! Say that sin is yours! Say it! Say it. *Say it*!"

"Yes!"

I had broken. Somehow the word didn't seem so nasty and vile on my own tongue. It tasted sweet and full of promise.

"Yes, I want him."

My mama moved faster than a shadow to me, her eyes bent on me with a blackened fire. Fire and blood and snow—was all I saw in her eyes. *Fire and blood and snow.*

"What you're playin' at ain't wise," she said quietly. "I got a wicked feeling on it."

"What do you know, Mama? You don't believe in sin and wickedness. In the right and the wrong of things. You just live, and live, and keep on believing in nothing."

Mama clicked her tongue and cocked her head to the side with a decisive hiss. "The earth ain't nothing, Jaelle. The earth bears you. It raises you from the ash and stone. It gives you food to eat and air to breathe. Water to heal and fire to raze. It's everything."

"Ain't nothin' but devilry and darkness," I shouted back in her face through gritted teeth.

Mama smiled, a crooked, wicked smile. The shadows creeping across her face were sinewy and strong, blackened vines of the dark's own making.

"You wanna see the darkness, daughter?"

Her gnarled hand grabbed hold of me and pulled me to my feet. The room was spinning, but she cared little for that. Mama dragged me away from the warmth of the fire. Away, and out into the night, where the cool shafts of moonlight broke upon my aching head. They settled there in my eyes and on my skin.

Mama left my side and traipsed her way out into the field with its high-topped, flowing grass, its flowering vines, and wild lilies. All of them hauntingly pale by the light of the moon. She stood amid all of it, her hands raised to the star-studded night, basking in the darkness and the light as it shifted and changed with the wind. I watched it swirl around her body, molding to her until she was both the moonlight and the night. She turned back to me.

"Come on then, child."

She had called me a child long ago, when in her eyes I showed promise for the work of her own hands. Long before the little church's beckoning and my baptism in the river. She had called me her own, her child, her daughter. Once, long ago.

She smiled and waved at me. "Come on."

My bare feet led the way through the grassy field, and I stood at my mama's side. The tall grass swayed in the sweet-scented wind, brushing against my cool skin. I closed my eyes.

"Feel that child?" Mama's voice swallowed up the silence and made the air around me feel warm and safe. The words wrapped around me, soft and gentle-like. "It welcomes you as the daughter ya are."

Daughter, not enemy, not traitor—friend.

She kept talking, her voice folding me into a delicate mess, a rivalry of chaos and control, all pushing up inside of me. She had put me under her spell, captivated my senses and calmed every fear. My eyes remained closed, but I felt the ivy amongst the grass begin to stretch up to my fingertips and twine about each one of them. Then, up my arms, covering me whole. Round and round, it wrapped itself about my flesh with a velvety touch. It was gentle and kind, and with it came a flickering surge of that power I had felt only in small doses. It teased me, tickling instead of the stroke of levin-fire I imagined it was capable of. With a sigh, and my mama's chanting heavy in my ears, I let whatever come that would. The moonlight took me, swept me into its arms and raised me up. My bare feet barely touched the ground, my toes grazing the deep-rooted soil.

Leanabh leamsa, tha thu.

I breathed it in, the softness of the voice on the air that melded with the gruff grunting chant of my mama. To me, it was all the same, and the sound burrowed deep inside me. The voice faded into my flesh and Mama's chant was done. My feet touched the ground once again. My eyes opened, and I saw my mama before me. The moonlight stained those dark eyes of hers in an eerie cold that seemed to cover my body. The whole of me was coated in that silver-white light of the moon, full of that power that itched to escape.

My mama smiled at me, placing both her hands on my face with kindness. "See, child. The moonlight speaks to you."

The tugging at my breast pulled a little harder as I watched my mama dance and sway to the rhythm of the wind. It was the ghost of her youth and wily spirit. That tugging pulled even harder now, but I hadn't a mind to listen. Still the moonlight called to me.

I left Mama there to dance in her darkness and tiptoed my way back into the house, where the cool shadows soothed my throbbing heart.

12 Mama and Her Mother

Great Ma, my mama's mama, was a hard and vengeful woman. Colder than Mama's icy veins and more bitter than a rotten crab apple. The hardness of the world had made her like that. But she was a leader among the mountain people, just like Mama was now. A wise woman, almost a goddess, cherished as the wild moon and the steady sun. She was important, and Mama clung to that.

Mama's mama wasn't just a mother to her. She was a teacher and a guide, spreading her sacred knowledge like flower seeds to the broken soil. Mama was the earth, tilled and ready to be planted, ready to bloom and grow into something wild and strong to please her. She soaked in every last bit of that know-how until she knew the earth and all its wonders better than she knew herself. That's how Great Ma liked it.

Great Ma died on Christmas Day back in '41 in the middle of a snowstorm. Her body was found in her favorite rocking chair. The one in my possession. It was an honor to be given something of Great Ma's, so it was told to me. I didn't care for the fact that she'd been dead in it. Sure, to most, dead was dead. But in these parts, ghosts and hainted things were real.

When Mama was very young, Great Pa gave her a moonstone necklace. Great Pa had mined the moonstone himself in the old days, when mining took him away from his family, and the treasures and trinkets he brought back were as good as gold and more precious than any money.

To Great Pa, it was a sign of his love for his young daughter. To Mama, it was a priceless treasure. She wore it day and night, never taking it off for even a second. To Great Ma, this gift to his favorite child made her green with envy. To her, the moonstone amulet was a sign of power and protection, of clarity and something else. Something that had its roots in the supernatural forces that Great Ma believed were governing everything. The sun and the stars, the earth and its movements, the luck and loss of people. Great Ma sensed something different about this precious stone, and she said as much to her husband. Despite her complaints, Mama kept the stone.

After a spell, Mama got very sick. Great Pa cared for her, while Great Ma looked on, rocking away in her rocking chair in a dark corner. She watched and waited for her baby child, the youngest of her brood, to die.

"That one will be the death of me," Mama heard her mutter from the shadows. "Let her die then, I'll not be sorrowed. Bury that stone with her, deep down in the earth."

Perhaps, she did want Mama to die. Perhaps, she knew something that no one else did. A sign, a vision of the future, that kept her hellbent on her little girl's imminent death. Perhaps it was for an earthbound and selfish reason that she wanted the child dead and gone. There were whispers all over town that Mama was not Great Pa's child. Whose child she was, Great Ma wouldn't dare to tell.

Seeing that his little daughter was ailing and sure to die, Great Pa begged his wife for an elixir of life made from her store of wisdom and roots to save the child. But Great Ma wouldn't budge from her chair in the darkness. So it was that Great Pa gave her the back of his hand.

"This be your child, woman," said Great Pa. "And you'll save her, or I'll not suffer you under this roof no more."

Great Ma thought about it long and hard, her eyes twinkling with the blazing flames of the fire. Now Great Ma was not one to bend to the will of any man, but that pitch-black night, something in her split in two and left her broken and raw. She looked down at her child sick with fever and tears ran from her cheeks like a deluge.

Quickly, she made a draught of her very best roots and herbs, things that Great Pa didn't understand, but still he watched her so that she didn't add something deadly to do the child harm. Great Ma brought the mixture to her daughter's lips and made her drink, whispering words soft and low. Great Pa couldn't hear the words, but as Mama drank the last of the potion, he heard his wife say with her hand on Mama's amulet, "Fire and blood, girl. Fire and blood."

Great Pa watched as Mama's eyes shot open like a bolt of lightning had struck her. Deep, uncluttered breaths rolled off her pale blue lips. He was pleased, so very, very pleased, and wrapped his arms around his beloved child.

Great Ma...she was anything but pleased.

Staying with Mama again was like peeling back the sticky layers of time and sitting in the mess you had made. I remembered that awful smell of rot and earth that seemed to penetrate every one of my senses, through my skin to the fleshy parts of me, the longer I stayed. I remembered the way she made me feel as I watched her toil at her work, a bundle of boiled nerves that were ready to burst. I remembered the look of her when she was lost in the ways of her mama before her, and her ma before her. Such an otherworldly look, as if the moon itself sat constant and still in her eyes. A flurry of fire lay there too, flickering back at me with all the daring and defiance of a morning star that refused to fade away with the dawn.

I remembered it all, and I hated it. But something kept me from leaving. I felt a tugging on my body, invisible vines that seemed to rise from the earth and cling to me. That earthy power that played about my skin and pounded at my breast was intent on getting to the very heart of me. I was hesitant to let it in. Mama sensed that, and with every new day, she was more insistent that I help her with her work.

Reluctantly, she taught me the way again. The way of mixing draughts and concoctions, learning which herbs and roots and flowers were best for every need and desire. The way of preparing talismans and charms, reading the movements of the earth and the moon, the weather and the seasons, and the stars. We lived for the earth, drank it in and slept in its embrace, and thanked it for its gracious gift of life.

Being with Mama and her ways was intoxicating, and the more time I spent with her, the more I began to forget life before her. My waking moments were waves of heightened consciousness and my dreams at night were distant memories of a nightmare. Most of my dreams, anyway. Some were cool and soft and sweet, and those I fell into with all my heart.

One night I dreamed of Elijah. It was a passionate and pleasurable sort of dream.

The color red. Skin on skin. My name on his lips in the dark. Moonlight flashing in his eyes like fire.

I awoke from the dream blushing like a fool. I sat dumbstruck in the darkness, ashamed of my own dark and dirty mind. I waited there in the silence of the night for God to smite me down for thinking such sinful things about a preacher man, but He didn't.

I was beginning to think in the quiet parts of my mind that perhaps all that hellfire and brimstone they shouted about in church every Sunday was nothing but talk. I hadn't seen it. My Great Ma had been a wicked woman, but when she died and they put her in the earth, the earth welcomed her back. There were no tongues of fire to ravage her body. No devils snatched up her soul on that dreary winter day with all her family standing around her open grave, wishing ill upon her, and spitting on her coffin as they left. Yes, she had been wicked, but neither the elements nor God above seemed to care. She passed from this earth in silence and dignity, like a body should.

Perhaps God didn't care what my dream had been.

"If you're intendin' to sin in them dreams of yours, girl, at least do it quietly. You're liable to wake the dead and rattle them bones with all that moanin' and carryin' on."

My mama's voice in the darkness of the room we shared frightened me. I jumped nearly to my feet, my breath catching violently in my throat. I could hear her throaty, gurgling laugh in the shadows. The creak of her bed as she turned her back to me. Then the room grew quiet again.

My whole body burned with embarrassment. I laid back down, too afraid that what I had dreamed would suddenly become flesh and blood in the night.

I'm dreaming once again. I can sense how deep the darkness drapes over me. Over everything. Slowly the darkness lifts just a little. Nightfall on the town. A mist carries me down the long dirt road to its center where the church and its gloomy churchyard stands.

I walk through the moss-covered stones and wooden crosses that pockmark the sweetly green grass. A chill runs through me; spooks and ghostly specters are the stuff of my nightmares. It was different when kinfolk made their way to their door on a cool summer's eve, but this...this was liable to take the very breath from my lungs and stop my beating heart.

I stop. Don't know why. Something—perhaps the mist—bids me stop. At my bare feet, there's a rotten mound of earth. The grass has long since died upon it, and the creepy crawly things of the earth, the kind that eat the dead, litter its soil. It smells of death. The mist swirls swiftly around me, and from within the foul wind that carries it, I hear Aunt Millicent's voice.

"*The earth here is dead, girl. Best be wary of its fruit.*"

I awoke as the sun rose. A cold morning breeze filled me full of shivers and a sense of dread.

13 Mama's Soul in Mine

"Folk's is talking, Kit. You'd best be wary. They say you've swept her up in your witchin' ways, intent on stealin' her soul for the Devil."

Otho, the man speaking to Mama at her worktable in loud whispers, was a man everybody knew for his gossiping ways and his tall tales. Like the boy who cried wolf, it was hard to take anything he said as gospel. My mama knew as much and gave him a devilish grin, a spark of mischief and delight in her eyes.

"There's no devil in what I do. You know that well, Otho, else you'd have stopped comin' ages ago." She met his fearful gaze with a glint of ire. "And your wife'd be all the worse for it, what with that damned colic and all."

"Besides," I spoke up. Otho seemed startled that I even knew how to open my mouth. I gave him a smile rooted in that same devilish mischief of Mama's. "What's to say *I* didn't bring the Devil with me?"

That set a look of fear in Otho's eyes, his scruffy face turned ghostly white. I nearly laughed with the pleasure of it. Mama cackled out a laugh as she handed him a small leather pouch full of the healing balm needed for his ailing wife. Otho snatched it up, saying not a word more. He shuffled quickly to the front door.

Before he left, he said, "Them church folk is a-talkin' too. The preacher's wife's got her eyes on ya."

Mama glanced up with a spiteful arch to her brow. "What's that woman got agin me? I've not touched a blessed hair on her head."

"Just you be wary." Otho slammed the door behind him with a decisive rush of cool morning air.

Mama's laughter trailed after him. She looked at me with a twinkle in her eye.

"A mind after my own," she muttered. The twinkle flickered out quickly and she hid her face, whispering, "A soul after my own, I swear."

Mama cleared her throat, and she looked at me again. She held out a basket of canned goods, pushing it toward me.

"Get ye gone, then. Go on. These won't sell themselves."

Mama sold goods to the local market. With her reputation in the town, I was surprised that Mr. Tillman allowed her to barter and trade at his store. Of course, Mama traipsing down Main Street once a month was an event for the wide-eyed townies, one that nobody wanted to miss. All of them immediately whispered prayers of protection to the Lord and crossed themselves if they had a mind to, for even to look on a witch was bad luck. For all their fear of curses and bad omens, it didn't stop them from looking though.

I was the one to walk down Main Street on that cool summer morning. A rolling fog off the mountain crept along with me into town. It was early but the morning busybodies were already out and about on the street, their eyes gawking wildly as I came barefooted into town.

I could feel their judgement bearing down on me. All those eyes, all those vengeful, bitter hearts bent on me. I clutched to Mama's basket with all my might, my other hand clasped tightly around the moonstone. I prayed for some courage to light a spark in me. As if in answer, the misty wind curled up around my body, enveloping me in a cloak of mystery and whispers. Then something wild in me broke like a flooded dam, filling all my insides with a vengeful and vindictive fire. It warmed me until I felt all aflutter with it. I stood tall, my head held high.

My feet led me to Mr. Tillman's store, and I stopped under the green-frilled awning to take one last look at them all. There they were, all of them, gawping at me like some wooden-headed ninnies that had just seen the boogerman. I gave them a wicked grin, pulled the store door open, and went inside. After the cool breeze outside, Tillman's store seemed stuffy, the air stale and sanitized. Everything was stacked too neatly, the aisles of goods too straight and narrow, and not a warm body in sight. My eyes scanned every bit of cramped and dusky space for someone, anyone.

"Mrs. Bennett, how are you this mornin'?"

Mr. Tillman nearly made me jump at his greeting. I turned to him with a weak smile. He was a great big bear of a man, nearly as tall as the large shelf of tobacco behind him at the counter. I bet he could raise his hand without effort and reach his fingertips to touch the ceiling. The thought of him wiggling his fingers in the air above him with that pixilated smile of his made me grin.

"Just fine, Mr. Tillman, I reckon."

He smiled back at that. Mr. Tillman wasn't one to judge a body by what or who they worshipped. He saw the good in everyone, no matter the circumstances of their life. As long as they had money in their pockets, he was willing to accept just about anybody.

"Every friendship has a price," Mr. Tillman would always say. "Mine just happens to be those coins jingling there along with ya."

Ding!

The door swung open, its little jingle bells clanging away. A tall shadow passed through it. Bathed in the hazy sunlight, it approached me at the counter. Blinking blindly in the light, it took me a minute to see.

It was Elijah. He smiled warmly at me; a sanitary and unsuspecting version of the look he had given me not so long ago. I didn't like this one. It turned my insides into a cold, bitter mush that dripped down to my toes with the drabbest feeling of nothingness I'd ever felt. I didn't smile back. I caught myself staring and quickly turned back to the grocer.

"I brought things from my Mama, Mr. Tillman."

Mr. Tillman snatched up one of Mama's jars, looking hard at its contents with a bit of confusion. "What's it to be this time, eh?"

He gave me a mischievous smile and a wink behind his smudged glasses.

"Elderberry jam."

He picked up another jar. "And this 'un?"

"Plum."

He nodded with a shake of his head. "Some kind of witchery in every jar, I suppose?"

I blushed bright red. I could feel Elijah's gaze on me, distracting me.

Mr. Tillman went on, "I can't figure how your mama makes these jams and jellies taste so damn good. Pardon, Preacher, folks just is eatin' it up by the barrelful."

Elijah edged nearer to my body, the heat of him brushing my skin in a fiery embrace. He hadn't even touched me. I knew I was in trouble. I leaned nearer to the counter, my whole body pressed up hard against it. Mr. Tillman kept talking, but I didn't hear him. While he mindlessly chattered on, he grabbed up the basket and took it into the back. I heard him in there, mumbling to himself as he always did.

"Can we speak, Jaelle?"

Elijah's whispered words tickled my ear with a warm breeze, making me tremble all over. I didn't turn around to him. I didn't dare. His hand brushed mine, soft and low so that no one would see, though there was really no one *to* see. Mr. Tillman was still chattering away in the back storeroom with Mama's jars of jam, and here I was thinking all the sinful things a girl could about the man behind me.

I peered around the counter to make sure Mr. Tillman was well occupied in the storeroom. Then, I whispered back, "We *are* speaking, Brother Wise."

I heard him chuckle just a little under his breath. I knew he was smiling at me. I blushed hard.

"So, it would seem, then."

That chuckle again. Warm breath on my neck. Shivers down my spine.

"Your mama wanna trade for somethin' or just take the cash?" Mr. Tillman yelled out from the storeroom.

It shook me from my sinful daydreams, and I blinked away those visions from behind my eyes. "Just the cash today, Mr. Tillman."

Mr. Tillman peeked his head out and gave me a nod before he bobbed back out of sight.

That was Elijah's cue to get even closer, his lips gliding across my ear.

"When?" he hissed.

Tremblingly, I answered, "When what?"

He breathed in deeply. "Please let me see you."

My heart leaped in my chest. I stood stock still, afraid that if I even breathed, his mouth would part from my skin and this moment would be over.

"Please," he begged.

There was that power again tugging at me from the inside, only this time it was different. This was a different sort of power. This power wasn't just hungry, it was wholly unsated. The longer he lingered next to my skin, the more agitated my insides became. I would have told him no right then. I would have run to escape his touch and the heat it carried. I would have—were it not for my heart. It beat as fast as a jackrabbit in spring, leaning ever so much toward that preacher man, until I just couldn't breathe.

I dared to turn to him. His eyes were alight with

fire. They were eager, as if he would bend the knee and bow before me. Worship me. That power inside me liked that idea, and a smile crept across my lips.

Leig leis adhradh.

"Elijah—"

He didn't let me say more.

"Please?" he begged.

I shouldn't let him do that. I shouldn't let him beg, but I did. My body tingled from my head to the tips of my toes to have him near me. My heart skipped a beat, and I felt that earthen power fill the space where it had ceased. It seeped up from the wood floors like the strong pull of fresh vines in spring, twining all about my flesh as he drew nearer and nearer.

"Please?"

My mouth opened to speak.

"Tell Kit that'll be all we need for a while. Till next month, eh?"

Mr. Tillman glided into the room without a notion of what had just transpired between Elijah and me. The smile was swept right off my face, and I felt Elijah pull back from me, stepping a foot away.

Room enough for the Spirit. Room enough for the Lord.

Mr. Tillman held out a bundle of cash and coins. It took me a minute to realize I was to take them. Slowly, I reached my hand out to get the money. Casting my eyes downward, I grabbed up Mama's basket from the counter. I hurried out without a glance at either of them.

The wind swept up to meet me as I hit the morning air, now hot and heavy with the promise of rain. I was flustered all the way back to Mama's, but I didn't speak of my meeting with Elijah to her. Not a word.

"What's with ya, girl? You look like hell."

My mama didn't mince words when it came to me. With Elijah on my mind and the remnants of that power still clinging to my bones, her criticism was the final straw.

Standing up and lit like a spotlight by the fire, I said matter-of-factly, "I'm going home, Mama."

It was the first time in my life that the woman looked truly disappointed. Not at me, but because of me. I felt a sense that she had cherished this time with her only living daughter and knew its value in the weight of things. I was of value to her now that I understood her. Understood her love and hate, and her ways. But I had to go. Something else was calling me back home. For good or bad, I had to go home, and she knew it. She nodded, and that was that. I packed my things and took to the road toward my house.

14 Dreams of the Present Turn Me Cold

It wasn't long before I heard from Sheriff Roy that he'd let Jeremy go. In fact, it had been a while since he'd left jail. Since he hadn't come home, Roy suspected that Jeremy had run off to avoid any more trouble with the law. Word was spreading fast around town that his run-in with Sal Temple was more than a drunken tiff. Whispers abounded about what had driven them to fight. It seemed that my husband's little secret wasn't so secret anymore. Despite it all, I had to make things right with the Temples. There would be no bad blood between us if I had anything to do with it. Not even with the talk about town.

On a clear afternoon, I walked the few miles to the Temple farm. I hadn't any idea what kind of greeting I'd receive when I stepped up to their door. All the same, I waited in the wary silence for it to open. It took a long time for the door to creak open just enough for me to catch sight of Sal in the shadows. He looked bleary-eyed and drunk. The stink of booze dripped from him, even through the small crack he'd left for us to see one another. It made my stomach roll with sickness, but I tried to smile.

"Afternoon, Sal."

Sal said nothing in return.

"I come to bring my apologies for my husband Jeremy. I know what he done wasn't right and it should be him here makin' amends, but—you know how he is."

"I can't rightly imagine," Sal said sternly. His tone was cold.

I glanced over toward the barn with its fresh, gaping hole. I nearly cringed.

"I truly am sorry, Sal. I cain't pay for the damage he's done, but there must be something I can do."

The light on the porch shifted and I saw Sal's face. It was tear-ridden and pale, and he looked at me with such a deep sorrow. Sorrow and shame and pity. I cleared my throat.

"Is Missy at home?"

His face swiftly changed. Hate remained where sorrow had been.

"She ain't here. She left. For her sister's a couple of towns over."

"Oh, well—"

"You best get home now, Jaelle. You best get home."

The door slammed shut in my face. Like looking through a tunnel, as the wind swept around me, I saw—

The color red. Skin on skin in the flashing light of a motel sign. Jeremy's name on the air, loud and breathless.

Trembling, I turned away from the door and made my way back home.

I awoke that night from a dream. It was a passionate and empty dream, full of things I shouldn't feel. The cool night air washed me clean of those clinging thoughts. I took a deep breath, wiping the sweat from my brow. As quickly as I had pushed those thoughts away, they returned all the stronger. Passion and desire, and the moonlight was urging them on. It was calling me out onto the dusty road paved with starlight that I could see just outside my window. Calling me. *He* was calling me. I could feel it, and this time I couldn't let it go.

The moonlight led me down the long, dusty road, the wind sweeping up urging my bare feet forward. It led me straight to the Narrow Way. The church loomed in a ghostly shadow over me. I felt the weight of it and peered up in the darkness at that big iron cross atop the steeple. Before I knew it, my feet led me into the church. A shadow followed me as far as the door, but no further.

It was strange to walk the little aisle toward the pulpit in the dark. The silence was heavy, and the moonlight streamed in red through the stained-glass windows, painting me and everything around me the color of blood. I walked up the steps to the pulpit and stood there. The empty pews were a ghostly congregation amidst all that silence.

"Repent!" I cried out.

My voice echoed emptily on the air. It was an empty word on my lips with none of the fire of Brother Wise. A creaking sound above me raised my eyes upward. The large wooden cross above my head swayed and swayed. There wasn't any wind, not a breath of air to move it. Quickly, I stepped down and made my way out of the church to Brother Wise's doorstep. It was still night, and I shivered in the cold. My mind was racing.

My heart told me to leave. To walk right back down that old road and just keep moving. Away from Elijah, away from Jeremy, away from Mama, away from everything I'd ever known. That was good and fine and all talk. For the life of me, I couldn't make my feet leave his front step. For all my fitful desire, I just stood there on that stoop. I didn't knock. Didn't raise my balled fist to even try. I just stood there, staring at my own reflection in the two crescent-shaped windowpanes in the door. My reflected face was ghostly pale and frightened, split in two by the glass pane, two halves of a very divided whole.

A cloud had drifted over the hazy moon, but even

that blanket of misty fluff could not hold back its light. It was cool and serene, and it soothed me to calmness. I recalled what I was about, what had brought me here in the first place. My fist rose to knock, but again I held back. I wouldn't call for him, not like that, raucous and abrupt, shattering the stillness of his peaceful slumber.

    I called him with that prickling power which had settled into my very blood and bones. I let it slide easily from my own flesh, yearning for it to push past the wood of the door and into the quiet of his room. I blushed to think of him there as my heart called him. His room was such a sacred place where the likes of me didn't belong. The place left empty beside him was not for me. It was made just for one prissy green-eyed worm of a woman, whose smile always seemed out of spite. Those eyes were always watching the womenfolk of the congregation too, watching and judging. I always felt it. I could feel it now, her grim eyes upon me, seeing all and calling upon her god of justice for revenge.

    In the windowpane, I watched half of my face cringe. I didn't want to think of Mrs. Prudence Wise and her green, green eyes just now. I sighed hopelessly. This was foolish, and I was a damned fool. I had half a mind to turn away right there and then, but the door quietly clicked and crept open.

    In the slippery darkness, I saw Elijah. He stared back at me, all wide-eyed and hungry. I fancied that he'd heard me. Heard the longing I had sent out on the hainted moonlight to his head resting upon that forbidden pillow. I thought of so many things to say, but looking him dead in the eye stopped my thinking right in its very tracks. There he was—Mr. Elijah Wise—Eijah, standing right in front of me. The dirtiest grin I'd ever seen was spread wide and wild across his face. That fire was glinting strong in his eyes, but I didn't mind. For the moonlight was in mine, easy and cool. I would quench that fire if it killed me. If it took all of me to do it.

The house was dark behind him, but he—*we*—were basked in the gossamer white light peering through the tall trees that surrounded the parish house. His house, his home, our—I couldn't let my thoughts go there.

His eyes were intent upon me as he offered his hand. There was a moment of my own hesitation, as his last sermon ran through my mind.

Truly I say to you, if you have faith the size of a mustard seed...

Faith the size of a mustard seed. Did I have any faith at all, when I was standing there with him, prepared for any kind of sin? I took his hand.

You will say to this mountain, 'Move,' and it will move; and nothing will be impossible to you.

He pulled me in tightly, his arms an open sea that welcomed me. His mouth was a lightning bolt, a beating pulse against my skin in fast kisses, deep and unsated. He filled every part of me. And I let him.

It is dark. So dark and black and horrible that I can't see a thing. The wind whips about my body so violently that I'm nearly bowled over with the power of it. I shake all over. My body is bare.

There's a hiss. Something slithers at my feet. Twines about my legs. I can't move for fear. Up, up my legs, it slides. Up my thighs with that ugly hiss. Across my stomach, my breasts, around my neck.

My mouth flying open, I start to scream. It jams itself into my mouth, reaching down my throat until breath escapes me and I'm choking. Choking to death.

I woke up with a start, the hint of that dark thing still draped over me, but the fear of it had already dissipated. It was a dream, nothing more. Dawn was fast approaching. I was still in Elijah's bed, burrowed deep within the cool cotton sheets beside him. The heat of his body pulsed next to my bare skin.

Naked. Just as the good Lord intended in the beginning.

A sinful smile spread across my face. The morning air was quiet and still, Elijah's steady breaths the only sound as he slept. My hand gently fell to my chest, reaching for my mama's moonstone to feel its soft power against my skin.

It was gone.

I shot up in the bed, feeling around me for it within the sheets and under the pillows. Frantically, my hands moved across Elijah's side, but I couldn't find it. I shivered in the sudden cold. That icy cold was like my dream. I tugged at the coverlet and hugged it close to my body.

"See, girl. Even the moonlight can deceive you."

Aunt Millicent. I could feel her before I could see her. There she was, creeping amidst the shadows in the corner of the room. She *was* the shadows, draped in them and made of them. She smiled at me with a wretched, deadly look of pleasure.

"You'd best find the shadow that brought you," she hissed.

There was that tugging against my body. That power that always seemed a breath away from my skin, toying with me. Only this time, there was something wrong. It was urgent and strong, a flicker of danger in its wake.

"Find it, girl."

Quickly, I jumped out of bed and pulled on my shift dress. I tiptoed my way out of the room, not taking a second to glance back. I went through the house without really looking at anything. Something was pulling me away, and I let it. Out of the door and into the front yard of the parish house, I went. My bare feet seemed to know the way, as they led me into the church's graveyard.

The churchyard was blanketed in a thick and soupy fog, one that was unnatural here in this place. Everything about the air, the cold and the mist seemed unnatural. Afraid, I kept going, the pull was growing stronger. Suddenly, my feet stopped on a bare piece of earth. My toes sank into the dead grass and soil. My head cocked to the side, I stared down at that little bit of earth with a curious cringe. It wasn't right.

Aunt Millicent stood before me, staring down at it too. Her face was dark and troubled. She looked at me.

"Dig."

I knelt with haste and used my hands to claw at the earth. I dug with a furious need, until my fingers touched something cold and dead. The feeling of it made me jump back. Aunt Millicent knelt now, a smile upon her face. She was pressing me to reach in and take out what had frightened me.

"Say to the mountain, 'Move,' and it shall be moved," though she spoke, there was another layer of voices beneath her, speaking in a tongue I didn't understand.

Her words hissed on the air, and then she was gone. I was alone, and there was a thing I just had to unearth, whatever it might be. Closing my eyes tight, I reached a trembling hand into the hole. I grabbed hold of that cold, dead thing and brought it up, quickly dropping it to the ground. I kept my eyes closed, wiping my hands on my dress until that cold feeling was rubbed out of my fingers. I had to look. I knew that. Slowly, I opened my eyes and looked down. There on the ground was a small burlap bag, tied off at its ragged ends. It looked old.

Carefully, I pulled at the string and the bag fell open, its contents spilling out. A swatch of red hair was among them. I knew what it was. My body sensed the darkness, the pitch, and the evil of it before I'd set eyes on it. I'd seen this kind of backwoods magic before. Saw it left on my mama's porch with all the ill will of its spiteful sender. Odds and ends, trinkets that amounted to a wicked curse. It was dark and very, very bad. I scurried away from it.

Sinner.

Out of the corner of my eye, a shadow shifted amid the tombstones and faded crosses. It made me shiver. Quickly, I scrambled to my feet, hurrying away from the churchyard and the home of Elijah.

15 Tongues of Fire

The smell of smoke woke me from a deep and dreamless sleep. The smell of rot and sulfur swirled all around me, a whirlwind of revolting muck and mire all pressed up against my face until I couldn't breathe. In the shadows, my Great Ma's rocking chair was just a-rocking away, a deeper shadow in its seat. Low laughter came from the chair. It shivered on the air with an icy chill of death.

The laughter turned into a howling shriek. The shadow dashed out of my window and into the night. I trembled in the wake of the haint. In these mountains, among the people born and bred from their roots, spooks and specters were a natural part of life. There were loved ones that visited for a spell, and then there were dark things like the boogerman. Just the thought of him made my teeth chatter in my head. I wrapped up tight in my covers and shut tight my eyes. My moonstone was gone, and with its loss, my luck had soured. Now, the boogerman had come, bringing with him the stain of Hell.

"What have I done?" The words hit my lips like cement, trudging out onto the air with every intention of breaking me.

Surely, what I had done with Brother Wise would send me straight to the fiery pits of hell. Perhaps the shadowy specter in the darkness I had seen was the Devil himself who had come to claim my soul in all its sin.

God help me.

It was in the early hours of Sunday morning. The

pale pink light had washed over everything in sight, coloring it with the awful stain of a brand-new day. I wasn't one to rue the morning or even one to fear it, but today, a fear so deep and heavy thrilled right through me. Every inch of me. I sat on the porch, rocking in my chair, just waiting for that fear to wash away. My eyes kept scanning the horizon for fire and a throng of angry Christians coming to judge me. They had to come. That's what happened in the older days when a woman was thought to have used her wicked wiles on a good and godly man.

That's what happens, isn't it?

The question tumbled around in my head again and again until I was sick. I couldn't bear the thought of walking up to the Narrow Way, a bruised and broken soul. It was the pride in me that wouldn't allow it. I wouldn't do it. I wouldn't confess my sins to a congregation of fitful, nosy people whose heads were buried way down deep in the dirt. They were the sinners to be judged, not me. My hand fell to my breast with a gasp.

Wicked, wicked thoughts! That's what comes of sin.

I sat back in the chair and rocked, trembling all the while. Darkness had crept into my mind. Pitch-black darkness and rage. Lust and envy. All those wicked things that preachers warned against. Everything that I had prayed to ward off in my own life for so many years.

Sunday had come and I was once again fearful of the judgment of the Lord.

Behold, I was brought forth in iniquity, and in sin did my mother conceive me!

My mama's ways were perilous on that straight and narrow path of God. I knew that. I had always known it, and no amount of temptation and heartache could prove it otherwise. Mama was a witch, a sinner, a devil in the eyes of God. Her ways were not my ways, and they were not God's.

Against you, you only, have I sinned, and done that which is evil in your sight.

The moonstone had left me just as the darkness had crept in. A darkness I had let inside. I had to be rid of that ever-creeping thing. Had to be rid of the stink of shame upon my skin. The feel and the taste of *him*—Elijah.

I know my transgressions, and my sin is ever before me.

The little church was calling me. Calling me home, far away from the cluttered mess of earth and vines and visions of my mama. Far away from that shadow that seemed to be draped over my horizon. Coming for me, full of fire, blood and snow. I could feel it and see it as clearly as day. No more night, no more moonlight, I was a child of the Light, a child of God. I had to be.

Ruith.

I ran straight to the Narrow Way, just as the church bells began their last call to the faithful from far and wide. There I was, standing in the shadow of that tall, tall steeple, its iron cross glaring down at me with all the judgment and the fury of a summer storm. It was unlike me to be afraid of this place, to fear my feet stepping onto its solid ground. Now, my toes sank down deep in my shoes, praying for the shifting dirt and roots, and the gentle power of the earth. As much as I desired them, I held back. That was not my god. It was no one's god, but the wicked. That's what Brother Wise taught.

Brother Wise—*Elijah.*

His name sank down deep into the pit of me, souring there like a bittersweet poison bent on killing me from the inside. I would see him again. I didn't want to, not now with his touch and the smell of him still clinging to my skin. What we had done was anything but holy. There in his home within the shadow of this hallowed place. There where God was watching. Watching Elijah and me.

The thought of God's eyes burning down on us in that moment made me want to retch. My body began to turn of its own accord, away from the church and back to the dusty road toward home. Away from Brother Wise and the eyes of God. Suddenly, I felt myself swept up by the arm and led right up the stairs into the church.

"Jaelle, honey, I was plum worried about you, what with Jeremy in jail and you alone with a babe comin' and all. I promise you. I'll not leave your side for a minute. You hear, not for a minute."

I turned to find Mrs. Samuels beside me. She was a stern looking woman, cold in her features and less a woman than an overbearing and austere statue of what a woman should be. She never talked much, save for those she kept in her sacred fold, of which I was not privy. Yet today, today she had accepted me as her own.

Is this you, God? Do you accept me? Do you welcome me back into the fold of your right hand?

As we walked into the church, I heard a hush sweep over the pews, the chatter dwindled to a busy hum, as Mrs. Samuels pushed me down in one of the front pews. With her arm locked in mine, she kept a sharp hold on me. At the church's front and center, was Elijah. His fiery eyes burned a hole right through me, his face flushed, and his mouth parted enough to see that it desired mine.

At the edge of my sight, my eyes caught sight of Mrs. Prudence Wise. She was sitting near the choir. Her hair was choked back in a bun, her dress finer than any I'd seen this side of the mountain. Her gaze tossed wildly between me and her husband, a tug of war that at last she lost. Her face grew pale. Quickly, I turned away. My eyes went anywhere, but back to look at her.

The rest of the pews were already full to the brim with families and old couples smiling cordially at one another and whispering their greetings. Everyone seemed so happy. So carefree and burdenless. They didn't feel the shadow that I did, nor the guilty pleasure of another man's touch.

The organ at the front of the church blared to life with a wrenching whine as the hymn began. The choir droned on in their lifeless dirge, out of tune and singing far too fast for the young organ player to keep up. One old man in the congregation called the sound "a cacophony of heavenly noise that would raise Lazarus all over again." I smiled just a little. The old man was right, even if I didn't understand all those fancy words.

Elijah glided weightlessly to his high-back seat of polished red wood, deeply carved with an elaborate cross, and sat down as if he hadn't a care in the world. Not a modicum of sin pushed down upon his heart. He was content and seemed right happy with himself, the sun glinting down from the red-hued stained glass upon him. A smile was stamped prettily upon his face. I watched him. I couldn't help it. As he sat there in his preacher's spotless clothes, his hair slicked back and not a curl in sight.

His skin glows in the silver shafts of pretty moonlight as he hovers over me. Reddish brown curls crown his head, and his eyes are alight with that fire. Meant for me. It's meant for me. His soft voice whispers my name. Jaelle.

I felt naked before him, as if all my innards, down to my spirit, were laid bare for him to see. My sin. My desire.

Mrs. Bateman sighed in my ear. Sitting on my left in all her hefty glory, she was already restless and fiddling in her purse for her noisy peppermint candies. As she dug in the cavernous hole that was her purse, she whispered my way.

"Roy told me all about your Jeremy."

My, what big ears you have, Mrs. Bateman!

She was always a ready ear for the latest gossip. The latest whispers of the community, those damning details that would make a preacher's eyes pop. They were all like that, all of them within these pews. Ready to damn their fellow man. Ready to burn him and bury him six feet under for his sins. The thought came to me that I was not one of these. I didn't wish for the downfall of my brothers and sisters. I didn't run to hear the worst of their souls and wish them ruin.

You're not one of these, a voice pierced the air.

An icy cold wind that seemed out of place in this holy hothouse. The air was heavy with the scent of sweet lavender and wild mint, not the factory-made stuff that Mrs. Bateman kept in her purse. This was a raw, unaltered, and wholly different sort of scent, with hints of age and the dampness of old earth. It twinged around my nose with such intensity, it made me feel ill. I lurched forward in my seat, ready to purge what little sat in my stomach. It didn't come. Mrs. Bateman saw and quickly crammed a peppermint candy in my face.

"Here, this'll calm your stomach, honey," she whispered low.

I took it and jammed it into my dry mouth. The candy rolled lifelessly about my mouth, clanking against my teeth. My stomach began to ease, just as the smell of lavender returned all the stronger, this time with a note of sour rottenness I couldn't bear.

My mind grew hazy and the white walls surrounding me were patched with dim shadows. My eyes followed the shadows to the great wooden cross above the preacher's pulpit. Down below the high-rising pulpit was Aunt Millicent. Her eyes were black, wide and full of rage. Her hair was mussed. Her pale blue frock was stained with blood and earth. Her face was as white as a sheet as she looked through the faces in the pews.

Brother Wise had taken to the pulpit, and with an

apple-red face, he had begun his lusty sermon. All eyes were on him, glued to him like he was the Lord himself. His fiery words slipped from his tongue with such passion and noise that the walls themselves shook and trembled at the sound. Every man, woman, and child were deathly silent and utterly still as they listened.

Millicent stumbled down the long aisle, grumbling to herself as she passed the people in the congregation. Her worn shoes shuffled with a hiss, pew after pew. No one else saw her. Her lips moved endlessly; dried blood painted across them like ruby-red lip color. I leaned forward in the pew to hear what she was saying. My heart told me that I must hear it. Must heed it.

"Murderers! Vile sinners! Thieves and bastards! All of you! All of you whispering your sins in the dark, praying to the night that you'll not be found out. Your god will punish you. He will raze you to the ground. I promise you. The god of the earth will swallow you whole."

Her paper-thin and ghostly white features sharpened when she looked back at me and pointed a gnarled finger with trembling precision. The floorboards beneath my feet rattled and cracked. Thick ivy wrapped around my legs and twisted tightly with a vicious hiss. I didn't cry out. Didn't breathe. I just watched Aunt Millicent glare me down and spit upon the ground before her.

"Adulterer!" she screamed. "You gave yourself to a godly man and betrayed the power of your own people. The heavens will not take you and the earth rejects your body like the dead and rotten thing that you are."

The sound of her screaming rushed at me, a tidal wave of booming betrayal and guilt. All of it hit me in the gut. It wrenched my insides until I couldn't stand it any longer. The vines kept crawling up my skin, inch by inch until they were climbing up my throat. They reached for my mouth, my eyes, and ears. They meant to snuff me out. Snuff out the power in me.

"No," I whispered, though it felt as powerful and thunderous as if I had screamed it on the air.

I pulled myself free from those clinging vines and stood. Millicent watched me, her head cocked to the side with an odd sort of look. A look of confusion. Of surprise. Of fear. Her lips parted.

I heard the shifting bodies of the congregation. At the head of the church, I saw Mrs. Prudence Wise hurriedly excuse herself. All eyes were on me, staring with that same look. I looked at all of them looking back at me, my breath catching in my chest. Slowly, I sat down, feeling the eyes of Brother Wise on me. Millicent was gone. I sank down deep into the pew, praying to whoever would listen that his eyes would look away and never look at me again.

I managed to keep quiet for the rest of the service. No one else looked at me. No one, not even Mrs. Samuels, would speak to me. They were all frightened of me, and that, I thought at that moment, was a good thing. In a daze, I followed the crowd out of the church. As I stepped down onto the walk, the air was thick with the thunderous sound of a heartbeat, fast like a flittering bird caught in a net. I allowed it to lead me, away from the crowd, behind the church to the shadowed trees and graveyard.

I heard voices amid the tombstones and moldy crosses. I stumbled behind a tangled hawthorn and peered out to catch sight of Elijah and his wife. Their words were quiet but heated. I could just hear them from where I stood.

"You're acting ridiculous, Prudence. Get hold of yourself." Elijah grabbed hold of her arm, a hateful look on his flushed face.

She whimpered and pulled her arm away from his grasp. Eyes wide, she parted her mouth to speak, but something caught her eye. She glanced my way, eyes glaring daggers of spiteful green. I made myself scarce, hurrying back to the church, the crowd, and the safety of the sunshine. My heart beat wildly in my breast. Suddenly, I felt a brush of hot skin against my hand. I glanced back to see Elijah looking at me, his eyes full of fire and moonlight. Then, there she was, Elijah's wife clinging so close to him that there wasn't an inch of skin between them, her hand clamped down tightly on his. Her eyes were on me too, much sharper and greener than I remembered.

Damn her to hell.

I saw fire when I looked in those eyes of hers. Envy as wild as those flames. She was hell-bent on spooking me, but I wasn't afraid. I was filled with an irksome rage that burned until my body was fully afire.

I hate that woman. I hate her.

Fuath dhi gu ifrinn.

I didn't understand the echo in my mind, climbing the walls of my guarded thoughts to stain my conscience with blood-red shadows. I didn't understand the words, but I understood the feeling that had come over me as I watched Mrs. Prudence Wise. Something must be done about it. I let the crowd of churchgoers envelop me and lead me far away from Elijah and his wife, who were still standing in the shadow of the iron-wrought steeple.

***

Mama didn't answer her door. I heard the soft lilting sound of her voice chanting inside.

"Mama!" I yelled, my fist pounding on her screen door.

The chanting stopped. A shiver ran across my skin. The thrum of her magic spilled out onto the porch to meet me. It was defiant, a searing, violent wave rushing toward me. I was not unprepared. I met it with my own violent shade of power. When her face appeared at the door, wrapped as it was with shadows despite the sun overhead, I could see the worry in her eyes. She did not open the door.

"Mama—" I started, but she didn't let me finish. Not a word more.

"What you want, girl, I cain't give ya." Her voice was cold.

That shiver on my goose-pimpled skin got worse. I felt the tug of war between her power and mine, each vying for the upper hand. I leaned in close, as close to her as the screen between us would allow.

"How do you know what I want?" I whispered, scared that should the wind hear my words, Hell itself would crawl its way up to get me.

Damn her to hell, Mama. Damn her to hell with me.

Mama's eyes grew wide. "Thems dark thoughts you got, girl. I'll not have that sort here. And don't you be comin' round again."

She slammed the front door hard, so hard the screen door shivered and shook. The violence of it shook that shadow right out of me, and I stood in its wake, fearful of what lay just below my own skin. I left Mama's emptyhanded.

The sun was hot on the walk back to the farmhouse. I didn't notice, nor did I care. My feet shuffled up the dust from the road and I walked in a sickening daze all the way. The air rang with a wakefulness that droned deafeningly in my ears, along with the voice of Aunt Millicent. I could sense her heavy shadow at my back, following me at every step. Following. Always following. Cursing me all the way.

My feet stopped where the gravel met the grass of my front yard. I couldn't get them to go any further. Not when *he* was watching me from the front porch. Glaring me down with as much hate as a man could muster.

Jeremy was back. He sat on the porch just swinging away, his eyes bent on me with a crooked smile. I knew that smile well. I knew what it meant, trouble.

"Cat got your tongue?" he said.

That's when I saw the shotgun tucked under his arm.

With a flick of his wrist, it was up and aimed at me. I said nothing. Just stared down the barrel of his shotgun. He wasn't going to get a word out of me. He chuckled with a wicked sneer spread across his face. It made me sick to look at it. He knew that. There was something else there in his eyes—fear. He blinked long and slow, and it was gone just as quickly as it had come. A shadow of it remained. I could sense it. This man was afraid of me.

I cocked my head to the side, observing him in silence. He didn't like that at all. Didn't like me looking at him in any way other than with my own fear. Fear of his power, his strength, his rage. He rose to his feet when I still didn't answer him.

"Just you go on a-lookin' at me that a-way. See where it gets ya."

Coming to the edge of the porch, he stared down at me, the sun beating down on him with its own rage. I was glad of that.

"Answer me, dammit!" the man screamed.

In the hot sunlight that beamed down on his head, I could see his thinning hair, the baldness underneath shiny with sweat. He was getting old. It made me smile. He swung to slap it off my face. I felt the air rush past my face along with a steady ringing in my ears. He had missed and tumbled forward, falling into the dirt and gravel at my feet.

Watching in silence, he moaned, gripping the gravel with both bloodied hands. He reached up to me, wanting me to help him to his feet. Just so he could tower over me once again and beat me senseless. I didn't lend him a hand. I kicked off my shoes so that I could feel the cool earth below them. A shadow loomed over me, cold and ever so dark, yet it comforted me.

"*Mallaich an t-amadan*", it said to me. The words played over and over in my mind, making me brave.

I stepped over his body. I went up the front steps and into the house, slamming the screen door behind me with all the force my small hands could muster. I didn't look back at him. I didn't want to know if he was alright. He was, I was sure of that. He always was and always would be if I didn't do something about it. I could hear it on the wind again. Feel it in the bones of that old house. In my own flesh and bones. It rattled and raged all around me until the house shook with the sound. It was time.

Kill him.

16 Night Terrors

That night, I watched Jeremy drink. Watched him gulp down bottle after bottle until he was wobbling on his feet and slurring his words. I didn't say a word, didn't complain, didn't worry. I just let him be. Rocking in my great ma's old chair, I waited and watched in the shadows.

My great ma was a wild woman and a witch. She was feared more than my mama in her time, feared and respected for her power and her knowledge. Her prized possession was that chair I'd been given It was a gift from her lover when she was a young woman.

Jeremy sat across from me with his booze in his hand, staring into the fire. It was chilly on that late summer night; not chilly enough for a fire, at least not for me. I think he liked to watch the flames, the crisp wood burning, as if there was some pleasure in a burning thing. For the life of me, I couldn't reckon why. He took a swig of his bottle and turned his beady black eyes to me. The fire was in them, twinkling there like some devilish star. It gleamed out at me with a fierceness that only he could design. A master of dark shadows and cruelty, a master of me.

Is he, child? A voice rang in my head.

I was careful not to turn my head toward the looming shadow standing just in the lighted doorway that led to the kitchen. I knew it was there. I could feel its eyes on me in the darkness. They were watching me, watching him. I kept my eyes on Jeremy. I could feel the shadow coming for me, hear its shuffling footsteps whining on the floorboards. I could smell the old earth and the stink of it. Suddenly, it was at my back, leaning so close to my head, I could see the shadow in the corner of my eye, burning like night as it choked out the day.

We are the children of the mountains and the ancient earth. Not like him. Not like any of them.

I trembled as an ice-cold breath brushed against my ear.

What bears us up from the roots and sod gives us power. Gives us strength. You have it, girl, inside of you.

I turned my head toward the voice.

"What y-y-you l-looking at, b-bitch?" Jeremy's voice broke the sliver of connection that lay between me and that shadow.

My eyes focused and saw him glaring at me sharply, bottle still in hand. He quickly rid himself of it, chucking it into the fire. The little bit of booze left in the bottle hit the flames with a hissing whoosh and the fire licked the underside of the mantel. The smell of alcohol and smoke fluttered on the air, stinging my nose, filling my mouth until it was all I tasted.

I shook my head. "Nothin'."

"T-t-that's right," he stuttered.

Jeremy always had a bit of a stutter when he was that drunk. I didn't know him as a child, so I could only wonder if it was something he had outgrown, or his tongue just got stupefied and stunted when he'd had too much to drink. Either way, it was a sure sign for me that he was good and wasted.

Inside you, girl, is a whole world of power and strength and magic.

"You oughta b-be glad I'm b-back," Jeremy just liked the sound of his own voice in the silence.

Inside you is the light.

"You got n-nothin' without me."

The light of a thousand ages of earth and stone.

"Nothin'. Might as well be d-dead without me."

All the strength you need lies inside you.

"You t-tried to k-kill me with them witching powers of your mama's."

Strength to kill.

"But look at me, s-solid as a d-d-damn oak tree. Solid and strong."

Kill.

"Ain't nothin' that can send me under the earth."

Kill.

"Not even you, woman."

Kill him.

"Do you hear me, woman!"

The sound of both voices collided in my head, crashing like waves on the sea, ugly and bitter and wild. Out to get me. Out to make me afraid.

Jaelle.

"Jaelle!"

A fire so angry that my heart nearly stopped inside me rose up in my chest. Up my throat to my mouth, where I tasted sulfur and rot. I screamed as it left my lips and raged into the air with a wild force that nearly knocked Jeremy down. The lights flickered, the fire shivered, and across the room, the window shattered. With the power released, it left me. I cringed, clamping my cold lips shut so that I wouldn't vomit.

Jeremy only laughed. He wasn't afraid. He stood up, towering over me in the shadows, and shuffled toward me. His darkness crept over me, stalking me until it hung on me, like his stench as he stood over me. His body clung to its drunkenness. His eyes were dead sober, glaring down at me. Looking into me. A god that knew my sins, knew my weaknesses, knew every inch of my body and my soul. I looked up at him, chills running across my skin, burrowing in deep until the very flesh of me felt dead. Dead and buried in the ground.

Kill him.

I felt that power prickling at my fingertips.

"I..." I muttered.

Jaelle.

I felt it building and building beneath my skin.

"I..."

Kill him, Jaelle.

But I let it slip away. I looked away and stood up. "I'm headed to bed."

He let me pass. I could feel him watching me, feel the buzzing energy of his anger flush against my cold skin, making it colder until it was numb.

One step. Two steps. I nearly made it past the threshold.

"Where you goin', girl?"

My body rocked, the wobbling of my feet making me feel dizzy and unsteady. I didn't turn to him. Didn't even look his way.

Stomp. Stomp. Stomp.

I could feel his breath on my shoulder, all hot and full of stink that curled around my nose and mouth. He was breathing heavily, the warmth of his mouth nearly touching my skin. I stayed perfectly still. Not a move. Not a breath. Nothing he could hear or see in the dark.

"I ain't finished yet," his warm words breathed across my bare neck. A rush of touch whispered over me.

"Mmm," he mumbled with a groan of desire. His fingers grazed my arm, gentle-like though his callused hands were rough. They prickled down my skin with their roughness, and I shivered.

Jeremy chuckled in the shadows. "I ain't never had a woman walk out on me. Not never," he whispered gruffly.

Again, my body trembled at the hotness of his breath on me. His hand lingered on the skin of my arm. Suddenly, he gripped me tightly and whirled me around to face him. Sneering at me, he slapped me hard across the face, knocking that shadow right out of me with the force of his hand. The power and the rage behind it. I clung to the wall. My face turned away from him, I spit blood onto the floor. I felt the heat of his hand on my cheek as it burned with such intensity that I winced with the pain.

"Don't you turn away from me, witch!"

With that, he ripped me from the safety of the wall and forced me close to him. He grabbed me by the neck to make me look him in the eye. His eyes were full of devilish delight. He grinned at me with a hiss and brought his face to mine. He breathed me in deeply, a hound on the scent. When he'd had enough of that, he pushed me away, into the hallway, where I hit the wall again. My head banged hard against the light floral wallpaper and my fingers clawed at it until it peeled back when I pulled myself up. I heard him laughing behind me.

Stomp. Stomp. Stomp.

"Lord help me," I whispered in the shadows.

I prayed. Prayed to God so hard that I thought my lips would bleed and my insides would turn outward in their leaning toward the Almighty. I prayed as I listened to Jeremy coming.

"Jesus—"

I didn't get to finish my prayer. Jeremy's hand grabbed hold of my head and slammed it against the wall. I saw stars. Not the shiny, glittering kind in a velvet black sky, but the kind that burned into the back of my eyes and made me sick to my stomach.

"Heaven or hell, where's your god now?"

The words sank heavily into my head, seeping down deep into the blackness of my mind. He let me go and I stumbled away, pushing the screen door open and tumbling onto the porch. I still heard his laughter trailing behind me. Down the steps I went, landing on all fours like a dog in the dirt.

Dazed, my head spinning, I turned my head upward toward the real stars. There they were, twinkling and dazzling, something heavenly among the hell of this earthly night. Though they were a million miles away, I reached out my hand to touch them. My fingertips tingled with the echo of their light as it pulsed across my skin, burrowing down deep there until I could feel the power of that light in my veins.

To the stars, I cried, "Help me!"

Slam! The screen door screeched shut. Jeremy's fumbling footsteps came toward me. I crouched low on the ground, praying the earth would cover me and swallow me up.

Clomp! Clomp! Bam! I watched as Jeremy's feet tangled together on a jutting tree root and he went down. He hit the ground hard, out cold. My own sight grew dark and all the light, even that of those damned stars became faded, and at last snuffed out.

Meuran socair freumhaichte gu domhainn.

Before I even opened my eyes, I prayed that I was dead. I could almost feel the cool earth lying heavy on my skin, tracing around my body with each delicate grain. Burying me deep. I felt my body shift and that deathlike illusion faded. I wasn't dead and I wasn't under the ground. It was night, and I awoke on the grass just past the porch. I willed my body to move, and with great pain, I was able to shift my aching limbs to a sitting position. My hands cradled the life inside of me, tears crawling down my face.

"Please," I whispered, my voice gravelly and weak. "Please be alright."

But I felt nothing moving.

"Please."

Beneath my fingertips, a gentle thump beat against my skin. My baby. My baby was alive. My breathing came fast, my heartbeat pounding in my chest as loud as thunder. There was not a cloud in the sky above. Only those twinkling stars. I felt the earth moving beneath me, moving and flexing. Vines reaching up from the soil and creeping past me, toward Jeremy. Those slippery vines twined around his limbs, then, they swallowed his body up until there was no more of him.

My head sank to the ground with a heavy sigh, my eyes closing. A groan sounded next to me, noisy and full of phlegm. My heart sank to my stomach. Jeremy was alive. The vines were gone, not a wisp of them left. Jeremy's hands and face were scraped and bruised from his fall, adding to the cuts already there from his accident. A large cut ran across his forehead, bleeding heavily. His head lay in a puddle of vomit, his loud, heavy breaths making ripples in the muck near his mouth. He was still out cold.

Cursing under my breath, I scrambled over to him. I shook him hard, but nothing made him stir. There wasn't a way in the world that I could drag him up those steps and into the house. There was only one person I could think of just then who might help me. I got to my feet, though my whole body ached, and I made my way into the house.

Slam! The screen door hitched behind me as it shut, startling me. I was as jumpy as a grasshopper. With my hand clinging to the wall, I made it to the telephone. There I stopped, hesitating longer than I needed to. I had already made up my mind, but something just kept pulling my trembling hand back. Finally, with a deep breath, I grabbed the receiver and spoke to the operator.

I didn't know the hour. I was sure it had to be late. As if it read my mind, the stuffy old grandfather clock in the parlor chimed the hour. Ding, Ding, Ding. Three. It was three in the morning. With a sigh, I waited for the phone to ring. It did. Almost immediately, there was an answer.

"Hello?"

A flash of heat colored my cheeks. I took another deep breath, my hand trembling as it held on tightly.

"Elijah?"

I hung up the telephone, my breath coming a little easier, though my head was aching something awful and my heart was all aflutter. Elijah was coming. But that didn't ease my mind. Nothing would ease my mind until something was done about Jeremy.

Something must be done, Jaelle.

With my head all in a daze, I made my way to the kitchen. My hands had a mind of their own, reaching into the drawer for that big knife. My feet had a mind of their own too, tiptoeing out of the house to Jeremy's body. Whispers in a stunted wind surrounded me. A suffocating wind that seemed to steal the breath right out of my chest. The whispers were sharp and full of an ire that matched that of my own heart.

The shadow at my back brushed against my skin. I raised the knife, my hands steady. I gripped the knife tightly and prepared to bring it down on good ol' Jeremy. The whispers swirled around me with a rotten scented wind. They urged me to move. To do it, to get it done. A shard of moonlight beamed on the knife's metal.

Jaelle.

I glanced up at the knife hanging in the air. The moonlight was only headlights. Cast in their blinding light, a mountainous shadow stood just beside the big black car. I dropped the knife. A tear from my eyes fell silently to the ground.

Elijah didn't say a word when he found me standing, bloody and bruised, over Jeremy's body. He must have flown down the road like the Devil was at his heels to get there. He didn't say a word as he helped me drag him into the house and into my bed. It wasn't until we sat in the kitchen over a cup of tea, the early rays of sunlight peeking through the dirty windows and the dusty curtains, that he spoke.

"Jaelle—" he started soft and low.

He stared into his chipped teacup with all the

intensity of a winter storm, blustery and cold. I didn't say a word. I let him mull over whatever words were desperate to tumble from his lips. He bit his bottom lip hard to keep them close. His hand kept busy stirring his tea.

"Jaelle, for the life of me and the love of all things holy, I cannot let you stay here with that man."

His eyes raised a little, glancing over at me with such a look of pity, I could barely stand it. He started to say more, but he thought better of it and bit his lip again. His face was something new and strange to me. It was flushed with the pink-white light of dawn, brimmed along his elegant brow with a veil of sweat, and crested with a flurry of wispy curls. He hadn't had time to slick them back, and the delicate ringlets clung close to his head like a crown. The light rested there too. He looked regal and noble and full of a godly fire that I had never seen in a man. It nearly took my breath away. He was…beautiful.

The Devil can take an awful pleasing shape when he's a mind to deceive.

Aunt Millicent's old saying floated about my head, a hainted wisp of old faith and twisted roots that dug deep into my chest. It pained me. But the look on Elijah's face pained me more. His eyes pierced me like a bolt of lightning, fiery hot and levin-quick. They made me shiver and I couldn't help but look.

I had nearly forgotten what he'd said, when he spoke again, this time more adamant. As he did, he reached trembling fingers to my face and brushed away the mousy brown wisps that framed my thin cheeks. His fingertips brushed my skin. My lips parted, a deep breath fluttering from them.

"Do you understand, Jaelle? I'll not leave you."

Looking at him with those dark brown eyes so deep that they burned black, I fell. My heart leapt from my chest toward him, burst forth from its fleshy cage and flew to him. His face was so near to mine. The warmth of his breath washing me with spirit and life. He was close enough to touch. As he edged even nearer, his lips brushing mine, my hand reached up, fingertips tingling with that now familiar force that pulled me to him. Prickling and panging with a fitful desire, my hand settled on his chest. He took a deep breath, heavy on his lips. His heart beat fiercely there, his breaths rising and falling with such intensity beneath my palm. His lips hung heavy over my mouth. Not kissing me, just stroking the flesh of my lips. My mouth instinctively opened to welcome them, but he was gentle and soft and oh so very, very pleasing.

I breathed in the warm, sweet breath of him, taking it in like the very life of me needed it. Needed to drink it in. Needed to taste it.

"Elijah," I whispered so quietly.

I was afraid he didn't hear it. But he must have because he pushed into me and kissed me hard. I felt my body sinking down, deep into an oblivion of want and need so fierce I couldn't catch my breath, couldn't feel my heart beat. I couldn't feel anything but the touch of him.

From my belly came a decisive kick. It shook me from the inside out, rattling at my heartstrings until they were about to break. I pulled back from Elijah. His eyes searched mine with confusion and fear as he licked his reddened lips hungrily. He wanted more of me. My hand left his chest and gently cupped my belly.

The baby, my baby, had kicked. The feeling still echoed in my heart, and I willed it to come again, pressing my belly with urgent, anxious fingers. But it didn't. My heart sank. My baby had kicked me as I sinned with this man of God. It had protested my sin from the bowels of my womb.

Elijah still clung to me, his skin burning hot against me. I wanted more than anything to cling to him again, to taste the passion of his lips. But I couldn't. Not with the babe in my belly bearing witness. I pulled away further, ripping from his touch, the warmth of his skin, and my hands gripped tightly to the chair I sat in. I didn't move. Elijah looked disappointed. The kiss was not enough to fill his insides full of fire. I wasn't enough for him. Not now, when he seemed to need so much of me.

My face fell. He saw it and reached for me, but stopped, his hand quivering in the air before me. Inches away from my skin. Seconds away from my heart. His eyes went cold as he pulled his hand away. His face turned down, staring at Jeremy's blood spattered across his pant legs. He tried to wipe it away with a frustrated sigh, but the more he bothered with it, the worse it got.

"It'll happen again, Jaelle," he said with a touch of ice in his words. "That I promise you."

It had. Again and again, over and over, until my body had gotten used to the pain, to the expectation of pain that always came with the rage and the wanting. Elijah looked angry when I didn't answer. Was this man any different than the one upstairs? With his angry desire and his hungry hold on me.

Yes.

That was all my body could muster.

"It's got to stop, Jaelle. You've got a child to think of, and I—"

He stopped himself. I wasn't sure of the reason. He looked jilted and a little ashamed. His eyes kept drifting from me, ebbing and flowing like stubborn waves on the water, aching for the shore but too afraid to leave the sea. Quickly, he rose to his feet.

"A man like that does not deserve you. Does not deserve to stand beside you in this life. Does not deserve to live."

He seemed to regret the words as they left his lips. His fingers gripped the back of his chair so hard the wood groaned beneath his touch. This touch that a moment ago had been so gentle and soft against my own skin.

"An eye for an eye, Jaelle," he said.

He made his way to the door. His hand pushed the screen open, but he seemed fitful and unwilling to leave. Not just yet.

"So sayeth the Lord."

Then he was gone.

17 What Didn't Come With the Dawn

An eye for an eye.
     The knife was back in my hand. I gripped it so tightly, my fingers felt icy cold and numb. The early light of the morning grazed my feverish skin as I stood over Jeremy in the bed that we'd shared for so many years. The light nestled into the nooks and crannies of the mussed and empty side of the bed beside him. The place where I should be now if I were a good wife. My head cocked to the side at the thought.
If I were a good wife.
If I were a good woman, I would have left long ago. If I were strong enough. If I were brave enough. If I were smart enough.
My bare feet pressed hard into the floor, feeling every last sinewy grain, every worn and rutted spot where too many lives had been lived and rubbed away. Though there was no life left in it, that earthy force of power trickled up from the floor into my toes and straight up my body. It grabbed hold of me, waking me from a daze, and I remembered the knife in my hand.
An eye for an eye.
"An eye for an eye," fell from my lips.
I edged nearer the bed. He was still dozing off his booze and his fall. The bruised bump on his forehead was still oozing blood onto his yellowed pillowcase. Not even where we rested our heads was white and clean, worthy of the children of God that we were. That we were supposed to be. Everything we had was soiled

and rotten. It was not fit for swine, not fit for us, not fit for me. There were other homes where I could belong. Ones with crisp white cotton bed sheets that eased a body down to rest, cool shadows and warm spaces to live and breathe and be.

As he turned onto his side, Jeremy snorted and groaned in his sleep shattering my thoughts into a million pieces. Breaking me like he had always done. My hands had a mind of their own, lifting the knife up above my head with steady aim now. Breath came slow and deep. My body knew what it was about, even if my mind was slow to catch up. I decided not to think, just let my body do what it would. Elijah wasn't here to stop me now. I wasn't sure he would if he *were* here.

The knife rose higher. Higher. My lips parted, took in a shallow, stuttered breath.

"Jaelle," Jeremy gasped out in his sleep.

His eyes were still shut tight, a pained look on his face. The sound of my name on his lips startled me. I dropped the knife, and it clattered to the floor. I waited, my eyes closed, expecting only rage.

But nothing came.

I peeked down at the bed. Jeremy was still fast asleep, the gash on his forehead bleeding more now. There was a tear creeping down his cheek. In my heart of hearts, I wanted it to be for me, but it never would be. Never.

I turned away from him with a heavy sigh, grabbed the knife and left the room. My staggered footsteps led me to the shade of the orchard trees. The sun was already climbing high in the sky. I made my way to the center tree on its little hill, resting the palm of my hand upon its rough bark. My nails dug in deep, splintering the bark until it crumbled away.

All I could do was breathe in the light of the sun. The clouds swept past casting shifting shadows about my feet. I closed my eyes, tears falling fast, and waited. Waited for God to strike me down. A lightning bolt, a falling tree, a crashing wave, a mighty storm, anything.

But He didn't. Nothing happened. Nothing stirred but me. When my eyes opened again, they were met with shards of light that pierced through and blinded me.

"God help me," I said softly to the trees.

As if in answer, a gentle breeze brushed across my face. It was soothing and cold like the coming of winter. As it left me, I heard a hiss that made me shudder. With it, a single leaf, already brown and dead, fell to my cheek and fluttered to the ground.

"God help me," I said again. Stronger this time; louder. "But I have to do it."

The wind bellowed and blew in answer. I knew then that God was not in the wind. The gods of my mother twined about my body instead, and they made me strong.

PART THREE

FALL

She weeps bitterly in the night, tears on her cheeks, among all her lovers she has none left to comfort her, all her friends have dealt treacherously with her. They have become her enemies.

Lamentations 1:2

Witch Hazel
(BEAD WOOD)

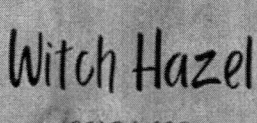

a shrub with fragrant yellow flowers that is widely grown as an ornamental – flowers in autumn

its leaves, twigs and bark can be used for many purposes and have many benefits

heals rashes, burns, bruises, and inflammation

wards off evil and heals broken hearts

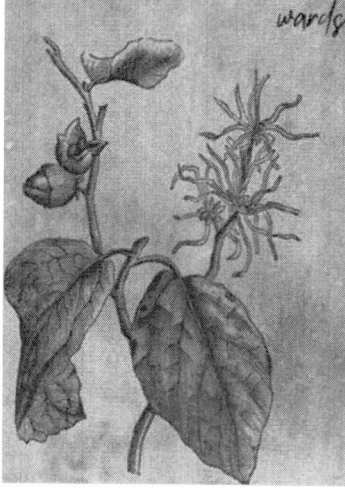

18 SUMMER RAIN MAKES WAY FOR AUTUMN PAIN

The dog came around with the cold weather. At first, it stayed at the edge of our property, way out in the fields, pacing in the tall grass like a shifting shadow. Before long, it had passed into the orchard, hanging around the trees. I watched it from the porch, coming closer and closer with each passing day. The closer it got to me, the more that fear crept into my heart. There was an eeriness about the critter, something that didn't seem quite right. A sliver of Mama's magic perhaps, a deep-rooted shadow draping over me from afar. I took it as an ill omen and left it at that.

Then, one morning, it was on the edge of our lawn, its paws planted defiantly on the cut grass. It was a black dog, pitch-black like midnight, and big, its long fur mussed and matted. The autumn leaves clung to its knotted fur, and it looked as if it had come straight from one of those ghost stories that my mama used to tell me on stormy winter nights. The ones about monsters in the blackness, looking in windows, peering in to watch you sleep and steal your soul.

This was no red-eyed monster coming for me, but it still brought a chill to my bones that even the cold autumn air couldn't. Something was coming. Something flying on the approaching winter wind. It was a night shade amid the day, one that I couldn't ignore. I feared that dog like I feared the Devil and the dark. One day, I found it at my doorstep, lying on the ratty welcome mat. It looked up at me with the bluest eyes I had ever seen. It terrified me, and yet I opened the door wide and let it inside.

The dog made itself right at home. It led itself to the kitchen as if it knew the way. No corner held a surprise, just a subtle knowing. I gave it a bowl of water and a leftover chicken sandwich from Jeremy's lunch. It eyed me all the while with those blue, blue eyes, looking deep into me. I sat in turn and watched it from the kitchen table.

The loud rumble of a truck broke the eerie quiet. I stood up to peer out of the kitchen window.

"Jeremy," I tried to yell, but it came out as a stunted whisper.

Still, he came running to take a look. It was strange standing at his side, getting such a close look at him. His days-old crusty stubble and mussed hair. The tension that stripped his features of any meanness. All that was left was fear.

"Shit," he muttered, rubbing an unsteady hand over his face. He turned to me, and said, "Stay," like I was some kind of dog.

I stayed as I was told and watched him scramble from the kitchen. From the window, I watched him standing restlessly on the porch steps.

"Hello, Pa," he mumbled with a sloppy tongue. It was barely midday, and he had already been at the drink.

Then, there he was in the flesh, Mr. Levi Bennett, all three hundred pounds of him. He was a mountain standing next to Jeremy, and Jeremy...well, he was nothing but a foothill, stuck with stumbling stones and jagged tree stumps. A no-good eyesore.

Mr. Levi was a staunch and rigid man, set in his ways and stubborn. Didn't matter what your ways were, you could be damn sure you were going to follow his word no matter what. That's just the way it was with Jeremy's daddy, and Jeremy knew it. There was no talking to Mr. Levi, no compromise, only rules, only rules, shouting and punishment.

Mr. Bennett eyed his son with all the sharp disdain he could while the sun beamed across his head. Jeremy blinked up at him. Despite his years, before his daddy, Jeremy was just a young, dumb boy, waiting for a whooping at every turn.

"You gonna invite me inside *my* house, or make me wait, son?"

Jeremy was quick to open the screen door. The next thing I knew, there was Mr. Levi Bennett before my very eyes, standing in the doorway of the kitchen. He looked me over with a sour frown choking his clean-shaven face, his piercing blue eyes giving nothing but hate. He eyed my swollen belly and grunted as he turned back to Jeremy in the hallway.

"You sure that thing's yours?" His voice was gravelly and ice cold.

Jeremy gave me a quick glance before his face fell, and he stared at the floor. His daddy merely laughed and led the way down the hall to the parlor. They left the parlor door open. I sat and listened.

Jeremy's daddy started things off with a wallop to his son's face.

"You been on the drink, ain't ya? I can smell it seepin' off ya, and it's not but barely noon. You been drinking, son?"

"No, Pa."

"You gonna stand there and lie to your daddy, boy?" Another slap. "Answer, boy. And right quick."

"Would you care to sit, Pa? We can discuss things proper that a-way."

They must have sat. I heard the furniture whine and groan beneath the weight of Mr. Bennett's wide ass. There was a short silence, tense and electric. Then their voices started up again, muffled and low now. I crept to the kitchen doorway to listen, but that damned dog started fussing. Its low growling bit the air with a decisive rage.

"Shh!" I called back to it, but it only got louder.

The voices in the parlor were shouting now. Furniture shuffled. A fight was on its way. The dog jumped up, sprinting to my side, its growl piercing my ears louder than the fighting down the hall. That's when I realized the dog was waiting. Waiting for what, I didn't know. But as sure as day, it was waiting. We stared at each other for a long while, full of a silent understanding between us that I couldn't shake.

"What, old boy?"

Of course, the dog didn't answer or even act like it'd heard me. I had nearly given up the quandary that was this mysterious dog, when up shot its head, its ears prickling back as it listened. I listened too, but I didn't hear anything. Not a thing. The air was heavy and quiet, a thick heat rushing through the room.

Thunderous stomps approached, and the dog went wild. Barking and carrying on while Mr. Bennett made his way to the front door. He gave me a glare before he burst out of the house. His truck vroomed to life and squealed down the road.

The dog lay down low, digging its claws into floor, as it growled loudly. Its eyes were bent on the dark hallway just across from me. I looked that way, but I saw nothing but deep shadows and a deeper dark. It sent a shiver through my skin, despite the heat from the stove so close to me. The dog growled louder still; its teeth bared. It could hardly contain itself. I was afraid to move. Afraid of what might be lurking in those shadows. What monsters were there to get me. Perhaps the Devil had come to collect me for all my sins.

"I'm not afraid," I whispered, mostly to myself. My words settled on the air with a decisive beat.

Silence answered me at first.

Run.

No.

Run.

I won't.

Run.

But it was too late.

"You should be, woman."

Jeremy's gravelly voice hissed out from the afternoon gloom. It nearly made me jump right out of my skin. He laughed. I heard him before I saw him. Then, out of the shadows, he stalked, a cruel smile spread across his stubbly face. His eyes were red like he'd been crying. This was not a man who cried or showed any weakness. Yet there it was, one tiny speck of a tear clinging to his unshaven cheeks.

So, the Devil does weep.

I didn't have time to say a word before he was on me, pushing me against the hot stove. My hand landed on its surface to keep me from falling. It burned my skin in an instant. I could smell my flesh burning, the stink of something rotten in the air. I screamed and the dog echoed with a whining howl.

My cry was quickly silenced with the back of Jeremy's hand. I stood in silence, tears streaming down my face. I could see the dog out of the corner of my eye, keeping close to me and growling wildly. The sound of it rumbled in the air. I could feel it through the floorboards, shaking the very ground we stood on. Jeremy leaned in close to me, his breath rancid and full of fire. He breathed heavily on me, belching long and loud in my face.

"What did your daddy say?" I dared.

He sniffled and turned away from me. I breathed a little easier.

"Old man's dying," he said with little emotion.

"Dying?"

As he rummaged through the ice box, "That's what I said, dumb bitch."

He grabbed a beer, the last one and slammed the icebox shut with a bang. He snapped the cap off the bottle on the edge of the counter and took a long swig.

"Old geezer's got the cancer. Done smoked his lungs to shit. Stupid old man."

He leaned against the kitchen counter across from me, staring off into the distance. He took another swig from his beer bottle, a longer one this time, nearly finishing it off in one gulp. Another belch.

"I'm sorry," I said softly. My hand was throbbing like the devil. My back still butted up against the stove, but I didn't dare move. The heat was unbearable on my skin and sweat was stewing on my forehead. Little baby droplets slid down my cheeks to my flushed chest.

He snorted and downed the last of his beer.

"That ain't the worst of it. He's done up his will just for the occasion. Turns out the old man ain't leavin' me nothin'."

"What does that mean?"

He turned to me, his eyes full of disgust.

"It means, woman, that everything we own ain't ours once that son of a bitch is dead. This house, the farm, and the orchard, all of it's to be sold out from under us."

"But we had a good harvest this year. The trees, we done made it work."

I didn't like the desperate whine in my voice as I said those things. Jeremy didn't either. He made a face, one that I knew well. I shut up real quick. Clamped my mouth closed and locked away the key. That's how he liked it.

"You think that matters to him? To that bastard, I'm nothin' but a fool. The one failure in his life that he can't fix with money and a good name. Wouldn't matter if I made him a million dollars with that crop. He'd still make me out to be his one and only failure. Nothin' is enough for him. Nothin'."

He was growing fidgety, his body flushing with a feverish red that colored him like a patchwork quilt, all up and down his front. Then, as if the fever had taken him all over, he screamed in a fitful rage, the beer bottle in his hand getting the brunt of it. It shattered at my feet. I kept my body real still. Didn't move. Didn't jump, just kept breathing. Jeremy's body was trembling from his head to his toes with pent-up anger, I thought he'd burst right there in front of me.

    The dog was also at my feet. It had crept up beside me, dipping low, its teeth still bared and a deep growl rumbling from its open mouth. It was creeping closer and closer to Jeremy with a wild rage of its own. He screamed at the dog. The dog bayed back at him. The sound of both clashed and clattered on the air, ringing in my ears until they ached. The two collided, bare skin against matted fur.

    An eerie shadow crept out from both man and beast, full of energy and feeling, straight to my feet. Like a wave, it swept over me until I couldn't breathe. It was a rush, a mess of rage and that earthy push of power seeping up from whatever lay beneath the floorboards to my bare feet. The earth seemed to rise to meet me, that power floating across my skin. The sound of the fray in front of me began to fade away to a distant thunderous rumble and a voice overtook me.

    Àrdachadh an talamh gus coinneachadh riut.

    Invisible vines, tendrils like spiderwebs climbed up my skin, clinging tightly to every inch of me, every morsel of flesh and blood and bone.

    Bidh feòil is fuil is cnàimh ag èirigh gu na reultan.

    I breathed in earth and stone. I exhaled stars and spirit.

    Ruith.

    I didn't understand.

    Ruith.

    Run! Like layers of my own skin, the voice peeled away until the mystery of its words stuttered to life. And then—it screamed, *Run!*

    Jeremy screamed as the dog swiped at his neck with sharp white teeth. I saw it as if from a great distance, like a tunnel scratched with light and shadow. Jeremy grabbed the dog by the neck. He squeezed and squeezed, choking it until not a sound rose from the animal. When he was satisfied it was silent, he slammed its lifeless body to the ground. The body bounced just a little and skidded across the floor. There it lay, not moving an inch. The tunnel vaporized and vanished. All that was left in that shadowed room was Jeremy and I, looking at each other blankly in the silence.

Jeremy's eyes were not penitent, but wild. A darkness lay there, a piece of that raging shadow. He was huffing and puffing like a wild thing. His neck was bleeding pretty badly, a rivulet of blood streaming down his chest and staining his white undershirt bright red. He was glistening with sweat and stunk to high heaven with the funk of ripe death and grime. He just looked at me. A look that said he didn't care for the life he'd just taken. He just wanted it gone. Even though it was gone, he still seemed hungry and ready for more death, more blood as if he would never be sated.

I was in real trouble if I didn't move away from him right now. I stumbled back a step, and his eyes shifted from a dull darkness to a fast and sharp fury that was intent on me. He took a step towards me and stopped. His hands were trembling in the wake of his rage. I watched those hands, not his face, as step by step, he came for me. Those hands turned into fists not a breath away from me.

"You say one word..." he grumbled, but his voice trailed off.

Without another word, he left, banging the screen door behind him. He left me alone with his mess yet again. But this time, I wasn't going to clean up after him. This time, I walked away.

19 The Dark Ain't What It Seems

Jeremy buried the dog in the far southern end of our land. The south fields were often flooded and swampy, swarming with bugs and wild birds. A ruinous wreck of muck where nothing grew. No place for a living thing. No place for a dead thing either. Not a word was said about the dog after that.

Weeks passed and I didn't leave the house. I was too afraid of Jeremy, too afraid of all those people out there in the town, whispering and judging the way that they always did. I had enough of that at home. Jeremy's eyes were always on me now, always desperate to root out some secret wrong I'd done. He couldn't find one. Not one. My sin with Brother Wise was wholly unknown to him. It had to be, if he knew, he would kill me.

As the last veins of summer heat bled themselves dry and faded into the chill of autumn, my mind began to suffer with a penitential darkness that I couldn't shake. I missed Mama. I missed talking with her in the muddled dark of early morning. I missed her smile upon me as I pleased her with my knowledge of that which she shared. Her palsied hand upon my back to soothe me. Her words of wisdom mixed with a mischievous smile. I missed the pull of my moonstone and the voice that seemed to steady me.

I realized now what my mama meant to me. There was much more to the ties that bound us than just magic and earth. There were deep veins of what looked like love buried among those roots, and nothing in the world could rend them. I stayed away because I feared that bond, that pull toward her, and her second sight into my soul. She knew me, and that I feared.

Like the gentle tide to the moon's caress.

It went against everything inside me. Still, the pull and the desire for her love were always there. With each day that passed, I felt a rush of fear. A dark cloud was hanging over us, coming nearer and nearer with its lightning and its thunder. Something was coming.

Thig, leanabh.

Come, it beckoned. *Come.*

Folks said a storm was coming to the valley any day now, but it didn't worry me. I was bound and determined to visit Mama the very next day. There was only one problem—Jeremy. That night, while he pressed new stamps into his precious book. I came and sat down next to him at the table. I was quiet-like and sickly, but I kept my eyes on him, steady and firm.

He didn't even look up. He just muttered, "Whatever you're thinkin' on getting' from me, girl, forget it. I'm busy."

He pressed another stamp into his book, his fingers careful and steady, which caught me by surprise. Jeremy was neither careful nor steady about anything, not with that devilish drink raging through his insides every chance he got. I watched him treat those damn stamps like his children, the book like his lover that required gentleness and patience to be cared for right.

My heart fluttered wildly in my chest and my stomach churned. I wanted to smash it all to pieces and leave a flurry of paper and chaos in the wake of my jealous rage. He glanced up, hands frozen in mid-air, while he looked at me. He was annoyed. I could tell by that scrunched up, sour expression on his face that he was anything but pleased.

"Well, woman?" he demanded.

"Ain't seen Mama for a spell," I started in a quiet tone. "I'd like to go to her tomorrow, if you've the time to take me."

Jeremy's eyes had returned to his book while I spoke. He huffed and snorted something awful. A scoffing laugh, I reckoned, from the nasal racket he made.

"I figured you and that witchy woman was done. Ain't heard a peep from her since I got back and you ain't been askin' to see her." He glared me down. "Till now."

Another stamp in the book, oh so carefully placed.

"She's my Mama," was all I could stutter out.

Jeremy smirked, a devilish look glinting in his eye. "And you're a Christian woman, so I thought. Don't seem right." He paused only for a second. "I heard tell in the town about your Mama. Nasty, rotten things. That preacher's wife has sure taken a sharp tongue to her standin', and even those who hold fast to those wicked beliefs of hers are startin' to question what side of Heaven she's workin' for."

The heat from the stove roared through the room. It was too hot, and a ring of sweat had begun to pearl about my forehead. I felt my cheeks flush a violent red. He noticed and smiled.

"I never thought I'd see the day when you'd leave the Lord for the ways of that woman. The very same woman, I might add, who you swore up and down you'd never be like. Damn near hated the old bat."

He shifted in his seat with a smug look sweeping across his dirty face. Tears welled in my eyes, but I fought them back with furious intent.

Na leig leis an duine do spiorad a ghabhail.

I gripped the edge of the table tightly, my nails digging into the peeling wood. He wasn't going to best me. Damn it, he wasn't. I wasn't going to budge from this seat until I got what I wanted.

"She's still my mama," I declared, loud this time, so he wouldn't be mistaken.

A spark of that electric pull slipped from my fingertips and skidded across the table toward Jeremy. His eyes grew dumbly wide, and he nearly bolted out of his seat. Breathless, I waited, my eyes upon him and he stared blankly back. Now I had his attention.

"Something don't feel right, Jeremy. I wanna see her. Tomorrow." I was adamant now and ready to fight him, tooth and nail.

He didn't say anything for a long while, his mouth hanging open.

"Alright."

That one word was a shock to my system. I'd never heard him say it to me. Hell, not to anybody. But there it was, hanging on the air with a heavy punch. I nodded, still in shock. I got up from the table and left him. I didn't hear a peep from him for the rest of the night.

All I see is fire and blood and snow. The snow is thick, and it falls heavily. The smoke blots out the sun. I can feel the white-hot heat of the fire against my skin, so close that my flesh crackles and pops.

I am burning. Burning in the snow. And the darkness of death is creeping into every part of me. Coming. Coming. Coming.

"Where are you, girl? Lost in that head of yours with an aching in your belly." Mama's voice startled me to wakefulness. Or maybe it was the rotten pain in my belly. I couldn't tell. It was night, and the shadows were deep in my bedroom, where she shouldn't be. Couldn't be. Yet, by the all the saints in Heaven, there she was, rocking away noisily in Great Ma's chair. Though the darkness was thick and pitchy black, I could just make out her figure.

The chair rocked back and forth on the squeaky

floorboards.

"That bellyache of yours will kill ya." The rocking stopped. "Don't let it."

I squinted, trying to see her better. My hands grasped my belly as a sharp pain riddled all my insides, trembling way down deep.

A patch of moonlight peeked in through the open window, frigid night air tumbling in with it. I shivered wildly as the pain got worse. That little sliver of light shone eerily bright on Mama's face. Her eyes gleamed with it, an unearthly glint of fire in her pitch-black gaze. She turned to me, looking stern and full of fury.

"I done warned ya, child," she said with a shake of her head. Her wispy, white hair was a crown of gossamer glow as she set to rocking again. "Storm's a-comin'. I tried to warn you. Tried to, but you're just as stubborn as a damn mule. Gotta have that baby. Gotta have the preacher man. Gotta have love. Gotta have Heaven. You know what you got, girl, is too many wants. You want all the world to settle at your feet without you fighting for it. Don't work that way. Just don't work—that way."

Her pale face whipped around to look at me, those black eyes staring me down.

"Mama?" I managed to squeak out.

In a flash, she was off that rocker and next to me. Her bent form bowed down to meet my face, her rotten breath wafting heavily toward me. She smelled of stale death. A sliver of dried blood was caked onto her forehead. She looked like death, the very vesture of it in the pale moonlight. Sharp shadows that kept shifting across her face.

"Mama," I whispered.

I reached up to touch her, but she shied away from me with a hiss. The pain in my stomach was getting worse now. It tore through me violently with every breath. Mama seemed to smile at my agony.

"Don't you see it? The shadow be a creepin' up

your skin like poisonous vines. Grasping at you. Clinging to you, all rotten and spoiled. Dirty magic bends an ear to you. Makes you weak when you should be strong." She glanced down at my swollen belly. "It lays rot to the life inside you. And that's what he wants."

My eyes closed with the pain. They closed out of fear too. Fear of those black, beady eyes and the hate behind them. Mama grabbed my head in her hands and made me look.

"What are you trying to tell me, Mama?" I asked, barely above a whisper.

"Your heart's no good at deciphering the shadows from the light. You got dark through and through, and it's about ready to push up and outta you if'n you don't take heed."

"Mama, I—"

"Shhhh," she silenced me. "Listen."

I said nothing, giving into the pain now searing through me.

"Listen, girl," she said again firmly. "*Ruith.*"

She was gone.

I screamed as a flood of something liquid and warm rush between my legs. The moonlight shone down on me like a spotlight as frantically I peered down at the blood on the white sheets. Just then, I heard a tinny prickling sound at my window. It was snow, frail and icy white specks in the pale moonlight. Blood had come. The storm was brewing, and a tinge of lightning streaked across the sky.

Fire and blood and snow.

20 What's Lost in the Storm

The world was all splotchy gray and black, a feverish maze of shadow, light and sound. All I felt was that indescribable pain piercing my body like a knife. My cries got Jeremy's attention, and reluctantly, he came. He did what he could for me with clumsy, unsure hands. A man doesn't know about such womanly things.

More blood came. More pain. In my darkened daze, I watched Jeremy's face turn pale, his eyes wide, as he rested his cool, callused hand on my burning forehead. I winced, and his eyes narrowed, looking me over sharply.

"The baby," I bade my lips to move to say only this before my eyes closed again. I couldn't bear to keep them open a mite longer.

Jeremy sighed loudly as if he was setting his mind to something. Then, I felt the weight of his body lift off the mattress with a decisive screech of its springs. I counted his heavy, shuffling steps down the stairs.

One step.
Deep breath in.
Two steps.
Deep breath out.

My body settled into a restless ease. I knew he was ringing up the doctor and the doctor was going to come right quick. My baby and I would be saved. This damn storm rattling at my window would surely pass without a fuss. Jeremy's voice floated up to me, a haunting, muffled glob of sounds. With my eyes still closed, I tried to focus. Slowly, the words began to make some sense.

"Missy...Jaelle, she's awful poorly...think it's the child...coming early...no...NO...ain't gonna leave her...not now...promised...yeah...I know...can't let her...die..." The phone slammed down, making the wall below quake.

"Stupid damn bitch. No good." Jeremy's voice trailed off in my semi-consciousness. I began to slip into a dark sleep. The phone again. I fought to stay awake.

"Dr. Lee?"

More muffled words and then—

"Hello? Hello, Dr. Lee? *Hello?*"

The ice cold wind whipped against the loosened windowpanes with force.

Slam! Went the phone again.

"Damn it!"

Clomp. Clomp. Jeremy plodded up the stairs and into our room. I felt him standing over me, so I opened my eyes just a little. He was glaring me down with a cold and unfeeling stare. A body would freeze ice solid from such a look. I wouldn't have minded right about then. The fever had latched on hard now and my whole body burned as if it were on fire.

Fire and blood and snow.

"Phone's down. Gotta go for the doctor. May be a while. Storm's bad. I'll be back." Then he was gone. I slipped further into that black sleep as the storm raged outside.

It is dark inside my head, but I can hear Mama's voice as clear as day.

"You remember your Aunt Millicent, girl?"

I answer in the darkness, "Yes, Mama."

"How'd she die, then?"

"An ailin' babe was brought to her, nigh on dead. It died in her arms before she could do anything for it. Millicent was hellbent on saving the child and used the

old ways to try to bring it back to life. And the child came back, hale and rosy pink. The family was grateful and paid her handsomely, but Millicent made them swear on their lives that they wouldn't breathe a word to anyone about what she'd done. The family swore to God above that they would never tell. But they did."

"Word spread," Mama's voice interrupts me. "And them people was awful fearful. So fearful that they began to wonder if'n Millicent weren't with the devil. Them words got a lot of power to 'em. They can bend and break people. They can bend and break laws too. And they can bend and break you."

The darkness begins to flutter with patches of white, falling and falling all about me. And I see Mama, way out in the orchard, waiting for me. She's standing in the ice and snow, her bare feet burrowed in the drifts. Mama is untouched by the storm that rages about her, but the front of her dress is stained in blood that drips onto the snow.

"Mama!"

I'm on the porch now, and she is too far away. The icy wind whips wildly about me and I shiver in fear. Mama's hurt. She has her arms reaching out to me, pleading for me, screaming for me in the fury of the storm. I take a step toward her or try to at least. Step after step, until I am running. I am running nowhere fast, no closer to Mama. A sharp wind howls, swirling around me, and with it comes my mama's words.

"You know how she died? They hung her up in a tall, tall sycamore tree. They watched the life leave her body and then they set her afire. Like an animal."

I'm crying, "Mama, please."

Her arms stretch out to me, her lips moving fast. Still, the wind carries her voice to me.

"They'll kill you for what you are, Jaelle."

There's a tightness in my chest, a rush of blood down my legs to the snow.

"Jaelle!"

The cold came first. Then the blinding whiteness of the light. Bursts of bitter snow pelted my flushed face. I felt weak as I came to. I had made it all the way outside and into the storm, carried there by a dream.

"Jaelle!" Jeremy was calling. I turned, and suddenly, there he was, his arms wrapped tightly around me.

"Mama's calling me," I muttered in my daze.

He held me close as I collapsed into his arms. "No, she ain't." He whispered with a coldness that made the snowstorm seem like a summer gale.

My eyes fluttered closed as he picked me up and carried me toward the house. He stumbled clumsily in the snow, but he never dropped me.

"Her mama should be here, Jeremy. Gotta put your troubles with her aside. She might be dyin'. Her and your child with her."

I knew that voice. It was Dr. Lee. Despite his robust and booming voice, Dr. Lee was a teeny man, balding and always flushed a bright red. His spectacles made his eyes look big and buggy. I never did like the looks of them. It seemed like I was a bug under his dirty microscope and there wasn't anything he couldn't see.

I could hear Dr. Lee plodding along behind us in the snow, cursing all the way. A blast of heat hit my skin as we entered the house, and immediately, I fell ill. I groaned loudly as my insides churned. The pain was unbearable now. There was a deep pressure near my core that wouldn't let up. Jeremy tightened his hold on me as we went up the stairs. I was planted back in my bed and wrapped tight with blankets and cold sheets. Though my body was burning, I couldn't stop shivering.

Dr. Lee hovered over me with those bug eyes of his. I tried to look away but there was only Jeremy glaring down at me from a darkened corner. Both were watching me like I was a damn bug to be examined. Squashed. Obliterated.

Hands roamed freely over me. Checking my pulse. Feeling my forehead. The cold of a stethoscope on my breast, pushing into my hot skin. Hands moving down. Down. Pushing into the pain.

"She's losin' the child, son. I'm sorry. But we've got to make sure we don't lose her too." Dr. Lee rattled off a list of supplies he needed, while Jeremy stared at him with a dumbstruck expression on his face.

"But the storm is awful bad."

Dr. Lee looked at him harshly. "Go on, son—git! Do as I say! And you'd best go and git her Mama."

Jeremy quietly backed out of the room. In a few minutes, he was back with Dr. Lee's supplies, and then he hurried out again. His truck burst to life outside and rattled off into the distance. Then it was just me and Dr. Lee for a long while.

"Mama..." I whispered through the pain.

"She'll be comin', Jaelle. Don't you worry." Dr. Lee checked his watch, his face flushing a bright red with anger. "If that husband of yours would hurry it up." He turned to me with a distracted smile. "Don't you worry none, you hear?"

I wasn't worried. Mama would come. She would be here any minute to ease my pain and worry.

"*Finally*," Dr. Lee's words broke through my thoughts. "You're about as slow as molasses, boy. Get on in here."

"Mama."

I opened my eyes, but the first thing I saw was Jeremy, white as a sheet and stained with blood and soot, his red-veined eyes bigger than old Dr. Lee's. He pressed himself against the far wall, clinging to it for dear life. In his hand was my moonstone amulet bloodied and cracked.

Dr. Lee huffed. He looked madder than a swarm of hornets. "Did you get her mama or not?"

"I ain't got her mama," Jeremy eked out, quiet-like and wary.

"What you talkin' 'bout, son?"

Jeremy stumbled and stuttered over his words now, "S-s-she's d-dead."

That got Dr. Lee's full attention. He stood up, eyes as big as saucers. "What?"

Jeremy nodded, still stuttering all over himself like a drunkard. "D-dead. I s-seen her m-myself, all s-sprawled out like on the g-ground. Her house afire."

Dr. Lee sighed. Tears welled in my eyes. I began to shriek and wail.

The doctor yelled over the noise I was making. "Dammit, Jeremy. What the hell happened out there?"

Jeremy shook his head. Dr. Lee's eyes narrowed. "There w-w-was b-b-blood."

The room went quiet around me. The pressure inside me was almost more than I could bear. I wanted to push the pain right out of me. So, I did. I started to push. That got Dr. Lee's attention.

"I ain't got time for that now. Jeremy, call the police. I gotta tend to your wife." Before Jeremy was too far away, Dr. Lee yelled out, "Get the preacher man!"

Jeremy was all too happy to leave. Minutes later, I heard him on the phone with Roy. The line must have been restored, if even for an instant. The world was going dim again, but Dr. Lee kept shaking me awake.

"Don't go and die on me now, Jaelle. I won't abide that."

It seemed like there was a tug of war happening inside of me. There was Dr. Lee fighting to keep my body alive, whispering a quiet prayer over me. Then there was the smooth, easy darkness of death bidding me to follow. I felt the gentle hands of the doctor, a steady pulse of urgency in his touch. But the pull of death was tantalizingly sweet, rolling over my body like a calming wave. I hadn't expected for death to be so still and silent, so soothing to my soul.

I had nearly laid myself down in its shadowy pool when another touch set my flesh afire. My eyes jolted open. Standing over me were Dr. Lee and Aunt Millicent.

Millicent wasn't a bloody mess now. Death had not left its scar upon her body. She was youthfully old and full of life. Her eyes were agleam with a simmering fire, a spirit that could not be quenched. Though she smiled at me, her eyes were serious and full of worry.

"Ain't your time yet, baby child," she said to me. "Not yet."

The doctor paid her no mind. I was sure he couldn't see her like I could. He didn't see her steady hands rest on my stomach, where a fiery warmth began to emanate. I locked eyes with Millicent. She grunted low in her throat, a chant of ancient words I didn't understand, blowing her foul-smelling breath in my face. I lifted my head and strained to hear the words. I needed to hear them, to understand them.

Thoir anail beatha dhan sgàil seo. Anail.

"Breathe!" Millicent cried and pressed her hands inside my chest. The pain hit me like a shot. I screamed and the world went dark.

Even with my eyes closed, little patches of white light fluttered across my vision. A cold draft of wind tickled my face. It forced my eyes to open. The storm outside the window had passed, and crisp morning light gleamed out onto the snowy landscape. Everything was covered in white, as if the world was caught up in a great billowy cloud. It was quiet. Deathly silent.

"Jaelle."

The voice of Brother Wise shattered that silence with all the gumption of a wave of thunder. It rattled through me and shuddered across my skin in cold fear. I turned to the sound. He was at my bedside. Not another soul was in the room. With no one else to see, it looked like he had tears dotting his red eyes. His face was pale and unshaven, wisps of curls hanging about his temples. I wanted the light to catch on them and crown him like a halo, but it didn't. The light was scattered this way and that, a frayed flicker of fire on the holy man's face. It didn't suit him.

"Jaelle," he whispered again, but his voice was not his own. It was feminine and strong, the lilting sound of the word akin to that of my Mama.

He leaned close, took up my hands in his own, and squeezed them. He spoke in a hurried hush. "Please, listen. The Lord only takes what he will give again tenfold."

Funny, I didn't remember the Lord saying that in the Good Book.

"Do you understand?"

From the look on my face, he must have gathered that I didn't.

"A shadow has passed, but the storm is still coming."

Brother Wise was giving me the willies. I tried to sit up, but he took a gentle hand and laid me back down.

"Do you hear me, Jaelle?" asked Brother Wise. "The storm is coming."

"My baby?" I stuttered out the question, almost too afraid to hear the words hang heavy on the air. I heard them spoken from the doorway so heavy they choked me.

"Dead."

I turned to see Jeremy hovering in the shadows. He looked worse for wear, pale and splotched with blood. Mama's blood and mine. I moaned, sinking low in the bed. I remembered it all now. Mama was dead. And now, so was my baby. I began to weep, but neither man came to comfort me. I wept and wept, my belly and chest aching in my sadness.

"Jaelle," Jeremy said quietly. He looked awkward.

I didn't answer. I didn't listen. I just kept weeping.

"*Jaelle!*" Jeremy had had enough of my blubbering.

Quickly, I clamped my mouth shut. No more tears from me. No more wailing and grinding of teeth.

"Dear God in Heaven, let her grieve the child she's lost!" Despite his act of bravery in the face of Jeremy, Brother Wise seemed whiny, his voice strained and restless.

Jeremy didn't say a word. He just looked the preacher's way with as stern a look as he could muster in the early morning light. The preacher backed away, his head drooping low, and he left the room. I heard the screen door slam shut and knew that he was gone. There I was alone with Jeremy.

A patch of colorful light traipsed across the wall in front of me. My eyes followed it to Jeremy's hand. My mama's moonstone dangled from his bloodied fingers. Mama's moonstone, Mama's blood.

I dared to meet his dark, eerie eyes. "Get out."

But he didn't budge.

"Go on, then," I said. "No need to watch this broken bird."

Jeremy grabbed up the amulet. Holding it tightly, he gave me a smirk and shuffled out of the room.

This bird may be broken, but I was alive. Alive and full of fire. This broken bird was a phoenix. But could I rise from these ashes? All those broken parts inside me had left me undone. Even in the light of dawn, I didn't know if all those odds and ends could be patched up into a living, breathing woman again.

21 Jeremy

Jeremy wasn't born with a silver spoon in his mouth. His daddy came from poor mining folk, born and bred in the mountains and valleys. Jeremy came up from the earth and found the Lord amidst the roots and tendrils of a family divided.

His mother, Violet, was born wild, a daughter of the earth and stars, bred to be a healing woman. Mr. Levi Bennett fell under her spell at the age of twenty-two and never looked back. Didn't matter if his Christian ways clashed with hers. Didn't matter if she had sworn she'd never be tamed enough to marry. He wanted her, and young Mr. Levi Bennett always got what he wanted. Violet and Levi were married on a wintry January morning back in '11. Come the spring, Violet was born again and baptized into the church of Christ. Mr. Levi Bennett liked the look of his squeaky-clean new wife and set upon her like a famished wolf. Jeremy was born in the new year, while the wintry winds blew, and the snow fell thick and heavy on the fields.

Mr. Levi Bennett had been dirt poor at the start. He worked in the coal mines for many years, spilling out the life from his lungs with each passing day down below. But the life of a coal miner wasn't enough for a man like him. He saved and saved, and just about killed himself, until he could buy a plot of land. The farmhouse and orchard came with it, and he learned to tend the dead trees until there was life in them again. The farm and the orchard burst into life. Everything was right as rain at the golden trough of

Mr. Levi Bennett. His pockets grew heavy and overflowing with his fortune, but other than a girl child the following year, his family was the only thing he couldn't seem to grow. No more live children came.

Violet Bennett had once been strong and sturdy as the earth, but the loss of her children broke her spirit. Instead of clinging to the two she did have, she pushed them away. Jeremy reached for his father's love and instead he received the back of his hand and the sternness of his word. Jeremy was relieved when his father went away to the Great War. He prayed that he wouldn't come back, but that left him with his mother. Either way, there was little love and much fear.

His father came back, all the angrier. Jeremy returned the feeling with his own rage, rending any ties the two had forever. Jeremy grew up into a man, very little like his mother and a lot like his father. He ducked out of the next war by paying off Dr. Lee to fail him in his physical exam. Said he was flat-footed and near-sighted. Jeremy wasn't either. He could shoot a house fly straight out of mid-air one hundred yards away, so he said anyway.

The army didn't get him, but I did. I met him coming out of church services on a right pretty spring day. I was walking home when his truck sidled up beside me, moving slow so that he could look me over. He put the window down, his arm resting on the door, and he gave me one hell of a smile. It about knocked me off my feet.

"Hey, there." His voice was all raspy and full of warm allure. It must have been all those cigarettes he smoked. A younger, dumber me took those two words and turned them into a fantasy come true.

"Hey, there," I said back, blushing wildly. I kept walking and he kept driving slowly beside me.

Here was this handsome man looking at me like I was the only female in all the world. One that he wanted. One that he couldn't live without. All this was spinning inside my head, and all he'd said was hello. I cleared my throat and kept my eyes down while I walked. There was a long awkward silence that came thereafter. I thought it would never end.

"What's your name, little miss?"

My name. He wanted to know my name.

"Jaelle."

He nodded with a wink. "Jaelle. You got a back name to match that front one?"

There was a small, wispy voice at the back of my brain. A niggling in the folds of shadow and silence that seemed to warn me against him. I couldn't quite hear it, but from the feeling in my gut and my chest, I knew I shouldn't give him my name. Of course, I didn't listen.

"Reid. Jaelle Reid."

"Jaelle Reid!" he yelled out the window, as if he were announcing me to the world as his own. "Mmm. Rings like a church bell on the tongue."

This man had a fire in his eyes when he looked at me, and a passion on his lips that I already knew would not be satisfied. His overly friendly words made me blush even more. He saw that and smiled. I think he liked making me restless. He reached over and opened the passenger side door, his smile spreading from ear to ear.

"You come on now, and I'll take you home."

I stopped. His truck stopped beside me, idling with a steady purr that I could feel through the soles of my shoes. My toes squirmed in my sweaty, too-tight dress shoes with the kitten heels. They were once white but had long since become a tarnished, tobacco-stained yellow. My dress too had been worn by at least three other bodies before me. Its printed pattern was as faded as my smile now, worn out and barely seen even in that bright Sunday sun.

He saw my face change and gripped the steering wheel tightly. "Now, I ain't no stranger if that makes you fearful. My ma knew yours a-ways back, so I've heard."

"Really?"

He nodded again, his smile returning. He looked confident then, sitting up straight in his leather seat with that prideful grin.

"A-ways back. Now, don't that make us friends already?"

There was that voice again, pushing against the folds of the back of my mind and urging me to listen. The sight of this beautifully rugged man in front of me, and the warm sun beating down on me, made me melt into a puddle of nothingness. Whatever the voice was saying, I couldn't hear it. I didn't want to either.

So, I smiled wide like the dumb little girl that I was, and I said, "I reckon."

"I reckon," he echoed. "Alright then. Git on in here, Miss Jaelle."

I hopped right into that truck, and we sailed off into the sunlight.

***

"What the hell were you doin' out there at her place in the middle of a storm, Jeremy? That's what I'd like to know."

Roy's voice was muffled, but loud. Loud enough for me to hear upstairs in our bedroom. Jeremy didn't answer. Roy sighed, loudly. The man just could not do anything quietly.

"Damn it, Jeremy. What the hell am I supposed to do with that?" he said.

Jeremy was silent. Roy kept on talking in an admonishing tone.

"Look at you! Covered in her blood and the woman's just lying there with her head bashed in. What the hell am I supposed to think? Huh?

It was Jeremy's turn to sigh, more of a groan from

deep in his throat.

"Well?" Roy demanded. "You've gotta have somethin' to say to me." He dipped his voice down low. "I could hitch your ass right back into that cell again, Jeremy. Now, you listen up, and you listen *real* good, you hear? You tell me the truth; did ya kill her?"

It was silent.

Roy must have slapped Jeremy in the face from the sound of it. He seemed desperate to get a rise out of him, to get any kind of emotion or word from my husband. Roy needed something, and Jeremy had no intention of giving him what he wanted.

"Jeremy!"

Roy really was desperate. Here he was with a possible murder on his hands in a town where the biggest thing to happen was a tiff at the annual church picnic when Mrs. Balk accused Miss Green of stealing her recipe for potato salad. This man of the law was in no way ready for a real, honest case of murder, and he knew it.

"Fine, then. I'll take your silence as admission of guilt." Another long and weighted sigh. "Son of bitch, Jeremy. What were you thinkin'? 'Bout everyone in town is that woman's enemy, but you—you had it in for her since you was courtin' Jaelle. Everybody knows it too."

"You gonna take me in, then?" Jeremy finally spoke.

I listened hard, my heart pounding in my chest. Roy must have been thinking. Not a word was said by either of them for a long while.

"You know we've been friends since we was young'uns," Roy started, clearing his throat again, as if the words just couldn't make their way to his lips. "You're like my brother."

My heart beat nearly out of my chest. Up and out onto the air.

"You was never there. You understand me? As far

as I know, you was here the whole time with your wife while she was ailing."

"What about Doc Lee?"

Another pause. Roy was spinning himself a web of deceit and lies every second he was silent.

"You don't worry 'bout Doc. I'll handle him just fine without your meddling. The man owes me a favor anyways after last fall."

The word around town was that last fall, Doc Lee had gotten himself into a heap of trouble. One of the elders' wives claimed he had made advances toward her when she came to him for an ailment. He was plum drunk, so she said. Roy had handled that right quick. After all, he was pals with Doc, and a pal was a sacred thing around here. Akin to brothers, or even stronger than blood. It was passed off as a sick woman's fancy, and nothing more. After all, women are touchy, too sensitive at times, and a mite loud in their protestations against their men. Roy kept his friends close and out of trouble. He would do the same for Jeremy, whether he was guilty of killing Mama or not.

"What about the witch?" Jeremy asked.

My body was helplessly tuned in to the voices downstairs. Roy's breathing was quickening, while Jeremy's was as steady as a rock. Even from my perch up in my bedroom, I could feel the tension in the air between those two men. Quick as thunder and jagged like the lightning that chased their brewing storm.

"I'll deal with her. But you were never there, do you understand, Jeremy? You. Were. Never. There. And get rid of that charm, for god's sake."

Dear God, no.

The screen door slammed shut. I laid myself back down, sinking low into the bed, and waited. Soon the screen door slammed again. Footsteps off the porch, past the orchard, and out to the open fields. I lifted myself to see out of the window. From there, I saw my husband out in the furthest field, where only months past I had prayed for the earth's blessing. He was digging in the snow and damp earth with his bare hands. I watched him dump a small bundled up something, along with the moonstone into the hole he'd made and cover it up again. He stared down at that piece of earth like something would come up out of it to grab him. But nothing did, so he headed back to the house.

I wept as I watched him walk the fields. Perhaps losing the baby was God's punishment for my lustful sin. Perhaps losing Mama was the earth's punishment for betraying everything it meant, everything it had given. If God and the earth were against me, what did I have left?

Jeremy had nodded off thinking that I was asleep in the bed. He was propped up in Great Ma's rocking chair, his head drooping low to his chest while he snored. The snoring had wakened me. I just laid there and watched him sleep. What was he dreaming of? Whatever it was, he looked troubled. Frightened, maybe? I could see it draw back the lines on his face, staining him with shadow. I smiled. I was glad of whatever terrified him. Maybe Mama was poisoning his dreams from wherever she was in the spirit world. I could only hope.

Suddenly, he jolted awake, nearly falling out of the chair. He caught me staring at him and he sank back down in his seat. We looked at each other for a long spell.

"You gonna live?" he demanded, though his voice was shaky and uncertain.

"I reckon," I answered. "You?"

He seemed unnerved by the question. I liked that too. He squirmed just a little, a shiver perhaps running down his spine. He looked pale and a little gray in the morning light.

"I reckon."

"My great ma died in that there chair you're sittin' in."

I watched him squirm a little more and clear his throat. He put his hands in his lap and scratched at his ragtag jeans. He kept his eyes on me. I kept my eyes on him.

"I reckon there might be some awful bad luck clinging to it. Best be careful where you sit." I smiled. He didn't look pleased because he knew what that smile meant. It was a flag raised in battle, and the war between us had just begun.

PART FOUR

WINTER

"You shall not suffer a witch to live."

Exodus 22:18

Poison Hemlock
(Devil's Flower)

a large European biennial poisonous herb (Conium maculatum) of the carrot family that is naturalized in the U.S. and has finely divided leaves and small white flowers

if consumed, it causes paralysis, and soon after, death

Death alone it brings. Death and ill fortune. Be wary of its use.

22 In the Wake of the Storm

I watched the remnants of the storm melt and fade away from my bedroom window, where I perched for what seemed like ages. Doc said what I needed was bedrest and some tender care. Jeremy was all too happy to maroon me in that bedroom of ours upon pain of death. But he didn't need to go that far. My body was weak and the last thing I wanted was to leave. I was far too ill, and the claws of death were slowly stretching up my body to claim me.

Sorrow had overcome me. Pain had overwhelmed me. I wanted to die. To be buried in the field along with my baby and the last piece of Mama I had left on this earth. Jeremy must have known that I wanted to die. He must have known the power he held over me now. It was his hand that kept me alive against my will. It was his hand that had the power to end me too, but he knew that would make me happy. So, there I was, his prisoner

I was awoken by the sound of knocking at the front door. It was fast and hard. Whoever it was sounded eager and a little frantic. There hadn't been many knocks on our door since the baby died. I didn't care. I didn't bother to sit up to look out of the window.

Jeremy's footsteps stopped at the door. The front door creaked open. Muffled voices. A familiar voice that I couldn't quite capture in my sleep-ridden daze.

As I faded back into sleep, I heard, "Stand down, Mr. Bennett."

Elijah. My eyes shot open with the fierceness of a lightning bolt. A white-hot heat flushed my body, but with it came the echo of pain. My body couldn't yearn for him. It hurt too much. I turned my head away, squeezing my eyes shut tight. I prayed that I wouldn't hear him again. That my body would obey and let him go.

Go, Elijah. Please, just go.

But he didn't.

"You cannot stop me from ministering to one of my fold in this most grievous time for her. For you both. Please, Mr. Bennett—Jeremy—please."

Please, Elijah. Please, don't push him.

There was a long, hard silence.

"Elijah," I whispered faintly, my eyes still shut. "Go."

The sound of Jeremy's shot gun exploded on the air. It became deathly still.

"My woman don't need the likes of you or your god. Ain't you heard, her people's nothin' but heretics and witches. That ain't somethin' the likes of you should care for. So go on and git now, or this here rifle'll make you leave."

Silence.

Elijah was stubborn and hesitant. I could feel the heat of him from where I lay. His fitful rage climbed the stairs to meet me, rushing at me in a wave of hot whispers. I kept my head turned against them. I didn't want either of them. My body clung to them in such violence it was hard to bear.

Footsteps off the porch and onto the gravel walkway. Then they abruptly stopped. He must have turned back.

"You cannot keep her from the Lord she loves. He will find her."

Jeremy said nothing. A moment later, I heard the front door slam again. Jeremy's heavy footsteps climbed the stairs. The air was cool again, but my body was still restless. I hoped he wouldn't see the desire that had swept over me and the pain it had caused. A slick veil of sweat had collected on my brow. I didn't have the strength to wipe it away, and anyway, there wasn't time. Before I knew it, he had crossed the threshold of our room and stood just inside the door. His dark eyes barreled down on me with such ferocity I could barely stand it. The rifle was still in his hands.

"Preacher man called on you."

I clamped my mouth shut, so tight that my teeth ached and chattered.

"You wanna see him, don't you?"

He got no answer from me, but that didn't satisfy him. He plopped down into Great Ma's rocking chair with a sigh.

He rocked forcefully in that noisy chair just to get on my nerves. It was working. He stopped rocking and planted his feet firmly on the floor. He leaned forward with a sickening smile.

"You want him, don't you?"

I squirmed beneath my covers, desperate to get away from that stare and that gun. My lips parted, downturned in a thread of a sour frown. It made me sick to death to look at him. My silence was enough of an answer for him, and he leaned back in the chair, rocking once again. The sound was unbearable, but I kept quiet. Jeremy gripped the arms of the rocking chair so tightly that the old wood whined beneath his fingernails as they dug in deep. That rage was for me and me alone.

"Belike you've wanted him for quite a while. I seen it in those snake eyes o' yours. Always watching him. Always pining for him like a damned schoolgirl in pigtails. Listening to his longwinded preachin'. Followin' wherever he leads like a damned sheep, foolish and stupid. You think you hide that lust and desire of yours. But I can see it crawlin' all over you, even now. You're a mite sinful for a godly woman, ain't ya? Mite lustful in the loins for a man you can't have."

Something wild in me stirred, and I answered

through gritted teeth. "I done had him."

Jeremy sat up straight. The rifle found its way to me, pointing at my heart with all the certainty of his rage. I stared down the barrel of what might have been. He could have killed me. I'm sure he wanted to, but he didn't. He just glared me down all quiet and brooding something awful. His face was beet-red. He was fuming, but he didn't say a word. He just got up from the rocking chair and made his way to the door.

He stopped there at the threshold, his back still turned to me, and he said, "What you got here ain't good enough for you?"

I thought about not answering him, but that fitful fire in me kept on burning.

"This ain't no home, Jeremy. And you ain't in love with me anymore 'an you are with her."

I could hear his teeth grinding together. His fingers gripped the rifle tightly. One hanging off the trigger with ease. "Her?"

Missy. I wanted to name her. Something stopped me. Instead, I said, "Whatever trollop you got hangin' in the shadows waiting for you. You go on to her. I've no need for you."

He gave a throaty, gurgling laugh. It was a menacing sound, cruel, deep and dark.

"You've a need for me yet, if you intend to survive." He turned his angry eyes to me. "Just remember that—Wife."

"I know you killed my Mama, Jeremy."

His eyes narrowed. They looked fearful and wild.

"If'n she was killed, it was her own doin'. Her ways was wicked, and your ways are her ways. You'll meet her end before long. I promise you that. God promises that."

"What do you know about God, Jeremy?"

He stopped. "More than you."

He clomped back out of the room, disappearing into the shadows like a ghoul. I wasn't afraid. I should have been, but I wasn't. I just laid my head back down on the pillow and closed my eyes.

Patches of wakefulness and sleep came upon me in rugged waves. Even in my waking moments, dark dreams twisted reality into a mush inside my brain. Jeremy would come and go, a grim shadow standing over me. The angel of death, my husband, and my warden. I wanted to make him leave, but I didn't have the strength or the words. I was glad to sleep then in those brief seconds between nightmares when I could rest.

I don't remember if days or weeks or months passed after that encounter with Jeremy. All I remember is the noonday sun like a dagger sheering across my face and the sound of Jeremy's truck rattling to a stop near the house. A brief silence while the engine settled noisily, and then a car door slammed. The passenger side door slammed a second later.

My eyes burst open. A girly laugh climbed up to the window from the front lawn. A familiar one at that. Still, I waited in silence, my heart nearly tumbling to the pit of my stomach. The front door opened. Jeremy's voice boomed in the front hall, shattering what silence I was clinging to so desperately.

"Make yourself right at home."

Another giggle. It made me want to vomit.

"Don't mind if'n I do, Mr. Bennett." The female voice was playing coy, every syllable of every word dripping with honey. My own mouth went dry, a bitter taste cleaving to my tongue. Missy's clatter always seemed to rub me the wrong way, no matter its sweetness. I should have been surprised that this harlot was here inside my house, but I wasn't. I had dealt a hard blow to Jeremy by challenging him, word for word, I'd aimed daggers at his manhood, his worth, his deceit. Now, he was going to play just as dirty.

A woman's high heels on the stairs. A hesitant

shadow at the doorway.

"You still ailin', Jaelle?"

Missy was reluctant to come in. I coaxed her to my bedside with a gentle smile. With all the courage I had in me, I took her by the hand. I held it tight. She looked at me nervously, batting her eyes to avoid my stare. My own eyes bade her to bend down to me. She obliged, leaning in close. She looked uneasy so close to me. I smiled. Her eyes grew wide.

"You've got eyes for my Jeremy," I played it like a game, smiling all the while. I toyed with her, wearing as wide a toothy grin as I could muster.

She swallowed hard, her wide eyes growing wider. Her rosy lips turned down swiftly into a frown. "Jaelle, honey, I—"

I squeezed her hand tighter. She squirmed beneath my touch, but I didn't let her go. I held on tighter than a bloodthirsty leech, drinking in her mask of cheap cosmetics and fear.

"Jaelle," she said again. This time with a great amount of unease, every bit of which I enjoyed.

"Go on, now. You can tell me. We are friends, after all, Missy. Ain't we?"

"Y-yes," she stuttered quietly.

"Yes, you fancy Jeremy. Or yes, we're friends?"

She blinked, her mouth hanging open wide enough to catch flies.

"Yes...we're friends."

I patted her hand, holding it so tight I saw her flinch. Still, she didn't say a thing. "Bosom friends, then."

She blinked again, slower this time, as she nodded dumbly. "True and lastin' friends."

I sighed like that was enough for me and laid back down on the bed. I kept my eyes on Missy. She tugged her hand away from mine with one big, exasperated breath. She looked at me and her eyes flashed like lightning with rage.

I feigned innocence. "You come to visit me. That's right good, Missy."

"No, Jaelle. I come to stay for a while. To care for you. Poor Jeremy's plum tired out of caring for you by himself. I'm here to ease the load and keep you company."

I gritted my teeth beneath a weary smile.

"Ain't that good of you to think of Jeremy and me. Lord knows, his load is heavy. And you'll be such a wonderful distraction for us." I spoke with all the sweetness of a summer rain ready to burst into a deluge to flood the bitter soil and she knew it.

Her smiling eyes and wholesome, dough-like face were spoiled. Rotten in the crisp, eager sunlight, and growing putrid. Veins of shadow played about her face. Missy stood up and slowly backed away. She kept her eyes on me as she did, as if at any moment I would leap out of my bed and eat her up, like a hungry wolf ready to gorge itself on a smaller, weaker, and more annoying critter. To her, I was a monster, a vile creature that was worse than a devil. I was the woman in the way of what she wanted, and I hadn't died.

Maybe I was being punished for my sins. By God, I was going to see that Missy was punished too. Somehow, I would see it done. Missy turned her back on me to leave.

"Missy?"

Reluctantly, she glanced back.

"This is an old house, liable to fall down around you if'n you don't take care. The walls are thin. You can 'bout hear a fly buzzing in the next room over. No secrets to be kept in this house then. None at all."

She looked angry and wild. She nodded and crept out of the room on her tippy toes. I nearly laughed. If I could put the fear of God in that woman, belike I could do anything.

23 A Place For Everything...

The winter season grew warm, as if the wintry storm and foot of snow had never happened. When the snow was gone, I could plainly see the little pile of disturbed soil. The place where my baby was buried, along with Mama's amulet.

I heard they buried Mama on her own land, out behind her house, in the shadow of a willow tree. No gravestone to name her, no cross over top to bless her. She too was just another pile of upset earth, nothing that anyone would remember. After a while, not even me, once the spring rains had doused the soil and bid the long, tasseled grass to grow.

Mama and my baby were not meant to be remembered, and Jeremy had made sure of it. I wanted him dead for it. Dead and buried way down deep so even the Devil himself wouldn't recall where he was laid. Way down deep where the worms and all the underthings of the dark would eat him up. Turn him into nothing but new soil. Then he too would not be remembered. He deserved that. He deserved worse, but that would satisfy me well enough.

I spent those long, dark days thinking on that, letting my rage fuel me as my heart and body eased into a thrumming wakefulness. A steady and consistent flame burned low within me, and a whispering voice beckoned me in the dark with the constancy of a gnat in the summer heat. It was the spark of life left in me from the storm. It wanted to catch fire and spread to every inch of me until there was nothing but anger and fire. A fire that could burn.

A fire that could kill.

I waited, and while I waited, I watched what went on around me. Oh, and there was plenty to see. Jeremy never came to see me once Missy arrived. I was glad of it. The last thing on this earth that I wanted was to see his ugly face. For a while, Missy went on like nothing had happened, like I didn't know of her longing for my husband or their secret trysts behind closed doors. But like I said, the walls of that house were paper thin, and it didn't take long to decipher the racket coming from the other room.

Jeremy had always been a quiet lover for me, but with Missy, it was all wild and ravenous crying and moaning. Not only were they loud about their lovemaking, but they were constant. Day after day, oftentimes more than once, the walls would be a-quaking and a-shaking in the wake of their violent love. Day after day, I sat in that room and listened. I couldn't help but listen. It was the only cursed sound in my hellish silence.

After they were done, I could hear them laughing and carrying on, breathless and panting. Then the door would open, and Missy would come in, her dress all wrinkled and her hair a mess. Her lips would be swollen, and a slick veil of sweat shone on her body. She would blush just a little, barely able to meet my eyes. I hated her.

Without Mama, I felt utterly alone. At least with her moonstone, I had felt connected to my past as much as my present, or even my future. The roots and tangled vines of her magic were ingrained in my flesh and blood and bones. In those dark days, I needed her near me. Mama and Great Ma and Aunt Millicent. They were the steadiness in the chaos, and at times, they were the chaos. I felt at war with myself for needing them. For desiring their ancient earthen wisdom, their surety that like the seasons, all the ill-making and evil would pass away into dust. It was hard to think that anything would be good again. Not when Jeremy and his whore still kept me captive in this house, ailing and alone, while they worshipped each other like golden calves in the desert. Theirs was a barren desert, their lust was the fire that kept them thirsty, and I was the watery oasis where neither one would drink again in friendship or in love.

"Jaelle," Missy had come to check on me after another romp in the sheets with Jeremy down the hall.

She looked at me with a sickeningly sweet smile, one as proud as a peacock. She had found herself a bit of pride knowing that she was set above the woman of the house in Jeremy's eyes. Of course, I couldn't understand why rutting with a fat, filthy buck like Jeremy would bring her more pleasure than that of her husband. Sal was a good man, and he was blessed with fortune in a place where most people had so little to their name. How could she choose less when she had always known more? Did she think that by picking Jeremy she was gaining something? I didn't answer her. I just kept glancing out the window, my hands planted firmly in my lap so as not to slap her when she came near.

Nearer, still she came, smoothing out her crumpled dress and minding her hair that had fallen into her face. Little curlicues of blonde brushing her flushed cheeks. She sighed, distracted and a little annoyed.

"Jaelle, you ain't said nothin' in a week. You've hardly ate." She cocked her head to the side with a silly smile, like she was Mother Hen, and I was her unruly chick that must be put in check. "What's the matter? You don't like my cookin'?"

Missy's home cooking was about as scrumptious as hog swill on a hot summer's day.

"I haven't a taste for anything," I said at last, "least of all bad cookin'."

Missy's eyes batted wildly as she took that in. It festered there in her gaze, spoiling her smile and laying it to waste. She huffed like the spoiled little child she was, her fat face wrinkled and scrunched into a disgusting mess of emotion I didn't care to see. The wheels inside her head were turning awful slow, and she struggled to say a word back in her anger. At least, I gathered from her look that it was anger. It was such a dumb and fretful face she was making; I had to stifle a laugh.

Wouldn't want to hurt her feelings now, would I? No. Not now.

She was as red as she could be now, stifling all that fussy rage. With a frail and trembling hand, she brushed away the scattering of blonde hair from her sweaty, flushed face.

She started to stutter out something, but stopped herself, choking on her own words. Her hands were balled into fists, her fancy wedding ring flashing in the sunlight. Flashing like her ire, golden but deadly. Missy thought better about those words hanging off the edge of those swollen red lips, and with another girlish huff, she whipped her plump body around and stomped out.

I heard her downstairs moments later, crying her eyes out to Jeremy while he tried to calm her down with all manner of coaxing and kisses. But nothing did calm her. She was surely vexed and would have none of his tenderness, which was wearing thin fast.

"Stupid, damn bitch," I muttered from my bed, praying they could hear my mutterings all the way down the stairs.

After all, the walls were thin. I knew then that Missy would surely wear out her welcome just as quickly as she'd come. He would grow tired of her, tired of her whiny, nasal voice and her thick, pasty skin. Yes, I knew my husband would grow sick and tired of that hussy and come back to me. And when he did...

God help him.

24 AND EVERYTHING IN ITS PLACE

When Doc Lee visited the next day, it was like nothing was wrong in this house of secrets. This den of sin. God would surely blush and rise with His holy vengeance to rend every bit of us if He stepped foot inside. Doc Lee wasn't one to shy away from the raw and ungodly. He had seen it all in his many years. Although he went to church each Sunday morning, I doubted he believed anything that wasn't written on the side of a bottle of booze.

As Doc examined me, I listened to Missy and my Jeremy, going on and on about me as if there were some actual concerns for my welfare. They chattered incessantly, playacting all the time.

"She ain't ate for days."

"A powerful grief done took hold of her and she just ain't right, you know? Doc?"

"She looks right close to death, Doc. Will she be alright?"

I kept my mouth shut. I was weak and tired; if one of them were to blow on me, I'd perish. Doc Lee was annoyed for both of us. He stopped what he was doing, turned to Missy and Jeremy, and gave them a look full of daggers and spite.

"I ain't come to hear from you two. I come to hear from her."

The "her" being me, though he never did call me by my name. Perhaps he thought it would conjure up something terrible if he did.

I'm not a devil. Just a woman. Broken, like a flightless bird.

Doc Lee looked at me with that same dose of annoyance and said, "Now, why ain't ya eatin'?"

I motioned for him to come closer and whispered in his ear. Out of the corner of my eye, I saw Missy lean in too, trying desperately to hear my words. Doc Lee burst into gut-bellowing laughter. His head reared back as he held onto the pot belly peeking out of his tight-fitting flannel shirt. He really ought to have gotten married. The man needed a proper woman to care for him, to make sure his meals were hot, and his clothes fit just right without any wrinkles or holes.

He turned to Missy and Jeremy, who'd just about turned whiter than a sheet, a wide toothy grin on his face. "Seems the vittles ain't to everybody's likin' round here," he said with a chuckle.

Missy grumbled under her breath, her sharply pointed nose crinkling with displeasure. Jeremy looked anything but pleased. He gritted his teeth, his lips pressed firmly together to temper his rage.

"If she don't like it—" he started.

Doc Lee whipped around to him with a glare behind his smudged and dirty glasses. "Listen here, Jeremy Bennett. This woman done birthed a child."

"A dead one at that," Jeremy muttered.

Doc Lee cleared his throat and ignored the snide remark. "*And* nearly died doing it. You get her what she wants—anything she wants—and don't you be a-griping about it neither. Ya understand?"

Jeremy was spitting mad now, but he choked out, "Right, Doc."

Doc Lee didn't look satisfied with that answer. He looked a little worried as he glanced back at me. I saw the wheels in his head churning with that worry, like he wanted to carry me right out of that room with him and just drive away. Like he knew what was coming for me. Instead of doing anything, he just gave me a weak smile.

"Don't you worry. You'll be right as rain in no time

at all." He patted my trembling hand, not noticing how much it shivered in fear beneath his touch. Perhaps he just didn't want to notice.

"Don't worry," he said again, as if to say it twice would make it so.

I had little trust that it would. Doc got up off the bed and edged toward Missy and Jeremy to speak with them quietly. Their words were muffled, fluttering to me with a vacant echo.

"This is your woman, Jeremy." He gave a sour glance toward Missy, before he added, "And it is your place to care for her."

Jeremy was quiet. His answer to everything these days.

"This is *your place*, son," Doc emphasized, grabbing his big black doctoring bag and heading toward the door. "You take care of her."

It was meant kindly, but it came out as a warning hiss. Then he was gone. Missy let out a laugh, her belly flapping with each bellowing gust.

"Seems old Doc don't know her like we do. Seems an awful shame. He'd be best to take care of things for us. Ain't that right, Jeremy?"

"Quiet!" Jeremy roared.

Missy shut up right then and there. That smile swiped right off her doughy face. He looked frightened. They met one another's stare in the heavy silence. They didn't say a word, but I could see it in their eyes. They were planning. I kept my eyes and ears open the rest of the day, preparing for their act of war against me. It was coming.

Much later that day, Jeremy had left the house. Missy came in with a steaming bowl of something that smelled as foul as cow manure. She pulled up my rocking chair and sat herself down next to me. She tried to smile, but it was a frail and flaccid thing. Not worth the trouble to put it on her painted face. Her eyes were set on me. She was determined.

"Now, Jaelle, it ain't right that you ain't eatin' even a bite. Won't you just take one teensy bite of this here porridge for me? Just the one?"

She danced the spoonful of muck in the air before me. A mother hen to her little chick. Her smile got wider, and she jammed the spoon to my lips. The warm metal tapped against my teeth hard, but I wasn't budging. Not a drop of that hot mess was going to fill my insides. With a desperate cry, she grabbed me by the face and tried to pry open my lips. Still, I wouldn't budge. My mouth was an iron trap that the likes of her would never unseal.

She threw the bowl across the room. It shattered, the muck flying everywhere. It even landed on her fancy dress. Tears welled in her eyes.

"One way or the other, Jaelle. One way or the other, I swear to God, you will eat." Then, she was gone. Huffing her way out of the room. A cow in a violent tempest.

Whispers filled the air with the electric pull of lightning in the dark of my room. It was night now, and the whispers on the other side of the wall had been going on for some time. Soft and low, but still, I could hear them. They weren't the lulling whispers of two lovers in the dark. They were the hissing sounds of two sinners conspiring toward a greater evil. Yet they were quiet. Too quiet for me to understand.

"You know what they're saying, don't you, child?"

My mama sat in the moonlit corner, half full of shadows so I could not see her face.

"Murder," she hissed with delight. "They've a mind to kill you."

I shivered in the sudden cold that had come with her.

"That chit of a woman, Missy, wants you gone. Her husband just about done tossed her out on her ass for her lustin' ways with your Jeremy. Word's gettin' around in town that she's nothin' but a damned hussy. Not the goodly woman everybody was led to believe she was."

Mama stopped her rocking and leaned forward in the chair. Her face was lit by the moon, eerie and bright, and her eyes gleamed with an unnatural light.

"They mean to murder you, don't you understand? And then, they'll run off together to God knows where, so long as no one knows their names."

I spoke up then, my voice frail and weak in the darkness. Barely above a whisper, "How will they do it, Mama?"

She chuckled, leaning back into the shadows. "Silently, child. No blood, no mess. Not a whiff of suspicion hangin' on them."

"I don't understand you, Mama."

"Poison. They been trying for a while now, but you ain't ate enough for it take its effect."

"They been tryin' to poison me?"

She gurgled out a laugh again, a deep, raspy, and death-like sound that made me shiver and shake. "That old rat poison in your cellar does more than kill the rats, child." Her chest rattled like it was her last breath on this earth. She came forth from the shadows, her head now bashed in good and blood streaming down her face. "It'll kill more than rats, you understand?"

I nodded, shivering again at the thought.

"Don't let the spring come round again with such a shadow on your back. That aching in your heart. Not when there's a way." She said it again, "There's a-way, Jaelle. Now."

I nodded. I understood her.

"But you need yourself some protection."

My hand instinctively grasped for the amulet around my neck that was no longer there.

She made a face in the moonlight, a look of disappointment. "Find it. And do what must be done."

Her body was peeled back into the blackness, and she disappeared in a wisp of eerie moonlit mist. Still, her voice carried on the air to me with a hiss, "Find it."

I nodded to the nothingness.

The moonlight lit the way out into the fields, my bare feet tiptoeing gently in the dead, damp grass. It had been easy to slip out of the house; the two conspiring lovers had swiftly fallen asleep in each other's arms. I peered through the crack in their door to make sure.

The air was crisp and cold, my breath rising in misty clouds that fluttered up to the stars as I walked. The moon was bright and ornery, fighting back the puffy gray clouds that kept crowding around its hazy orb. It filled my heart with hope and a tremor of something else. A vibration of thready courage that wrapped itself around my flesh inside and made me wild for action. For the thing I was about to do. I was weak, but I was ready.

I reached the little mound of upturned earth at the edge of our land. I stared at it for the longest time, the moonlight capturing its eeriness, its quiet rage. There beneath that broken ground was all the hope and devastation of a lifetime, and it longed to be above the earth once again. I could feel my fingertips pulsing with the power of the moonstone already. I knelt; hands ready to dig. I could feel the moon and stars at my back, urging me onward, but all I could think of was God peering down from that same black veil of night. He was watching me; he had to be.

The ground wasn't sacred. It wasn't even blessed to receive the little life that had been in me for all those months. All those precious moments feeling the life inside of me move and grow and be. All that time of hope. All that time of constant prayer, wishing for a healthy child in my arms. Yet there I was clawing at the earth like an animal to reach my babe, and the moonstone that seemed to be the key to everything now. All my sorrow and all my strength. All the power I needed to do what must be done.

I dug for what seemed like an eternity, until my fingertips were numb with the damp cold. No matter how much I dug, all I saw was an empty black void down below. No child. No moonstone. Exasperated, I leaned back for a moment, my eyes up to the sky.

"Please. Please just let me find 'em," I whispered.

Out of the corner of my eye, I saw my mama and Aunt Millicent watching from the apple trees in the distance. They were urging me to keep digging.

Dig, child. Dig. Dig.

So, I dug. I dug until my hands felt like blocks of ice, my fingers like splinters of piercing pain. Then, there it was. The amulet laid atop a yellow-stained bundle. My baby. I was afraid of what lay there beneath that dirty cloth. Afraid to touch it, though I longed to. With trembling fingers, I snatched up the bloodied amulet, wiped Mama's blood on my nightgown, and quietly fastened it around my neck. I felt its power pulsing on my cold skin with a satisfying warmth that made me dizzy, drunk on its prickling force. I sighed at the weight of it against my chest, happy to bear it.

But I wasn't here just for the moonstone. I looked back down in the hole. My stomach churned as I reached in with both hands and brought out the bundle. I cradled it in my arms like the child it had been. My heart was aching to look on the child I'd carried. I had to see it. My hand moved before I was ready and slowly peeled back the cloth. There was my baby, still covered in blood and almost black. Its tiny body was curled up like a kitten. It didn't nearly look like I had imagined.

My heart sank, racing in my chest. My stomach burrowed up to my throat, bile in my mouth that tasted of spoiled, rotten waste. I couldn't bear to hold my baby; not like it was. Somehow, my arms wrapped around it. I couldn't let it go back into the earth to rot into dust. Not yet.

In the dwindling dark of the night, I held my child until my heart was full of hatred and poisonous rage. When I was done, I laid it back down in the soil and covered it up with care. I gave it the earth's blessing, and the promise of blood and revenge. I prayed that God wouldn't hear.

As I walked back to the house, I felt faint and weary, my body struggling to keep upright. I made it back to the porch, into the house and up the stairs. I peered into the lovers' room. They were still wrapped in each other's arms, fast asleep and carefree in their dreams.

But not for long.

I smiled thinking of the plan I'd made, that Mama, Millicent, and me had made out in that field. If I was to die, then those two lovers would die right along with me.

25 Too Many Cooks in the Kitchen Spoil the Soup

When I awoke early the next morning, Mama's moonstone was still thrumming hard against my skin. Pulsing with the steady beat of my heart. I felt stronger and more alert. My body was on fire with a new breath of life. That deathly cold had left my limbs at last, and the pain had all but subsided. I felt a little like myself, but deep beneath my skin, nestled among the veins and muscles and fleshy parts, there was something dark. I had felt it slowly collecting over the long year, pushing up through the very soul of me. Now, it was rising to the surface, barely a breath away from breaking through my skin. With it came that secret voice. I feared what it would bring, but it felt good. That darkness was less shadowy than my own heart's hue. My heart had rotted into a decadent mush, a black mass of what was once beautiful and blessed.

Blessed to suffer. Blessed to die. Blessed to sin.

The words stained my mouth with venom and black thoughts. Yet, they made my insides shiver with delight. They seemed truer to me now than any gospel I had ever heard. I was a sinner. I was a fallen child of the Lord. I had fallen deeper than His Hand could reach.

Only Mama and her magic could reach me in those depths. Only Mama and her magic could understand how I had languished in that dark hole, dying slowly, while the world around me moved forward. I never moved. Only Mama and her magic could pull me out and give me strength. The strength of ancient roots that would raise me up. A raging power that had lived many lives. The lives of seasons, the lives of storm and sea, the lives of women like Mama and me. I was as much a part of those lives as they were a part of mine.

My thoughts were ripped from me at the sound of Missy moaning from the other room. The sun had only just broken through the wispy cloud cover hanging low above the hazy horizon, and they were already at it. That ancient rage rippled through me, tore a hole in my aching chest, and I knew then that it was time.

It's only right, Mama's voice echoed through the room, a soft hissing sound barely audible above Missy's disgusting noise. *It's only right, baby girl.*

"It's only right," I echoed back to the empty room.

With Mama's blessing, I slipped out of bed and tiptoed my way to the door. It was open just enough for me to peek through and take a listen. The house had gone quiet. Not a peep from the lovers down the hall. Not a sound from anywhere. I took this as my sign. I opened the door a little wider, just enough for me to slide through. I prayed that it wouldn't make a noise, but it squeaked as it swung on its rusted edges.

Damn. I waited a moment, just to see if someone would come because of the noise I'd made.

Wait.

Breath in. Breath out.

Wait.

No one came. I took a deep breath out and crept past Missy and Jeremy's room.

"I wish that awful woman was dead." Missy's voice was hard to miss in the deep stillness.

I stopped just past their door. I trembled in the cold and the rage I felt, but still I listened.

The feeling's mutual.

"Don't worry, honey. It'll be done soon."

I heard the bed creak and whine under the weight

of that hefty woman as I imagined she laid atop my husband's chest. He sighed heavily, an exhausted and weary sound.

Missy's voice came again, "I hate her. I hated her the first time I saw her. All mealy-mouthed and mousy. Can't say a damn word without blushin' and turnin' her damn eyes away."

Jeremy laughed and said, "That's how I wanted her. She'll damn near do anything I tell her to now."

A pause. "I ain't that a-way, Jeremy. Is that what you want me to be?"

"'Course not, honey."

I imagined she smiled at that.

"But 'twould make ya a mite prettier and pleasin' if you wasn't so gabby."

She's bound to get on your last nerve at some point. Just you wait.

Missy pouted, "I ain't what you want then? You want that mealy-mouthed little chit. Don't ya?"

Jeremy didn't say a word. I heard the springs of the mattress whine again. The old girl rolling off him, I supposed.

"I hate her...hate her. When Jeremy? When will it be over?"

"Just you wait, darlin'. It'll be done. I promise ya."

That darkness inside of me wanted to bust right into that room and catch them in their nasty plot to kill me. But that's not what Mama would do. So, instead, I just kept walking, down the hall and down the stairs.

I passed like a hainted thing through the house. I didn't make a sound. Not even my shadow dared to paint the walls. I ignored the mess—Missy couldn't keep house to save her life—and made for the cellar door. It creaked open with an anxious whine and I was washed in the darkness from below that gulped me up in one big hissing swallow. I was always afraid of the cellar. A childish fear, of course. It always seemed as if there was a smell of death and dark things down there. Like the boogerman himself would leap out at every step to get me.

Today, I wasn't as afraid. I figured that if the boogerman were down there lying in wait, he would know my wicked intentions for the visit to his lair, and he would let me pass. I prayed under my breath that I was right this time, and step by step, I crept down into the deep pitchy darkness. There was a bare bulb hanging at the bottom of the stairwell. I couldn't see it in the dark. I felt for its rusty pull cord. My fingers swam in the nothingness for what seemed like an eternity before they brushed the cool metal of the cord. I gripped it tightly with a sigh of relief and yanked.

The cellar was immediately showered in a yellowish haze of light. The musty air smelled of old clothes and moldy earth, like a grave. There was a hush over this grave. I let it sweep over me, breathed it in and stepped toward the furthest corner. That was where Jeremy kept his tools. A black toolbox sat next to a rusted out can of kerosene, which sat next to a box of rat poison.

My eyes homed in on the mildewed box of poison. Its top was ripped off. I lifted it off the shelf. It was almost all used up. I knew for a fact that we didn't have a rat problem, hadn't for a long time now.

How long had he been planning to kill me? How long had he been trying?

My grip tightened on the box, and I backed away to take it upstairs. The amulet against my breast began to pulse and thrum violently on my skin with a red-hot heat. I could almost hear my Mama and Millicent's voices whispering from it.

Not this, baby girl. You know the way.

I did know the way. A better way, thanks to Mama and Millicent. I put the beat-up box of rat poison back on the shelf and slipped up the stairs.

I stepped outside, wrapping my shawl tightly

around the goose-pimpled skin of my arms. Breathing in the cool, crisp morning air. It filled my insides and eased the aching in my bones. My heart slowed its jackrabbit pace just a little. I waited to listen. The two lovers hadn't gotten out of bed yet. I had time enough to get what I needed.

I went down the front porch steps and out into the yard. My footsteps were quick, despite the hesitance in my muscles with each movement. I went past the orchard and into the western field.

It must be here. It must be.

A lavender scented breeze brushed across my cheek, making me stop. Aunt Millicent. I closed my eyes to savor the scent of her. She was leading me.

Here.

Opening my eyes, I glanced down to see exactly what I had sought after—hemlock. It grew wild in these parts, blighting the fields with its poisonous, pretty speckled flowers that looked as delicate as snow-white lace. You couldn't cut it down; it grew back just as lush and spread just as quickly. Jeremy had thought he'd been rid of it all last spring, but here it was waiting for me.

I smiled to see it. After all, it was a pretty sight to see this early morning. It shimmered in the pale pink light, an ominous stain on its perfect white. A fitting sign. I took the hem of my nightgown and used it to pluck a handful of the flowers. I was careful not to touch its oily lifeblood. Like the forbidden fruit of Paradise, just to touch it was to die.

I used my shawl to bundle it up, a neat little package of death in my hands. My feet were frozen as I crossed the fields again. Up the porch steps and into the house. Even from the bottom of the stairwell, where I listened as quietly as a church mouse, I could hear Missy's steady snoring from the end of the upstairs hall.

By mid-morning, the house smelled of cinnamon

and spice. It brought my husband and that hussy stumbling down the stairs. They batted their sleep-crusted eyes with dumb surprise as they watched me bustling about the kitchen. I gave them a tender smile as I put the last sheet of my apple turnovers on the table to cool. I could still see the sweet heat rising from their gooey pockets, but that didn't stop Jeremy. He made a beeline for the nearest turnover, grabbing it up with a yelp as it burned his fingers. He dropped it to the table, his sad eyes watching as it plopped into a soppy mess on my tablecloth. I hid my anger with a simpering laugh. Missy glared my way, but I pretended not to see her. I only had eyes for Jeremy. He took notice.

"They're hot from the oven, silly," I said between giggles. "Figures. My Jeremy, always hungry as a bear in winter. Always got a taste for my cookin'."

He gave me a half-smile. "Your turnovers 'specially, Jaelle." He glanced at Missy with a cautious smile. She didn't return it. He cleared his throat, his smile quickly fading.

"Well, go on now. Both of ya sit," I said, pouring on the sweetness like thick honey off the comb.

Missy looked over at Jeremy, but Jeremy was ogling those turnovers. With a huff, she plopped her fat ass into a seat at the table. Jeremy licked his lips and rubbed his plump belly as he sat across from her. I was standing between them with a smile so wide, sweet, and bright, even the scattering of sun poking in through the curtains was no match for it. I could light up the room all on my own. Jeremy was soaking it up.

"Jaelle, honey, shouldn't you be in bed resting like Doc said?" Missy's tone was anything but friendly.

I skipped over to the kitchen counter where the rest of the apple turnovers had already cooled. I scooped up a few and skipped my way back to the table. Carefully, I placed two of the pastries on a plate for Jeremy and set it before him, like he was a king.

His eyes lit up like I'd never seen. I plopped the smallest runt of a turnover in front of Missy. She sneered at me until she realized that Jeremy was watching.

Time for some genuine playacting.

"Just a taste, right, Missy? We gotta watch our figures, don't we?"

Missy glowered at me. I just smiled.

I gripped the chair in between them with all the strength I could muster while I smiled away. Thinking I should look a little meeker and milder to keep up the act, I dabbed at my forehead with my apron and let out a heavy sigh.

"Doc is a good man, but the best medicine he don't prescribe is sunshine and a bit of exercise. These here turnovers kept me busy all morning."

While you horny toads slept away the daylight.

"And that sweet sunshine peering through the windows did the rest. I feel almost as right as rain, like he said."

"Truly?" Jeremy said with a tender expression.

It almost made me regret the hemlock seeds riddled all through the turnovers I'd just served him. But only almost.

Missy picked up hers, inspecting its golden, flaky crust with a look so foul, she might as well have vomited right there on the spot. My heart sank. I'd never, ever seen that woman refuse a bit of food when it was offered. Hell, I'd seen her raid my ice box countless times without permission, while she jabbered on faster than a jaybird. What was this now? Was she not hungry after all that fussing upstairs? Or was she jealous of the scrumptious delights I'd laid before my man? I sat down before an empty plate. Missy's eagle eyes noticed, and she scurried to grab a turnover. She shamelessly plopped it down on my empty plate and gave me a wicked smile. There was silence as each of us looked the other over, unwilling to break this fast alone.

Jeremy was the first to grow restless.

"Well, hell, let's eat," he croaked, settling his butt into the seat.

I watched him grab up a turnover, bringing it to his mouth with a greedy smile. His mouth opened wide. My heart stopped beating, as I waited for him to take a bite. A breath closer and the pastry would be in his mouth. Closer. Just a little closer.

I nearly jumped at the sound of the phone ringing to life in the hall.

Jeremy stopped; his teeth ready to gnash the turnover into tiny bits. No other sound came. Then, there it was again. Grunting a curse or two under his breath with an angry sigh, he slapped his pastry down and got up from the table. He cussed all the way to the hallway, letting another one slip just as he answered the phone. Missy and I listened from the table. Not a word was spoken between us.

"What is it, Mama?" A pause. "Mama, you need to calm down. I cain't understand ya."

A long moment of silence followed that seemed to pull the oxygen from the room and fill it full of shadow. My heart was in my throat, beating wildly. That darkness began to creep along the walls, crawling like new ivy around the doorframe. Something was coming.

A sigh from the hall. The phone slammed down with a decisive clank, the bell inside lifeless, void of a voice. Jeremy's lazy clomping came toward the kitchen. Slower now and sullen. I turned to Missy to get her reaction. Her cheeks were full of turnover, and she hopped out of her seat to grab another. My stomach turned sour to see her eat.

"Daddy's dead."

Jeremy stood in the doorway as white as a sheet. That shadow followed after him, climbing up the walls and inking the yellowed white of the room with its blackness. Jeremy's mouth hung open, stumbling to say more, but he couldn't.

"I'm sorry, Jeremy," I said quietly.

He stared out into space. I could see the wheels in his head colliding with one another in a disastrous muddled mess.

"I—" he started, and then his globby tongue got in the way. He swallowed hard and his eyes went dull. "I best get on over there. Mama'll need me to tend to things."

He turned his back on us.

Through a mouthful of my apple turnover, Missy yelled out, "You want I should come with ya, Jeremy? Women folks need a female touch when it comes to grievin'."

Her lips smacked and the food left in her mouth made a creamy mushing sound that made my stomach turn. Jeremy glanced back at her with a look I could only guess was disgust.

"Nah," he said. "You just stay here with them vittles. That plump belly o' yours would miss 'em if you was to leave."

Missy stopped chewing. Her eyes grew big and wide. I doubt that anyone had ever called her fat to her face. Until today. Jeremy turned to leave. The apple turnovers on his plate were cold now and uneaten. My plan was twisting sideways, and he was leaving me alone—with her. I couldn't let all my efforts vanish in vain. I grabbed a basket and wrapped up a bundle of turnovers. Quickly, I headed toward the front door, praying I wasn't too late to catch him.

I found Jeremy on the porch, his head in his hands as he leaned against the column. Just like that night in the spring when the storm came, and the apples grew. The apples that had made up our first harvest. The apples I'd used this morning to make the turnovers that would kill him. They had to kill him. I had to kill him.

The door creaked open as I slipped outside. He

whipped his head around to look at me. His eyes were red, redder than that night, but there wasn't a stain of a tear on his face.

"What you want, woman?"

I tiptoed toward him. Gently, I took up his hand in mine and set the basket in his hands.

"Tell your Mama to be well," I whispered.

Jeremy blinked, his face falling into a somber look of disbelief.

"After all I done, and you wish her well?"

He had used and abused me. Raped me. Lied to me. Cheated on me. Tried to kill me. And he brought that whore of his into our home to help him do it.

"You be well, Jeremy," I patted his hand with the gentleness of a dove, the loving kindness of a damned saint.

He nodded and tucked the basket under his arm as he headed toward his truck. I watched him drive away, hoping against hope that he wouldn't be back. That the poison would do its work on him and his whole damn family.

The sky was cluttered and dark now. A sharp wind was picking up, blowing the straggling copper-colored leaves right off the trees. Around and around, they spun up in the air, a cyclone of bloody red and rust that danced across the road and chased after the plume of dust left by Jeremy's truck. Despite the wind and the rustling leaves, it was ever so still. The sky was threatening to rain. A roll of thunder scattered over the land, trembling over the house until it quaked with the sound.

I heard a muffled cry. Something inside slammed down hard onto the floor. It was quickly followed by a flabby plop that I could feel even from the porch.

That must be Missy's breakfast disagreeing with her.

I couldn't help but smile. Mama's moonstone burned at my breast while my heart beat faster. I took a deep breath and went inside.

As soon as I walked through the front door, I smelled the sour, earthy scent of vomit. I heard her retching in the kitchen, choking and gasping for air as it just kept coming. I slowed my steps. I wanted to take my time. To savor every moment.

"Jaelle!" she managed to yelp out, a wet and cluttered mush of sound.

I slowed my steps further.

By the time I made it to the kitchen doorway, Missy was just about foaming at the mouth. She was down on her knees, sitting in a pool of chunky vomit, her body shaking uncontrollably.

"J...J...Jaelle!" She was vomiting blood now.

She reached out to me with bloodstained hands, but I kept my distance. She pleaded with her eyes. But when she saw my cool expression, the dark creeping around my eyes and the corners of my lips, her gaze shifted. Her face fell. She knew. She gripped the ratty, checkered tablecloth with all her might, a low rumbling scream forming in her throat. It was quickly garbled with another long spewing mess that landed at her feet. She tried to raise herself to her feet, knocking everything off the table with a crash. She fell with it and lay flat on her fat, bloodied face. Missy laid there for a long while, wheezing as white foam bubbled at her lips.

I finally stepped into the room. She couldn't move now, her limbs frozen in tremors. Her eyes peered up at me as I stood over her. It felt good to be above her. For once, it felt good to have the upper hand.

"He...ee," she gurgled out, but I didn't understand.

Quite frankly, I didn't care. I slid a chair out from under the table, and I sat myself down in front of her.

"He...ee," she gasped.

Another volley of puke cascaded from her mouth and settled in a pool about her head. A wave of rage overwhelmed me. I clung to my amulet with all my might. The heat of it made me sick and dizzy. I felt a weariness drift over me, remnants of my loss. But I was still upright; Missy was not.

"I do believe you're dying, Missy," I said with all the hate I had inside me.

She began to choke, her body heaving violently. I cocked my head to the side to look at her. I wanted to see her eyes when they looked their last at me. She was utterly pathetic. Disgusting, a pointless waste of flesh and fat. She'd made herself a glutton and a whore to satisfy her appetites. She'd made me a murderer. Now I soaked up that aura of death that hung about her like a cool draft.

"Do you want me to help you?" I asked.

Her eyes did the talking now, begging and pleading for me to help her. Slowly, I reached out my hand to her, close enough to give her hope, but far enough away to keep her from grabbing hold of me. An exasperated, wet sigh escaped her lips, along with a river of spit. I clicked my tongue with a shake of my head, pulling my hand back. Her eyes followed it with a lifeless groan.

"What a mess!" I said matter-of-factly. "Got my hands full with tidyin' up by the looks of it." I turned to her with a wicked smile. "Idle hands are the devil's playthings. Seems you've let him run wild in my home. The walls are thin, I said. Of course, you took that and ran with it. Ran right into my husband's bed, all while I was ailin', near death after death done took the little babe I'd placed every hope on."

I took a breath, holding back my tears from her sight. She was wheezing now, her chest rattling like wet bones with every labored breath.

"Death done took my baby. By the looks of things, it should've taken me too. But here I am, and there you are." I leaned in close to her head, careful not to let my long, loose hair drag in her muck. "Maybe I'll rot in hell for what I've done to you. If I'm lucky you'll rot right there with me."

With that, I sat back again.

The minutes dragged on like hours, and my mind began to wander into a cloudy daze. There I saw my mama and Aunt Millicent looking at the little scene of chaos at my feet. Smiles spread across their cheeks, wide and full of wicked pleasure.

Done good, girl. Done good.

I'd done good. As I heard Missy's death rattle rip through her chest, my heart leapt with empty joy. I waited. Waited for the hours to tick away and the news that Jeremy had finally found his appetite.

My fingers were trembling so badly that I nearly dropped the phone receiver. Before I'd even brought it to my ear, the operator's loud and brassy voice came through, startling me. I mumbled something, unaware of myself. I felt like I was floating on a cloud, far, far away. So far and so high up that I would never come back down.

Gotta get rid of Missy. Gotta clean it up.

I had to get rid of Missy. The sudden panic at the thought of someone finding her terrified me now. I was afraid. Afraid of that body lying lifeless on the floor. Afraid of Jeremy lying somewhere at his mama's, dead as he could be. Afraid that somehow all these dead bodies would circle back to me. I couldn't deal with Jeremy, but I could do something about Missy.

The phone rang now. I was beginning to think I was out of luck when a familiar voice crept across my ear pressed against the phone.

"Hello?"

The rich tone of Elijah's voice was muffled by static on the line. He didn't sound the same. He sounded weak, frail, and needy, a shadow of the man from the summer.

Words faltered on my tongue. There were no words. So, he provided them.

"Is that you, Jaelle?"

I nodded. A foolish thing to do since he couldn't see me. There was a long pause. I could hear his heavy breathing on the line, the sound of air moving. He was pacing.

Everything went still.

"I'm coming." That was all he said, and then the line went dead.

I waited on the porch for what seemed like hours. Then he came, his car rising out of a billowing burst of dust, a thick wave of leaves floating on the air behind him. He leapt out of the car and hurried to the bottom step of the porch. He was breathless; he must have rushed to get here.

He looked me over carefully. "You look cold."

I realized I was shivering. I'd left my shawl with Missy's body in the kitchen. I wrapped my arms around myself. He shook off his jacket as he tripped up the steps to me. Gently, he wrapped his jacket around me, his touch lingering on my body for too long. He was close, oh so very close, and I shivered from the heat of him. My moonstone pulsed with the beat of my heart, fast as a hummingbird. I couldn't breathe.

"There," he said softly, his lips brushing my ear.

My heart beat faster until I remembered the dead body lying just inside. I pulled away a little, but he was having none of that and forcefully edged closer, pinning me against the column.

"Please, don't pull away," he whispered. "You called for me. That must mean something."

"Jeremy's daddy died today." I changed the subject. After all, there was business to tend to.

His face sobered, but he kept his body close to mine. "I know. I was called to minister there, to give solace to his mother. She is a good woman."

Those words felt empty on his lips. Once they had been used on my behalf.

"Did you see Jeremy while you was there?" My heart was racing now, my head spinning. He hissed under his breath and then grew quiet. His head bowed.

"Must we talk about death now, Jaelle?"

A sigh trembled silently from my lips. No talk of Jeremy. No talk of death. Jeremy must be dead. He had to be. With any luck, his mama was dead too.

"Life is riddled with death. What does it matter?" I answered, my voice gaining some strength.

He looked at me with a strange sort of wonder in his eyes and leaned in close to kiss me.

As his lips pressed up against mine, I pulled back an inch, maybe more, and whispered, "I killed her."

Now he pulled back, though reluctantly. "What?" His voice was shaky and unsure.

"Missy. I killed her."

I watched his face fall. He said nothing for a long while. I waited for his expression to change to one of horror or regret. But it didn't. Instead, he said, "Take me to her."

We stood in the kitchen as the sun began to sink below the trees. I looked at Elijah. Elijah looked down at Missy, hands on his hips. He inspected every inch of her. He didn't touch her. The look on his face showed he was frightened, disgusted even. Still, he didn't say a word.

With a sigh, he broke the eerie quiet, plopped down in a rickety chair at the table, and looked at me sharply.

"Jaelle, we've got to take care of this."

I didn't understand.

"Shouldn't I just turn myself in? Old Roy won't be hard on me if I do."

He leaned forward; his hands folded together before him like he was praying. Perhaps, he was. Perhaps the Lord listened, because he said, "You aren't guilty of anything, you understand? They were plotting against *your* life. What else was there to do?"

He glanced down and saw that his right shoe was sitting in Missy's puke. He turned green at the gills and quickly slid his foot out of the muck.

Swallowing hard, he said, "Truth is, Missy had reduced herself to something of a harlot in these parts. It was her affair with your Deacon Johnston that caused his speedy departure. Seems she left her husband about the time of Jeremy's little accident at the Temples' farm. No one knew where she'd gone. She didn't tell a soul, but people sure have been talking. Now, I see she was here all along, hiding away in a den of sin and debauchery."

His eyes softened as he turned to me. "You should never have had to do this, Jaelle. You should never..." His voice trailed off and his sad eyes wandered over Missy's deathly pale body.

"I can fix this," he muttered. His eyes met mine, he was determined and brave. The color had returned to his face, the fire in his eyes. "I can fix this."

The sun was a red-hot fireball floating just above the horizon and falling fast. Elijah's car was warm and loud. Too warm and too loud as it rattled down the road toward Mama's house. I cracked the window, leaning into the rush of cool air that trickled across my face. It was Elijah's idea to take Missy to my mama's. We'd bury her in Mama's grave; a place no one would visit, and no one would suspect. It made my body ill, my mind sick with grief, to think that this Jezebel would be sharing a resting spot with my mama. But the longer I had to think it over, the more it seemed like the only way.

"What about Jeremy?" I asked. There was still that matter to discuss.

Elijah bit his bottom lip tensely, his hands gripping the steering wheel.

"Let his people tend to him," he said.

I nodded. He was right. If Jeremy died, it was none

of our concern. They'd probably chalk it up to grief, a busted heart left broken by his daddy's death. No one would think otherwise. No one would suspect.

"Jaelle—"

I looked at Elijah. He was already looking at me, his tender gaze afire with want and need. He was hungry for me, I knew that. But there was the matter of the body in the trunk. As if he too thought of this, the spark in his eyes quickly sputtered out and faded. He seemed somber once again. We pulled up to Mama's place just as the first stars peered out from the purple-veiled sky.

"Where?" he grunted as he shifted the weight of Missy's large body in his arms.

We had wrapped her up in an old quilt. One that I had made in happier times. One that nobody would miss. I had the shovel.

"Where, Jaelle?"

I didn't know where they'd put Mama.

I could see that he was tired, and Missy's body was awful heavy. The way he looked at me made my stomach twist and sour. I wanted this to end. All of it. I wanted to get back into the car and just drive away. But I couldn't.

"Come on," I said, and then began to lead us through the thick thorns and bramble. Mama's land stretched out a ways, but it wasn't long before I found the willow tree. We fought our way through the thick dead grass, Elijah huffing and puffing the whole way. By the time we'd reached the tree's drafty shade, he'd broken out in a sweat.

"Here," I declared, pointing to the sodden plot of earth, still naked and bare. Now that I was here, it was strange to stand above the ground that held Mama in. The moonstone thrummed at my breast, panging for the hands that had held it and blessed it.

Elijah plopped Missy's body down on the ground without ceremony. I was sure he was glad to be rid of the heavy load. He was breathless now and beet-red in the face, his back bent, and his hands on his knees. He offered his hand to take the shovel from me. I gladly gave it to him. I backed away from the grave as he began to dig, watching in silence as he moved the earth that held my mama. As I waited in the tall, dead grass, I grew frightened. It wasn't right to dig up the dead. Surely, Mama's spirit would jump out from the shadows and curse us. She might even rise from her grave, screaming like a banshee.

A sharp, cold wind fluttered past me, full of whispers, and I shivered where I sat. It was Mama's spirit. It had to be. My eyes scanned the land around me and caught a glimpse of Mama's charred rocking chair just a-swaying in the wind on what was left of her back porch. There wasn't a soul around, and the wind wasn't so strong that it could twist around that rotted wood and make it move. It had to be Mama. I sank down low in the weeds; the only sound was that of the shovel as Elijah dug.

"Mama," I whispered low so that Elijah wouldn't hear. Only the wind answered me. "Mama, please. I promise we won't do nothin' to you. I promise your grave'll be just as nice as it ever was. Just, please..."

The shoveling stopped and my head popped up like a prairie dog. Elijah threw down the shovel. Breathless and dripping wet, he began to unbutton his shirt. There was nothing underneath but skin and muscle. He shivered in the cold, glancing at me to see that I was watching. A faint smile crept to the corners of his lips, but it stopped there. His shirt was tossed to the ground. He went to pick up Missy wrapped in the quilt. His muscles tensed and rippled as he lifted the body and tossed her into the grave. There was a hollow thump as she landed on top of Mama's wooden box. The box that held Mama in. Nailed shut, good and tight, so she wouldn't get out.

"I'm sorry, Mama," I muttered as Elijah made quick

work of replacing the soil and packing it down tight once again.

I placed a piece of holly on the grave once he was done. It was for Mama, not Missy. Elijah was just standing there, looking down at that grave, his face flushed and full of wildness. His sweaty body glistened in the moonlight. I tried not to look as I held out his shirt to him. He reached for it and pulled me close. I could smell the musky scent of his body. He leaned into me, pressing hard against me. He breathed me in.

"I've heard about your mother," he said in low, husky tones, keeping a sharp hold on me. "She was wild like summer storms and full of magic."

"Who told you that?"

His smile faded just a little. "My wife. She hears all the juicy gossip from those gabby women you sit with on Sunday."

I pulled away from him, but he brought me back. His warm breath brushed against my cheek. "Are you?"

There wasn't a breath of space between us now. He hummed under his breath as he took me in. "Show me."

His lips were suddenly on mine, pressing hard, as if he wanted to pull the very spirit and life from me. I waited to fall again, to feel that heated passion as it swept over me. All I felt was fire. Wicked, sinful fire that licked my skin and scolded it for its wanting. My eyes opened for an instant and caught the remnants of a shadow skirting behind the remains of Mama's house. A shiver ran down my spine, as I watched Mama's old chair rocking again on its own. Something dark was in the air, something black, rotten, and evil. I didn't like it one bit.

I pulled away, but Elijah pulled me back into him. The wind whipped around us, icy cold and smelling of death. He smelled of death, and it was rubbing every inch of me. I wanted to vomit. I wanted to run. But I just let him kiss me there in the moonlight. When he was done, he led me back to the car.

The drive home was long, and it felt like an eternity next to that man. My mind was pushing me to speak, willing my mouth to open. I couldn't help the words that spilled out.

"Elijah—why?"

He looked at me with those deep, dark eyes. "Why, what?"

"Why are you doing all this?"

His face grew serious, his eyes sullen. He thought about it for a long while before he said anything back. "Because I believe that you're a good woman. Better than most. And I believe that God would have me do it." He thought about it for a moment, and then he nodded. He was sure of it now. "I know it."

That was enough for me. I turned away from him and looked out the window as the darkness closed in on us and the night came.

The kitchen was dark and full of creepy, crawly shadows along the walls. When the little cuckoo clock chimed the late hour, I breathed a sigh of relief. I was alone, truly and wonderfully alone. But it seemed so...empty. The phone hadn't rung in all those hours. No news of Jeremy. Perhaps his family was too shocked to send word. Perhaps they were dead too. I should feel sorry for them. I should feel pity for them and send a prayer up to heaven for them. But I didn't.

There was a certain sense of freedom in the emptiness of my heart. I felt free to feel true feelings, not boxed up emotions taken off a shelf for just such an occasion. All my life, I'd stored up feelings like Mama's collection of canned goods. I'd labeled each one and set it aside for a rainy day. ANGER. SORROW. JOY. Losing the child, I had felt as if all those saved up jars had been knocked off the shelf, shattered into tiny little pieces that could never be a whole thing again. Those feelings were lost to me. All of them save for vengeance.

God said, "Vengeance is mine," but I couldn't wait for the Lord. If I'd waited, it would have been me curled up dead on that floor instead of Missy. Part of me prayed that the Lord Almighty would understand. A greater part of me didn't care. I had done what I'd done, and there was no going back.

A flash of headlights skirted across the dark walls before me, startling me out of my thoughts and back into the present moment. I heard the loud engine of a car stutter to a stop just outside. A car door slammed shut. Footsteps up the gravel walk. Then, up the porch steps. The front door screeched open on its noisy hinges. Footsteps through the hall. Up the back stairs. Door after door above me banged open.

Footsteps stormed back down the stairs. Into the parlor. Down the hall toward me. I didn't turn around. I just sat there staring at the place on the floor where Missy's cold, dead body had been. I heard the footsteps stop in the doorway. I waited, barely breathing.

"What in God's name, Jaelle?"

My body froze.

"Jeremy?"

26 THE WAKE

Jeremy's father was dead. My mama was dead. My baby was dead. Now Missy was dead too. But Jeremy—he was alive.

And I didn't know how the hell he'd managed that. He didn't give me time to ask him. In a flash like lightning, Jeremy was in my face, his rough, callused hand wrapped tightly around my neck. He sneered at me, his teeth bared and shining white in the shadows.

"Where is she?" he growled.

"I—" That was all I could utter before he tightened his grip on my throat.

"*Where. Is. She?*"

His eyes were full of fright, red and swollen from crying. It was a look of panic, like a deer being hunted. It made me wonder. He had lost everything in one day. His daddy. His land. His livelihood. And his lover.

That's when his eyes dipped down to my chest, where the moonstone hung. His gaze met mine in disbelief, before a sigh tumbled out of his mouth, and he loosened his hold on me. He shuffled to the sink, leaning his body against it, his back turned to me.

"She left," I said softly. "Said she'd done grown tired of waiting. For what I don't know. A man done picked her up. She said she had a better lover waiting for her."

His hands gripped the sides of the sink tightly, his body tensing. Still, he was silent. Quietly, on my tippy toes, I turned away and headed toward the hall. I was nearly there, nearly free of his presence, at least for the moment.

"Should be you that left. Not her."

I glanced back behind me to find him already eyeing me. There was nothing of the passion or the fire in his eyes like Elijah. Nothing of love or comfort or care, like Mama. Only sadness and emptiness and rage.

"Why didn't you just leave?"

Leave?

Here I was, thinking he'd had me bound to him with a steel grip, and all the while, he'd just wanted me to leave him. I stood there, dumbstruck and looking stupid. My mouth hung open just a little and my eyes were as wide as a doe's facing a loaded gun. When all the lives you've lived and the worlds you've created in those lifetimes have crashed down and everything is suddenly clear, what is there to say? What could I say to the one that had made those lifetimes a hell? Deep in my throat, a ready scream settled into a sigh. All the rage in me sank down to my toes.

"I'm sorry." I said, turned around and left him in the darkness.

The truck was packed and ready. Early morning light scattered across its rusted-out paint and its dirty windows. I waited by the passenger side door, dressed in my simple black shift dress, the only black thing I owned. I caught a glimpse of myself in the side mirror. I looked anything but acceptable, but for Mr. Levi Bennett's funeral, it would have to do.

I was impatient, shifting in my muddied shoes that were already killing my feet. Jeremy was taking too long. It wasn't like him to be late, or to make me wait. I was about to call for him when he burst through the screen door.

"I packed the vittles for the wake, Jeremy," I mumbled as he passed.

He didn't meet my eyes. We both got into the truck.

He turned the key in the ignition and the truck vroomed to life. Down the road, we went, not a word spoken between the two of us. There was to be no radio, no country music sing-along, no whistling tunes on this ride. This was a somber trip, one that neither of us wanted to make. There was grieving to be done.

The funeral was short for a man that seemed to mean so much to so many people. Brother Wise blessed the ground Jeremy's daddy was laid in and said the words a preacher ought to say to comfort the mourners left behind in the wake of so much sorrow.

Elijah looked tired and ghostly pale, his eyes dancing my way far too often. Once I even saw his cheeks flush when he glanced at me, his eyes full of that fire that made me feel like sinking down into the sod where I stood. I tried to keep my eyes from glancing toward him. For all my effort I could still feel the burden of his stare pressing down hard on me.

I scanned the rest of the mourning crowd, hoping for a distraction. My gaze rested on Mrs. Violet Bennett, Jeremy's mother. She was a tiny, frail thing, made frailer by her grief. Her skin was so pale. It was almost paper thin with blue-tinged veins poking out of her bony arms. Her dress was fine, the finest fancy dress I'd ever seen. It had a beaded trim around the bust line that sparkled in the dappled sunlight. For all its finery, it didn't seem fitting to sparkle and dazzle like that at your husband's funeral. Be that as it may, it would have been fine if I saw her weeping like the rest of them. Her face was shrouded in a black gauzy veil, an accessory added to her rather decadent hat. All beadwork and ribbons. Black, of course, but certainly not plain. I'd never have the likes of that, not even if I were the one lying in the coffin.

Violet stood there, perfectly still, as they lowered the coffin into the hole. She stood alone, strangely silent and unshaken, poised and pretty like a mountain on the distant horizon. She was born of the mountains, bred of the earth. *My* people. She knew toil and strife; they were old friends, as they were for us all. She reminded me so much of Mama, and my heart ached for her.

"Amen."

We all silently filed out of the churchyard, headed for the wake. I saw Elijah look at me, his face full of want, but Jeremy took me roughly by the arm and led me to the truck before I could even answer his look with my own. I managed to glance back at the gravesite long enough to see Violet raise her veil as she took one final look at her husband's grave. Her face was whiter than a sheet, but there wasn't a single tear to be seen. Nothing of emotion carried on her wild features. I saw her lips move, and then I saw something gleaming about her neck. A moonstone amulet. Jeremy pulled me into the truck before I could see more. As we drove, I pondered what I'd seen, as my own amulet beat like a drum against my skin.

I spent the afternoon in hushed whispers while family and friends paid their respects. Wakes are funny things. Some of them can be joyful, full of laughter and remembrance. Others are crying and wailing affairs. This one was the latter. There was hardly a word said other than to bemoan the loss of Mr. Levi Bennett and all that was lost with him.

"He was a good, God-fearing man."

"Not a debt owed to anyone. Paid in full every last time."

"He kept this town a-runnin'. No doubt about that."

"His son, Jeremy, ain't he the spittin' image of his pa?"

"Spittin' image is the end of it. He's a no-good, son of a—well, he ain't his daddy."

"Lemonade?" I asked with a smile, and those whispers died down.

Eyes danced away from me, anywhere but on me.

Not a soul would take the lemonade I had to offer. Quietly, I retreated to the kitchen, where most of the womenfolk were preparing the food. Like anxious prairie dogs, their heads popped up to take a look at me, standing there in the doorway with my pitcher. The women crowded around Violet, as if to protect her. Violet glanced up as she prepared a platter of spice cake, patting powdered sugar all over the top. She eyed me with a sigh and then went back to her business with a huff.

"Ya'll best git, or I'll tan every one of your hides," she croaked. All the women turned to her in surprise. She stopped what she was doing long enough to yell, "Go on, and git! Go back to your husbands and your mamas and your gossip. Git!"

They all did as they were told, filing out one by one in eerie silence. I was the last to go.

"You stay, girl." I heard behind me.

I stayed, spinning around on my heels to face her. She didn't say a word. She didn't look at me. She just busied herself with the plates of food, arranging them just so until they were perfect. Mrs. Violet Bennett had nice things, and people with nice things were fussy about how they looked.

"You got a lotta nerve showin' up here today, girl," she said, her eyes still never met mine. "After what Jeremy told me you done. Took up with a man, he says. Tore his heart right in two. And him, thinking that dead baby of yours wasn't really his."

Rage filled my chest, crawling up my throat to scream at her, but I held it back. My face flushed something awful. She huffed to see it and went back to her fussing.

"Now, Jeremy ain't a clever boy, and he ain't one for tall tales neither." She stopped, looking up at me with a stern eye. "And I can smell a falsehood a mile away, especially from him."

Violet pointed a pokey, red finger at me. It was

steady and coated with powdered sugar. "So, you go on and tell me the truth. I'll see if it ain't solemnly true. You done cheated on my son?"

Faster than a fly to sugar water, I shook my head in answer.

She glared. "You got a tongue to speak, or are you too mealy-mouthed to answer me?"

"No, Mama Bennett. I didn't," I lied.

I waited for her to see that lie spread across my face, to smell it on me like she said she could. She stared me down, good and hard, for what seemed like ages. Her breathing came fast, her narrow nose flaring out decidedly. She was looking into me, into the very soul of me, to see if I was a truth-teller or a liar. In that moment, I wanted to pray to God, but I didn't think He'd listen. So, I stood very still and waited.

Finally, she sucked in a mouthful of air and said with a nod, "Alright, then."

That was all. She turned her back on me and grabbed up a basket—*my* basket—covered by a dirty dish towel. She ripped off the towel, and there were the turnovers, poison and all. My heart skipped a beat and jumped right into my throat, choking me. Thoughts raced as I tried to understand how those had gotten here. Of course, I had sent them along with Jeremy. He was supposed to eat them. They were all supposed to eat them.

Violet placed those turnovers on a platter in a neat little design. Pretty poison. Fancy and laid out like a treat. My stomach was sick looking at them. A veil of sweat had gathered on my forehead, slowly beginning to trickle down my temples as I watched her touch each one. The moonstone around my neck panged with a sudden urgency that frightened me.

Black wisps of shadow curled about Violet and the table topped with poison. They traipsed their way toward me. Inch by inch, they fluttered and flew, getting bigger and blacker by the second, until all I saw was the darkness. It wrapped around me, bursting into a veil of night that swallowed the room. I closed my eyes to ward the dark away, but I could feel it around me, thick and heavy like summer heat.

Seall.

I didn't want to listen to that voice. It frightened me.

Seall!

I looked as I was told. There in the darkness was a shadow deeper than the blackness of the night. A dark so deep it had swallowed up all the starlight and left a nothingness in its wake. The shadow crept nearer. I couldn't move. The shadow became a living person. A woman—her vividly red hair as wild as an open flame on a sunlit hill, her skin as white as fresh cream and dappled with freckles, and her eyes as green as ivy. She was terrifyingly pretty, and her gaze was darkly set on me.

Great Ma, Eilidh, as she was known to folk in her time. Sinner. Witch. Devil. Even those who believed in her practices were afraid of her. Fearful of the powers she called upon on moonlit nights.

She crept close to me, draped in the tendrils of shadow I had seen moments before around Violet. Her body smelled of rotten things and fire. As she drew near, the smell seemed to burn itself into every part of me. Pitchy blackness dripped from her, oozed from her fingertips like sour magic.

Eilidh took a long hard look at me.

"A leinibh m' uchd-sa, de 'n talamh, ciamar a thàinig thu 'n so?" her words sank on the air, heavy with sorrow and ire so deep that it panged at my heart.

My heart cringed from their power. There was something dirty and devilish underneath them. She smiled at my fear. Her teeth were rotten and black inside her mouth, the foul scent of sulfur reeking out with every breath. When I did not answer, the woman screamed. A shrill and awful sound that filled the darkness and rang in my ears like thunder.

As her cry echoed on the air she said, "You have betrayed the god of heaven and the god of the earth. Your roots run deep, and they are rotten."

She clicked her tongue and hissed under her breath. "You have abandoned faith in all things and made vengeance with your god." She smiled a wicked smile of black, rotten teeth. "How sweet that you would remember me with such a cruel and violent offering."

She placed her snow-white fingertips over my heart. It seemed to quicken its beats at her touch, pounding like a drum beneath my skin, rattling my ribs with the sound. Eilidh closed her eyes to feel it. The sound of my beating heart was everywhere around us. She smiled again, but as she opened her eyes, the smile cracked and faded.

"But remember, blood for blood."

"I don't understand," I whispered.

Her tongue was alien and strange to me. Her words were like daggers that struck without warning in the dark.

She sneered at me like a wild animal. "Blood for blood, child. You have power in you, but you will pay for it and the blood you've shed. Just as your mother and her mother and her mother before her." Eilidh shivered at the mention of our family. She pulled away, hiding in the shadows. "She will kill you like the creature you are. We are all beasts in the night. Remember this."

Like lightning, in a flash she was gone, and with her, all the darkness and that putrid smell. I was returned to Mama Bennett's kitchen, the sunlight piercing through the bright, clean windows. The air smelled of lavender and fresh coffee. Violet was staring at me with eyes as big as saucers. She looked a little afraid and very annoyed.

"What ails ya, girl? You nigh on fainted right there on my floor."

I blinked, trying to get my bearings. Great Ma's words rang in my mind, rattling about with the heaviness of her shadow, as if she were still there, listening. Watching through my eyes. Violet had the platter of poisoned turnovers in her hands, ready to pass them off to one of the women who had returned to the warmth of the kitchen.

"No!" I cried and yanked the platter out of her hands.

Into the stove and its fire, they went. I watched them burn, hissing as they turned to char. As the fire licked up every morsel of my rage, I swore I heard Great Ma's laughter ringing in my ears.

"What the hell is wrong with you, Jaelle?" Jeremy demanded.

I stood up straight, but I couldn't make myself turn to him. He did that for me, spinning me around with a steel grip on my arm. I winced, until I saw his eyes, fearful and wide as they glanced down at the charred turnovers in the fire.

He knew. He might not know what was in those pastries, but he knew what they were meant for.

It was me. I killed her, don't you see that?

I waited for him to say something, anything. He let go of my arm and stepped back.

You know what I can do. You know I can break you. Bend you. Kill you.

That sense of Eilidh played about my fingertips, my skin, and burrowed deep. Little waves of electric shadow thrummed there, and I liked it. I liked the power that came with it, the feeling of the impossible becoming anything I wanted it to be. I could clear the room of all these heretics and Pharisees. I could kill that man if I saw to it.

But I didn't. I walked out of the room without a word, and the shadowy pitch at my fingers' reach frayed and fizzled out. I bumped past the black-garbed mourners and their whispers trailed behind me. If they weren't already talking about me, they certainly were now. I looked pale and frightened, shivering in a cold that only I felt. I passed through the parlor, catching the eye of Brother Wise and his wife. Her green eyes flashed as they glanced over at me. She squeezed Elijah's hand. I quickly turned away and disappeared into the crowd, pushing through it until I could breathe.

I found myself in the washroom, the door closed behind me, muffling all those whispers and hiding me from all those eyes. Shallow breaths sank into deeper ones. The flush upon my skin began to cool; I felt safe, at least for the moment. The door behind me creaked open.

Elijah stood in the doorway. He didn't wait for permission to come in. In a heartbeat, he was at my side and taking up my hands in his. His hands were trembling. My breathing was fast. His breathing was faster.

He kissed me. The kiss was fragile but deep. I felt the desire dripping from his lips, dancing on his tongue as it drowned me. My fingers brushed his chest. His heart was hopping as fast as a jackrabbit, nearly beating up and out of his well-pressed white dress shirt. I pulled my hand away; it was too much to feel his passion, his need for me.

Not now. Please, not now.

But my heart fell in worship where his lips touched mine. The world around me melted away. Wrapped in his arms, Elijah was all I saw. All I needed. All I desired. He pulled away suddenly, looking down on me with a wild breathlessness.

"I love you, Jaelle. Lord knows, I love you," his words were soft, barely uttered from his lips, and yet they pierced me right in the chest. "Say that you love me. Please."

My mouth opened to speak, and the words tumbled out before I could stop them. "I love you."

He sighed, as if the weight of the world had just slipped off his shoulders. He laid his head against mine. "Say it again. Please."

"I love you."

"Say my name. Elijah."

"I love you...Elijah."

He sighed again, a little lighter this time, and smiled. Gripping me tightly, he held me close. Then his face turned serious and gray.

"Then leave with me."

"Now?"

"No," he shook his head, his eyes drifting. "No, not now." He stumbled over his words. "After Christmas. We can start over with a new year. A new life."

I knew right then and there that I would follow him to the depths of hell if he asked.

"How? Jeremy—"

He was quick to cut me off. "Don't you worry. I'll have a plan by then. Just promise me, you'll be ready."

"I promise," I said as I leaned my head against his chest, his furiously fast heartbeat trembling like distant thunder against my ear.

Elijah held me close. We stayed that way for a long while, the muffled sounds of my father-in-law's wake jarring our silence. Finally, he pulled away, tugging my fingers from around his waist. His expression was cold and distant now as he prepared to leave me. He did so without another word and slipped quietly through the door. I heard him join the crowd, expressing his sorrows and giving comfort to those who wept.

I wept alone in that burdened silence.

For the rest of the day, I was quiet. I did my duty at the wake and stood by Jeremy's side with as much dignity as I could muster. By the time people had begun to leave, Jeremy looked pale and tired. He said his thanks to everyone who came. When the last of them had left, I took myself back to the kitchen. Before I'd even gotten down the hallway, I heard a voice.

"Mrs. Bennett?"

I turned around to find Mrs. Prudence Wise blinking back at me. I had never heard her talk before. I didn't know she could. She wrung her hands vigorously until they were red. With a deep breath, she said quietly, "We don't know one another well, but I..." Her head dropped down, her eyes staring down at the floor.

A flash of fire. Those green eyes watching me through the flames, full of hate and delicious spite.

My body burned ice-cold as the vision left me. My skin crawled and my forehead beaded with a nervous sweat. When I came to, Mrs. Prudence Wise was looking straight at me, that same fire lighting in her eyes. The fear faintly pressed into her delicate features suddenly faded into a sterner, stauncher expression. There was nothing on her face that revealed her nature. Nothing but ice-cold emptiness.

"God save you," she said, her voice unwavering and chilly.

Without a word more, she left me. I rushed out of the house onto the porch. The air was crisp and cool, tempering the feelings that had overwhelmed me and made me question myself. All I saw behind my closed eyes was that woman's green eyes, flashing in the fire. Her voice rang in my ears.

God save you.

Would He?

I shook the thought away with the cold and stood up tall.

That narrow way ain't for you. The earth and its roots are better.

But it didn't ring true. The seeds of doubt had been sown by that damn preacher's wife. Now, my roots were dry and sour with her venom. I sighed with uncertainty.

"Better get on home now, Jaelle."

Jeremy's voice startled me out of my thoughts. He

was standing on the porch with his mama. He kept his eyes down. As his mama handed me my purse and hat, she gave me a look that pierced me down to my bones. It was as if she too saw the blood, the fire, the snow, and the danger in Mrs. Prudence Wise's eyes. She saw it all and faintly smiled. She wished us well and sent us on our way.

27 THE FEAR OF GOD

The roots are rotten.
I am digging again, the earth of the churchyard unsettled at my feet. In the hole I've dug is the pouch, seething in shadows and a pitch-black nothingness that hisses beneath my touch. Against my will, I'm holding that darkness in my hand. I can feel its power playing about my fingertips, wanting to get inside my skin. The heat of it is almost unbearable. Yet I wrap my hand around it tightly, unwilling to let it go.

My eyes glance up to see Eilidh kneeling in the muddy earth before me. Her eyes are fire, and her smile is sweet but wretched. A poisonous kindness that makes me sink into her. And I listen as she speaks.

"The roots are rotten. I have made them so. Look, child. Look what I have done."

Around me, I see the shadows of Jeremy, Elijah and his wife, Roy, and Doc Lee. It seems like the whole church, the whole town, is there in that churchyard. Their shadows are scattered among the wooden crosses and gravestones. They are screaming as fire consumes them. And Eilidh smiles. I look into her eyes. Deep into her eyes. And I see the past.

Eilidh in the arms of a preacher man, sinning before the eyes of God. Quickly that passion turns sour, and the preacher man turns into a great darkness. Rejecting her. Condemning her.

I see through her eyes as she digs up the earth of the churchyard by the light of the moon and she places her curse. Black veins of darkness spread from that place out into the land, to the church, and beyond.

Eilidh is still smiling, her hands buried deep into the mud.

"The darkness I have spilled here poisons the earth. And the earth poisons the shadows. And the shadows poison the flesh."

She leans close to me, smelling of hellfire. She flicks her serpentine tongue across her rose-red lips, laughter tripping from them.

"They are cursed. Burdened with the sin of my blood."

Eilidh rises to her feet and shouts to the wailing shadows, "You are all cursed!" She turns her wicked eyes to me, her finger pointing at me. "You are cursed, child. Death is yours. Beware."

"Why?" I whisper.

Her body shifts into shadow, and suddenly, she is glaring down at me just inches away. She cocks her head to the side, as if she's reading me.

"All must die by their wickedness if I must," she hisses.

She screams and all goes black.

I woke from the dream in tears, trembling in the dark. My hands grasped for my neck, desperately tearing the amulet from my skin, and throwing it to the floor. It slid underneath Great Ma's rocking chair.

The woolly worms had been right. The winter was full of snow and damp, stormy weather, a cold snap hanging over the valley with a vengeance. Sickness stormed every household, and not a body, young or old, was left untouched.

Jeremy and I remained silent all those days. I stayed out of Jeremy's way, and thankfully, he stayed out of mine. There were no harsh words, no beatings, no bruises. It was a new kind of emptiness, and it made my stomach ache with anxiousness. We already knew all each other's secrets. There was nothing left hidden, nothing left to say.

After that horrid dream about Great Ma and her own secret, I was restless. On an early morning in December, I perched myself on the porch railing and watched the sun come up over the hills. My breath puffed out before me in wisps of haze. I liked the cold. It woke me up and made my body alert. Though I shivered in the chilly air, it was good.

I eyed the FOR SALE sign sticking up from the snow. It was a bright red eyesore if you asked me. It had sat there for a while now. Not a single person had come to take a look, and that made Jeremy angry. I understood. It was a good farm.

A body would be plum crazy not to see that.

Still, no one came, and the FOR SALE sign stayed.

It was nearly Christmas. In fact, it was only days away. Most years, there would be a tall, fresh evergreen sitting in the parlor, all decked out with candles, popcorn and candy from Mr. Tillman's store. The whole house would smell of tree sap and vanilla. I'd be baking up a storm for the church's big bazaar making cookies of every kind, pumpkin bread, and cakes galore. Usually, it was hard to keep Jeremy's dirty hands out of the cookies as they cooled, but now, he wouldn't touch a thing I made.

This year was different. I wouldn't be going to the church service or the party afterward. Besides my misgivings about my faith, Elijah thought it best if I didn't go. We were days away from our big escape, and as he said, we shouldn't raise suspicion. As the sun peeked over the treetops, I smiled. Not too many more days of this view, this prison.

A bang from inside the house wiped the smile right off my face.

"Shit!" Jeremy was up.

I wrapped my shawl around my shoulders and went inside. I was hit with a wave of heat coming from the kitchen's monstrous stove. He was fiddling with the stove and burning himself in the process.

IN THE COLD COLD WINTER

Jeremy had grown old in those fall months, his sharp features turning flabby and his belly growing large. His hair had thinned and grayed, leaving funny patches of speckled white about his temples. His eyes were smoky gray instead of the blue I had always known, a lifeless color for a lifeless, soulless man.

With the fire going good, he dropped his breeches and warmed his bare bottom up next to the stove with a sigh. His bare skin glowed in the fiery light of the stove grate. He didn't see me watching him. Meanwhile, the breakfast he was cooking himself on the stovetop was burning. The smell wafted to his nose, and he sniffed the air. Then he sniffed it again. His eyes shot open, and with his breeches still down, he whipped around to take his pan off the stove, burning himself. He let out a yelp so loud that it shook the timbers of the house. The pan slammed down to the ground, runny eggs going everywhere.

While he was cussing and carrying on, I slipped into the kitchen and silently cleaned up his mess. I started a new pan of eggs for him. He watched, nursing his blistered palm, his narrowed eyes on my every move.

I glanced at him and said, "I ain't gonna poison ya, Jeremy. Settle yourself down."

I went back to fixing the eggs, but not without giving him a shameful glance at his breeches down around his ankles. A flush of red crept up to his cheeks and he pulled them up, tightening his belt an extra notch. He plopped down at the table. Before his backside had time to warm the chair, I'd placed a plate of eggs in front of him, steaming hot and smelling good. He eyed the plate with a wild look of hunger. I sat across from him with a cup of coffee. Out of the corner of my eye, I saw him sniff the eggs. Satisfied that they were safe, he dug in, spooning big mouthfuls in between gulping breaths.

Before long the plate was licked clean. He didn't

meet my eye, but he said to me, "Them eggs was sure better than mine."

I smiled at him over my coffee cup.

"A mite better than that whore's. She damn near burnt everything she set her hands to." He stared down at the white tablecloth. His eyes were thoughtful, sad and faraway.

"I don't care what you done before," he announced after that silence. "But I won't abide a loose woman under my roof. Understand?"

I did, but it wasn't going to change anything. Still, I nodded.

He shuffled awkwardly in his seat. "County's buying up the farm and all the land. I imagine they'll be using it for some damn factory this town don't need. All the same, we're out of here on the first of the year." He took a sip of his coffee. "Be ready."

"Where?" I asked.

He glanced up, surprised. "Where, what?"

"Where're we going?"

He shrugged as if it were a trifling matter and none of my concern. "Out west, I reckon. Omaha. Got good land out that a-ways. Good people."

What he meant to say was out west, there were people who didn't know us, or what we'd done. People who wouldn't gossip and chatter about us or our business.

"Alright," I said, staring into the stormy swirls of rich coffee in my cup.

He nodded; his eyes full of an emptiness I understood. We had reached the end of everything, and there was nowhere to turn back. He took a deep breath in and got up from the table. Moments later, the screen door slammed shut behind him. For once, I was content with the quiet that he left behind, because I knew it was the last of it for a lifetime.

That night the stars called to me. Jeremy was

asleep in the parlor, curled up in a chair next to the fire. I slipped out of the house into the night, my feet bare and a shawl loosely hanging around my naked shoulders. The air was biting cold, yet I shivered off my shawl to feel it run right through me. There were whispers on the wind. Calling me out into the darkness. Past the fields to the orchard. Bidding my body to follow where they led.

The frozen grass crunched beneath my feet. The feeling thrilled through my body. I gasped in the icy moonlight and exhaled wisps of spirit that floated up to the stars. I found myself walking among the ghostly silhouettes of the trees, bare and dead once again. Dead without, their roots quivering with life way down deep. I let their lifeforce seep into my flesh, warming me from the inside.

A gentle touch came upon the bare skin of my shoulder.

"Jaelle."

I turned to the sound, and there was Elijah. His skin was pale and shone in the moonlight. He was a shining star in the blackness, burning so bright that I couldn't keep my eyes off him. His dark eyes penetrated every layer of my flesh, right down to my very soul, and he smiled. It was a whisper of a smile, faint and jaded, but it was for me.

Elijah's hands gently washed over the bareness of my skin until it was nothing but goose pimples and shivers. I leaned into his chest, wrapping my arms around him. Breathing him in. The sweetness of sandalwood and fresh citrus. Yet there was a note of sourness like death that trickled from him. It tinged my nostrils and made my stomach churn.

"Elijah—"

He didn't let me finish. His mouth crashed hard into mine, his hands everywhere at once. Lifting the hem of my nightdress up to my thighs, the fabric sighing beneath the brush of his fingertips. He leaned me against one of the trees, the rough bark pressing against my bottom as he ravished the rest of me. With his chest pressed against mine, I felt the rapid pounding of his heart as he had me. His grip on me was hungry but steady, a gentle forcefulness that I desired with his every touch.

My head reared back with a gasp of delight, my eyes peering up into the cluttered sky of coming clouds and stars pinioned to the blackness of the night. His warm breath fluttered across my cheeks, flushing them with sweet heat. I closed my eyes, letting it wash over me.

A prickling chill touched my face. Small and bitterly cold. Then another and another. I opened my eyes to a million stars falling from the sky. White sparks of snow fluttered down to meet us in our ecstasy, and as he collapsed against me, breathless and trembling, it was eerily quiet and still.

Elijah's face lifted to mine. His face was paler, his lips tinged white in the cold. They too were trembling, tears forming in his eyes.

"She's dying." Those were the words he chose to close our tryst in the dark.

"What?"

He held me tight. "Prudence. She's been sick for some time now. I care for her, and she doesn't say much. But I know she's dying. And I..." His eyes traipsed across the snow-painted shadows. "I'll see her to the end."

He waited for me to answer, but I had no words to give him. My mind was struck with the lightning of his affection and the fire of its descent into nothingness now. This was not a promise of a future, but a farewell that would never follow with another meeting. Here and now, beneath these snow-capped stars and unearthly shadows, he was saying goodbye.

"Jaelle—"

But I didn't let him say anymore. I peeled myself

away from his hungry touch, away from his fickle heart and cold love, and I turned toward the house.

"Jaelle!" he called after me.

As I walked back through the trees, the snow was falling harder. I waited. I waited for him to chase after me and give me his love again. Promise it forever and ever. Elijah Wise did no such thing. The moon and stars were clotted by the coming snow. The silence was heavy and once again, I was alone.

28 Unto Us a Child is Born

Jeremy's mama was ailing. Word came to us late in the night on the twenty-third of December. I packed a bag for him to stay awhile. He was gone by dawn. He didn't say much to me as he left, but I could feel it in my bones. A storm was coming, and his mama was dying.

I prayed when he left, while the storm clouds clustered and filled up the skies. After the nightmare of Eilidh's curse, I couldn't help but wonder if Great Ma had a hand in his mama's ailment. My body longed to plunge into the ice-capped river by the churchyard and be cleansed. It didn't matter if I froze to death or drowned in its depths, so long as my soul was clean again.

The thrumming power of the moonstone had left me, and with it, the shadow of Eilidh. I felt fully myself and full of fear. All my life I had walked the straight and narrow way. But this year's troubles had changed me at my core, at the very roots of me. I knew the power of God and the lure of the Devil. There were shadows all around us, trying to get into our lives, our hearts, our spirits. I had let them in.

Now?

Now there was a man that I wanted and could not have. Elijah was what I wanted. All my hope had lain in him. That hope was now spoiled and frayed. I hadn't heard a word from him since that night beneath the stars, and I no longer expected to. I missed Elijah, even though that felt wrong. Then there was Jeremy. My husband. The man I'd chosen before God until the end of my days. The one whose flesh I was shackled to until I died. The one I didn't want.

An electric clap and fizzle, and the house went dark. Night was coming and the shadows were deep on this winter evening. Bustling through the darkness, I found the kerosene lamps and lit them. In the parlor, I built up the fire until it was white-hot.

There was a knock at the front door. One single knock, sharp and short. Nothing came after.

Run came the voice inside me.

It crawled up from the depths of my shadowy soul. Pushing me away from the door just as my hand reached to open it. The door swung open, and there was Mrs. Prudence Wise. She was dressed for the season in rich reds and greens, and even her hat was a play on the upcoming holiday. For all her joyful attire, her face was pale, almost gray, and her eyes wore sickly, dark circles beneath their shadowy stare. She looked frightened and small. Behind her, standing as her shadow was Eilidh. The preacher's wife tried to smile.

"Hello, Mrs. Bennett," she and Eilidh said together

Her voice was fragile and faint. She clutched her purse tightly, wrapping her arm around its body. It matched her dress, though the shade of red was a bit off, I decided as I looked her over. She nearly shriveled beneath my gaze.

"May I come in?" It was more of a quiet demand than a question.

I realized I was doing nothing but staring. I dropped my eyes and opened the door wide to let her in. She stepped hesitantly inside the house, and I led her down the hall to the parlor. It was dusty and not fit for company, but I didn't care. This wasn't company, this was a nuisance that must be endured. I motioned for her to sit. She did so gingerly, still clutching that purse to her body like it was her protector. Seeing her up close, she looked all full of tremors and frazzled bits. Her hair, usually neatly pulled back, was in a messy bun with a scattering of pokey pieces striking out everywhere. Beneath her coat, I caught a glimpse of a dark stain on her dress, darker than its red material.

I sniffed. She looked at me blankly.

Finally, she said, "I've come for recompense, Mrs. Bennett."

I'd heard that word a thousand times on Sundays, usually in reference to great sins that had been committed and wrongs that must be righted. I wondered as to what she meant by it.

My head tipped to the side with a curious expression. "Forgive me, but I don't reckon I understand."

Her jaw tensed. She sat up straighter and tightened her grip on the sofa cushion. "God sees you, Mrs. Bennett. Everything you've done. Everything you do here and now in this moment. So, you'd best be honest with me."

I gulped in air. My body froze. Her green eyes flashed with fire. In the corner, Eilidh as a shadow, was creeping ever closer.

"You've been with my husband, haven't you?"

I steeled myself so that not a whit of my expression would betray me. Still, my words trembled off my lips with sharp uncertainty. "He's been a good pastor, and he's come to my aid when my body was ailin' and my spirit was low. No different than any other member of the congregation."

I tried to smile, to reassure her. She wasn't having any of it.

"I see," she said curtly. "For all the times, he's been away from me, you must be very poorly."

"I lost a child in the fall. Nearly died myself. But Brother Wise ain't been here more than a handful of times. I can't account for all his time away from you."

The silence was heavy. The air between us was

electric. The subdued look in her eye had turned wild, the color of her eyes muted by that fiery rage.

"I thought I would like living here, good people, good earth. But there's a darkness over the whole lot of you. The land too. There are secrets and whispers everywhere. The air here smells of death. I can't get it off me." She looked at me with big tears in her eyes. "It won't come off."

Fear numbed my senses. I sat very still.

"You can sense things, I see that," she said quietly. "But I can sense things too. And there's something not right. Elijah knew. I know that he knew, but no preachin' of sin and God's vengeance could cure it. You people are cursed. You're all rotten. Every one of you leads the other into sin. To eternal damnation and the fires of hell."

"Isn't that the way of the world, Mrs. Wise? Everyone is a sinner that leads others into sin."

She huffed and those eyes of hers glimmered with self-righteous rage.

"I'll not listen to you," she said with a glower. "I've heard tell of you and your family. All of them were witches killed for their sin."

She stopped, choosing her words carefully. Exactly. "You lure righteous, godly men to the wickedest of deeds."

I shook my head and stood up, turning my back on her. "Your godly men are about as sinful as they come, and it weren't me that done it."

"Are you saying he propositioned *you*, then?" she said it as if such a thing could not be so.

I turned back.

"My husband?" The words fell faintly from her lips when she saw me.

Her purse lay open now. I looked down. There was a knife in her hand, the blade pointed straight at me. Even with the distance between us, I could feel the cool darkness coming off that blade like it had already pierced my flesh. I didn't move. The blade was already bloodied. A shiver of fear tumbled all through me.

Elijah.

"Elijah." His name slipped from my tongue before I could stop it.

"Ah," she smiled grimly. "So, you know him."

I knew what she meant. Yes, I'd known him, again and again and again. My heart and body were full of him. Something which by the looks of her face, she'd never had. A deflated sigh fell from my lips.

"You killed him dead. Didn't you?"

She stood up straighter, as if she was proud. I could see a smudge of red now on her neck. It made me ill.

"Yes," she purred. "I tore out his heart with this." She raised the bloodied knife in the air. "And fed it to the fire. It's of little matter. He wasn't using it. Not for a long while now. It's warm in here." She put the knife down carefully on the sofa and shook her coat off with a lazy shrug.

Almost all her red dress was covered in what I could only imagine was his blood. At her breast, a shiny snowflake brooch was speckled in red. Her arms were scratched and marked. There had been a struggle. She grabbed up the knife again and gestured with it for me to sit. I did not sit, and that made her angry.

"So help me, Jaelle, don't make me hurt you before I've a mind to. I swear to God, I'll do it!"

I stood there, defying her. The knife trembled in her hand.

"People aren't angels," she muttered, her mind wandering away. "And they aren't devils either. They're something gray that's in between. Easily swayed by one or the other. But you—you're different. You and all your kind. You are the devil. As a godly woman, I must snuff you out like chaff from the wheat. Just like your mother."

I started to back away from her, but my feet wouldn't move fast enough. In seconds, she jumped up and ran toward me with the knife. A wicked shriek escaped her lips. I put up my hands in front of me to stop her. She knocked me down and straddled me, breathlessly stabbing at me. The knife snipped the sleeve of my dress in two and sliced through my arm. The blade just kept coming. Again and again and again, it hit the air. I felt the knife slide under my skin with a whooshing sound as the air left my body and the pain began.

With a cry, I rolled her off me and straddled her small form. She knocked the table over where the lighted lamp sat. The lamp wobbled and smashed onto the floor. The flame exploded, spreading across the floor quickly. It climbed in little fiery veins up the curtains and the wall.

Prudence swung the knife at my face, but I caught her arm and pinned it down. She fumbled with the knife until it slipped from her fingers and clattered to the floor. I used the weight of my body to keep her from moving as I stretched my arm out to reach for the knife. Beneath me, she kicked and shuffled, scrambling to get up. Though blood was streaming down my front, pooling on her and the ground, I was still stronger.

I stretched my fingers. Just an inch more, just one more. I grabbed the knife. I didn't hesitate. I plunged it into her chest and watched her eyes grow wide, the air in her lungs dissipating in a sighing hiss. She looked past me, the flames of the fire bursting in her dead eyes.

"It's snowing," she said.

I turned around to look out the window. The storm had started, a wispy curtain of snow floating through the air. It was coming down fast and hard, and the wind howled across the sides of the house. When I looked back at Mrs. Prudence Wise, I knew that she was dead. The light had left her, and the shadow had set in.

Jaelle.

The voice of Eilidh called me. Through the flames and the shadows of smoke, I saw her figure. Watching and waiting. I wouldn't go down on my knees. Slipping in my own pool of blood, I struggled to my feet and stared down the figure of my grandmother, that once had been a woman but now was only the dark itself. Her laughter answered my defiance. It cackled and crawled up the walls with the flames, nearly drowning out the sound of my heartbeat as it pounded.

"Go on and laugh, you bitch. Go on!" I screamed.

I could feel my body growing faint and fading into darkness. I wasn't going to die in this tinderbox. Step by agonizing step, I walked through the flames, through the house, my body igniting in a flurry of fire. My skin sizzled and burned, but I didn't scream. I wouldn't while that devil was listening, waiting for me to die.

I made it out of the door into the freezing air, and the falling snow. I collapsed in a sea of white and stained it red.

Fire and blood and snow.

My eyes caught a glimpse of a plume of smoke in the distance. It was the Narrow Way in flames. I knew it. Prudence had gone and destroyed everything.

Fire and blood and snow.

I lay there in the storm, staring up at the darkened sky as it showered crystal snowflakes on top of me. They kissed my burning flesh, and the fire smoldered on my skin.

Jaelle.

Three figures stood above me, shadows that were deeper than the dark. I smiled a wicked smile to defy them. I would be joyful as I died.

"Jaelle."

Another figure now hovered over me, tall and big.

Jeremy knelt to me, his eyes wide and full of fear. And what was that? Was it relief? He knew I was dying just by looking at me. His eyes left me and glanced at his father's house consumed by flames. I saw tears well in his eyes and fall silently to the snow, mixing with the stain of my blood.

"Damn it all to hell. Ain't nothing left. Nothing b-but f-fire and b-b-blood and snow," was all he said.

His voice faded away from me. I turned my eyes away. I didn't want the last of my life to be his pain. I prayed to the God of Abraham and Isaac. I prayed to the God of my youth. And I waited.

God answered.

There amidst the swirling wind and snow, I saw the little girl. The one I had imagined would be my own, in her little blue dress and crisp white pinafore. *My* little girl. There she was. Come to bring me to Heaven.

Have I won God's favor in this last moment? Have I been forgiven?

I reached for her. She reached out her fragile hand to me and smiled. Her mouth opened wide, black roots and darkness spewing from her and she screamed.

An Deireadh.

ABOUT THE AUTHOR

Keshia C. Willi melds fantasy and fright to create genre-bending stories that twist reality with every page. Raised in the mountains of Virginia, her writing has been a lifelong journey. Her latest novels, JOHNNY BE GOOD and BEWARE THE WOLF, were featured in Amazon's Top 100 Hot New Releases list.

Facebook: Keshia C. Willi Author
Instagram: @keshiacwilliauthor
TikTok: @keshiacwilliauthor

www.houseofhonorbooks.com
www.facebook.com/houseofhonorbooks

Be sure to sign up for the House of Honor monthly newsletter to keep up with all our latest releases.

PRAISE FOR THE AUTHOR

Johnny Be Good

Amazon Customer

5.0 out of 5 stars Johnny B. Good is a dark thriller that keeps you turning pages.
Reviewed in the United States on April 3, 2025
This book is riveting, a dark thriller that keeps you turning pages until the last page when you sit in shock at the ending. A moving story of an abused boy turned bad.

BOOKS BY THE AUTHOR

Tales of Ancient Fire
Fire Tales
Baneshelm

Johnny Be Good

Beware the Wolf

Made in the USA
Middletown, DE
31 July 2025

11466204R00146